PENGUIN CLASSICS

MICROMÉGAS AND OTHER SHORT FICTIONS

FRANÇOIS-MARIE AROUET (1694–1778), who later took the name of VOLTAIRE, was the son of a notary and educated at a Jesuit School in Paris. His father wanted him to study the law, but the young man was determined on a literary career. He gained an introduction to the intellectual life of Paris and soon won a reputation as a writer of satires and odes – a not altogether enviable reputation, for the suspicion of having written a satire on the Regent procured him a term of six months' imprisonment in the Bastille. On his release, his first tragedy, *Œdipe*, was performed (1718) in Paris with great success and soon after he published the poem he had written in prison, a national epic, *La Henriade* (1723), which placed him with Homer and Virgil in the eyes of his contemporaries. After a second term of imprisonment in the Bastille, Voltaire spent two and a half years (1726–8) in England, and returned to France full of enthusiasm for the intellectual activity and the more tolerant form of government he found there. His enthusiasm and his indictment of the French system of government are expressed in his *Letters Concerning the English Nation* (1733), published in France as the *Lettres philosophiques*, but whose sale was absolutely forbidden in France.

The next fifteen years were spent at the country seat of his friend, Madame du Châtelet, where he wrote his most popular tragedies and his *Zadig*, a witty Eastern tale, and started work on his *Century of Louis XIV*. After Madame du Châtelet's death in 1749, Voltaire was induced to pay a prolonged visit to the Court of Frederick the Great, with whom he had been in correspondence for several years. While there he completed his important historical work *Essay on Customs* (*Essai sur les Moeurs et l'Esprit des Nations*) and began his *Philosophic Dictionary*. Voltaire and Frederick could not agree for long and in 1753 Voltaire decided to leave Prussia. But he was not safe in France. After two years of wandering he settled near Geneva and at last made a home at Ferney. It was during the last, and most brilliant, twenty years of his life that he wrote *Candide*, his dialogues and more tales and his widely-read *Philosophic Dictio_____ _____ cting his ceaseless and energetic _____ ___s thing' – all manifestations of t_____ hodoxy

in Church and State. He died at the age of eighty-four, after a triumphant visit to Paris, from which he had been exiled for so long.

THEO CUFFE was educated in Dublin and at the Sorbonne. He has translated Saint-Exupéry's *The Little Prince and Letter to a Hostage* for Penguin, and is completing a new translation of Voltaire's *Candide* for Penguin Classics.

HAYDN MASON, Emeritus Professor in the University of Bristol and Officier dans l'Ordre des Palmes Linguistiques, was until recently General Editor of the *Complete Works of Voltaire* and previously Editor of the *Studies on Voltaire and the Eighteenth Century* (1977–95). He is the author of several works on literature, thought and society in eighteenth-century France, including a book on Voltaire's *Candide* and also an edition of that tale. A Professor in French at the Sorbonne (1979–81), he was President of the International Society for Eighteenth-Century Studies (1991–5). He is currently working on a number of studies of Voltaire's relationships with England.

VOLTAIRE

Micromégas and other Short Fictions

Translated by THEO CUFFE
With an Introduction and Notes by
HAYDN MASON

PENGUIN BOOKS

PENGUIN BOOKS

Published by the Penguin Group
Penguin Books Ltd, 80 Strand, London WC2R ORL, England
Penguin Putnam Inc., 375 Hudson Street, New York, New York 10014, USA
Penguin Books Australia Ltd, 250 Camberwell Road, Camberwell, Victoria 3124, Australia
Penguin Books Canada Ltd, 10 Alcorn Avenue, Toronto, Ontario, Canada M4V 3B2
Penguin Books India (P) Ltd, 11, Community Centre, Panchsheel Park, New Delhi – 110 017, India
Penguin Books (NZ) Ltd, Cnr Rosedale and Airborne Roads, Albany, Auckland, New Zealand
Penguin Books (South Africa) (Pty) Ltd, 24 Sturdee Avenue, Rosebank 2196, South Africa

Penguin Books Ltd, Registered Offices: 80 Strand, London WC2R ORL, England

www.penguin.com

This edition first published 2002
1

Translations (except 'Dialogue between the Cock and the Hen') and Translator's Note
copyright © Theo Cuffe, 2002
'Dialogue between the Cock and the Hen' translated by Haydn and Adrienne Mason,
first published in *Comparative Criticism*, 20, 184–7, 1998, copyright ©
Cambridge University Press, 1998
Introduction and notes copyright © Haydn Mason, 2002

Set in 10.2/12.5 pt Monotype Granjon
Typeset by Rowland Phototypesetting Ltd, Bury St Edmunds, Suffolk
Printed in England by Clays Ltd, St Ives plc

CONTENTS

v

CONTENTS

INTRODUCTION

This volume brings together a selection of Voltaire's short fiction under the headings of *Contes* and *Mélanges*. In a happy phrase, Voltaire's *contes* have been called 'the fables of reason'.[1] The description adroitly sums up that mixture of fantasy and rationality which characterizes these short stories. The protagonist in each one usually goes on a journey, literal or metaphorical. In so doing he acquires experience of the real world, both as actor and spectator. Travelling in a strange environment, he is educated, often by pure surprise. The knowledge gained will destroy belief in any 'system' that reduces the world and mankind to a formula, optimistic or otherwise. Behind the central character stands the author, ever present, guiding the reader towards a conclusion that, in a host of diverse ways, mocks at set patterns of faith. All around us complexity and contradiction reign. Once we begin to appreciate that, we may possibly start to show greater tolerance for others, avoiding dogmatic attitudes which bring only oppression and cruelty in their wake. The tales are 'philosophical', if that can be taken as epistemology and empirical enquiry, but not if it connotes metaphysics and unknowable truths beyond the sphere of human reason.

But how to define a Voltairean *conte* in terms of genre? No simple definition will suffice. For Voltaire himself was chary of providing a neat domain with clearly delineated frontiers. He used the term sparingly, and it was late in his life before any volumes by him bearing the term appeared; even then, it may well have been his publisher's idea. Stories like 'Plato's Dream' and 'Micromégas' came out first as *Mélanges philosophiques*; 'The Consoler and the Consoled' and 'The History of the Travels of Scarmentado' were originally *Mélanges de littérature*. As one can see from these titles, 'mélanges' (literally, 'mixture') is an even vaguer description. So any attempt at a tight genre-definition is doomed from the start.

The very looseness of the form helped to provide its inherent attraction, since it allowed for an unlimited mixture of registers and unfettered literary experimentation. The classicist Voltaire, who held the 'noble' genres of tragedy and epic in high regard, could afford to let his hair down in an area that had no traditional prestige attached to it. Besides, this love of story-telling appears everywhere in his writings: histories, philosophical treatises, correspondence. It was his way of giving indirect expression to his private feelings; indeed, it is not too far-fetched to see them as fulfilling a personal catharsis.

Story-telling, in fact, runs right through Voltaire's life. The first tales go back to 1715, the final one received its last revisions sixty years later. The diversity of the form is reflected in the *Contes de Guillaume Vadé* (1764), the first volume from Voltaire to include 'conte' in the title – where the first seven are in verse! Yet until very recently, editions of his *contes* were selected exclusively from his prose works,[2] despite Voltaire's frequent habit of intermingling prose and verse in many of his works and correspondence. So it is not surprising to find that the influences discernible in his *contes* stem from poets like La Fontaine as well as from prose writers. To recognize this fluidity, the present edition includes one of Voltaire's shorter narrative poems ('Cuckoldage'), which may serve to stand as a promise of the great comic poem *La Pucelle* to come in later years.

But that is not all, so far as we are presently concerned. Voltaire's polemical writings also took in *mélanges* (like *conte*, the French term is more useful than its equivalent in English). The author often dubbed them *facéties* (merry pranks). But the 'jokes' could be serious in their mischievousness. Some, like the 'Account of the Jesuit Berthier', develop a narrative in a way that makes them virtually *contes*. Others are in dialogue form. But all aim to shake the reader's conventional assumptions, to make him think for himself. Enlightenment is all. Satire, irony, dream-like imaginings, solid historical fact, parody: these are some of the tools which Voltaire uses in his pursuit of that end.

René Pomeau once described Voltaire as 'interminablement bref'.[3] The paradox admirably sums up the *philosophe*'s endlessly prolific capacity for concise statement, which has the incidental consequence that over a score of his writings can be included in this edition. Many are scarcely known outside France, yet they deserve recognition for the new insights they offer to those who have read only 'Candide' and perhaps 'L'Ingénu' or 'Zadig'. Together they show the author's vitality in casting his thoughts into ever-new combinations.

Although Voltaire never provided a definition of the *conte*, he made clear his intentions in *Le Taureau blanc* (*The White Bull*), published in 1774, when the heroine speaks for him. Her wish, says Amaside, is that 'sous le voile de la fable, il [le conte] laissât entrevoir aux yeux exercés quelque vérité fine qui échappe au vulgaire': 'beneath the veil of fable, it should allow the practised eye to perceive some subtle truth unnoticed by the common horde'.[4] The same point is made in the 'Conversation between Lucian, Erasmus and Rabelais'. Circumspection had been essential for Erasmus if he did not want to be murdered or burned at the stake. Rabelais, for his part, had decided that to act the madman was the only way he could pour ridicule on the religious and political injustices of his time. Voltaire was to take his own path of concealment.

It is through such approaches that the *contes* and the diverse *mélanges* can be seen as part and parcel of the whole Voltairean polemic. But the substance of these short works is bound up inextricably with the manner of their presentation. The greatness of 'Candide', it has been said, lies less in the actual arguments against Optimism than in the realization that they are demolished by 'l'obsession d'un style'.[5] The same observation applies to the works in this edition. Voltaire's bewilderment at the existence of evil in a Newtonian universe and his fight against *l'Infâme* (religious intolerance) have both passed into history. But the uniquely Voltairean style in which those preoccupations were couched remains, in all its protean variety.

The author's immediate emotions are transmuted: anger into derision, pain into jocularity. Bitter scores are paid off through ridicule. Comic effects are conveyed through a large diversity of techniques.[6] Cruel caricature of the Catholic Church as a Punch and Judy show ('Pot-Pourri'); or ironic portrayal of the Jesuit Father Berthier as central player in a farce of yawning, coma and convulsions: such are the modes employed. Reductionist methods are applied to human behaviour: the history of the world is construed in terms of constipation ('Lord Chesterfield's Ears': would Charles I have been saved from execution if Cromwell had not been intestinally blocked for the whole of the previous week?). The author creates a host of literary personae: those with whom he can identify (Micromégas, Scarmentado, the good Brahmin) or, more commonly, those he can assail in one form or another (the vindictive Acrotal, the perfectionist Memnon, the gross Bababec). He invents absurdist names (Merry Hissing probably takes pride of place in this edition). Writers are satirized obliquely: Fontenelle through the over-eager Saturnian, Rousseau, Descartes and Leibniz through their philosophies.

Through all this, Voltaire's ideal figure is, to cite the title of one of his essays, *Le Philosophe ignorant* (1766): the modest intellectual who stops short of dogmatic world-views, is free of the constrictions of the Church, and can get on with using his reason to penetrate accessible truths. By contrast, the only suitable response to the absurd little cleric in 'Micromégas' is Homeric laughter. The world and the human race are alike in being so full of contradictions that no overall body of doctrine can make sense of them. We must resign ourselves to living in uncertainty; and that uncertainty is the principle by which to exercise tolerance towards one's fellows: 'become honest men; exercise compassion' ('Dialogue between Ariste and Acrotal'). In a world of incomprehensible evil, pity and justice are the only decent response on the part of the *honnête homme*.

CONTES

Cuckoldage

This verse tale, mildly ribald in character, dates from around 1715. It demonstrates Voltaire's gift, even in early manhood, for parody. In his poem, an orthodox mythological account of the gods is transformed into the birth of the scabrous deity of the name of 'Cuckoldage'. The poet addresses his lady love as though he were in a conventional romance. Alas! she is married, so the only god who can help him is this disreputable instigator of infidelity. Voltaire is following in the line of La Fontaine's fables of the previous century, but here they are given a new treatment: sprightly, irreverent, in keeping with the aristocratic tone of the circle in which the author was moving. Already, if only by implication, Christian values are dismissed in favour of a pagan world of free love.

The One-eyed Porter

The suggestively erotic quality of the above poem is also a striking feature of this, one of Voltaire's earliest prose narratives, which we now know to date from about 1715 (although not published before 1774). This story was written to be read aloud in Sceaux, at the court of the duchesse du Maine, which was famous for its *divertissements*, and its essentially oral, improvised style is readily apparent. The magical, dreamlike tone shows Voltaire as under the influence, like many another contemporary writer, of the Oriental *A Thousand and One Nights*, which had appeared in French for the first time in 1702. The transformation of the poor one-eyed hero into a resplendent (and two-eyed!) young man comes straight from Araby. But the author conceals till near the end that it is all a dream, even though enough fantastic details have already been recounted to make one feel that this is surely a phallic wish-fulfilment. There is, however, also a darker side. The evils of life make their appearance in the first lines, never again to disappear completely from the Voltairean tale.

Cosi-Sancta

Like *The One-eyed Porter*, this tale originated at Sceaux in about 1715, as can be guessed from its similarly libertine attitude. But to this Voltaire adds an open tilt at Christian beliefs. St Augustine is cited as the source for the story that leads to the provocatively ironic comment which the author makes on female virtue. But what in Augustine's tale is a drama of sacrifice for love that leads to moral improvement all round is transformed by Voltaire into a mocking satire of morals when they are too rigidly held. Cosi-Sancta's troubles arise in the first place from her being a child of Jansenist parents who have inculcated in her a totally unrealistic sense of virtue. Voltaire delights in understated euphemism: the honeymoon night spent asleep; the danger to morality from mendicant monks; the brutally simple explanation from Cosi-Sancta's seducers as to what they want of her. One feels that already more than a hint of the black humour of 'Candide' is present.

Micromégas

Although it was not published until 1752, many of the essential elements of this story were apparently to be found in a tale entitled 'Voyage du baron de Gangan', subsequently lost, which Voltaire had sent to Frederick of Prussia in 1739.[7] In this tale the author had made comprehensive use for the first time of the imaginary voyage as an experience to broaden the traveller's view of life. The inhabitants of Sirius and Saturn move with ease through a friendly and homogeneous universe, made comprehensible by the discoveries of Newton about gravitation. Space is no more than a featureless landscape between two towns. Contrary to the Jansenist pessimism of Pascal in the previous century, the infinity of the cosmos is reassuring, since modern man has learned, thanks to science, to understand and exploit it.

The hero, as the change of title from 'Gangan' demonstrates, has acquired a new name redolent with possibilities. For 'Micromégas' is Janus-faced, looking out at once to the small ('micro') and the large ('mégas'). As seen by space-travellers, human beings are literally microscopic, invisible without the aid of a magnifying glass. Not only are they physically small; they and their planet are pathetically so: 'At last they made out a small gleam of light: it was the Earth. A pitiable sight, for people coming from Jupiter' (p. 24). Yet this obscure Earth, it turns out, contains a race capable of noble work – not, as they themselves prefer to believe, in metaphysics but in the more modest, though far more useful, activity of scientific experimentation. The Saturnian giant sums up the paradox: 'This atom has actually measured me!' (p. 30). From which the sage Micromégas draws the proper conclusions: one must never judge of anything by its apparent size. For even the tiniest of creatures, seemingly worth naught but contempt, may possess a God-given intelligence.

This *conte*, then, displays a general hopefulness more appropriate to Voltaire in the late 1730s than the 1750s. Humanity has a rightful place in the universe, provided it can recognize and accept that situation, and not pine for unattainable first truths. As Locke and Newton had shown in their different spheres of human psychology and celestial astronomy, the human animal possesses the unique capacity for empirical discovery of real knowledge about the world and subsequently for the rational processing of the resulting data.

Even so, the story contains its darker moments. In his wide travels Micromégas has not discovered true happiness anywhere in the universe. As for death, it infallibly comes at last, whether one has lived 15,000 years or a mere earthly life-span: 'Which, as you can see, is to die almost the moment one is born' (p. 21). The remark anticipates Beckett's trenchant statement that one gives birth astride of a grave.[8] Indeed, Voltaire's observation has been seen as the basic starting-point for the modern notion of death: material, scientific, a wholly natural event.[9]

So it would be imprudent to establish a simplistic contrast between this story and the later 'Candide'. But that said, one should recall that 'Micromégas' ends, not just in mockery of the pretentious little theologian but also with the expression of affectionate sentiments by the hero for the Earthmen he has encountered, while yet regretting their limitless conceit. The subtitle 'A Philosophical Story' makes clear where Voltaire is placing the emphasis. The tale is basically structured around two dialogues, the first between the two travellers, the second their 'conversations' with human beings. Apart from a cursory account of the personal troubles on Sirius that motivate the voyage, Micromégas is essentially a talking head, as is (even more so, though more fallibly) his Saturnian companion. Micromégas does not wish to be entertained with romantic fables; he wishes to *learn* ('I want to be instructed': p. 20). The discoveries made in this story are all related to man's cosmic situation. The problematics of social and moral relationships are still to come.

Voltaire has seized upon the use made of relative proportions by

Swift in *Gulliver's Travels*, a work much admired by him, which appeared during the *philosophe*'s stay in England. But he steers his narrative in quite another direction. Except for some ludic treatment of the space-journeys and the different sizes of men and giants, Voltaire eschews the fantastic. In its place he creates a universe devoid of Christian values where humankind, subject neither to the sins of Adam and Eve nor to the possibility of divine redemption, can still find for itself a meaningful niche.

The World As It Is

Voltaire's first *conte* to be published was 'Zadig' (1747). Thereafter, stories appeared regularly from his pen until the final years of his life. 'The World As It Is' (the title in French, 'Le Monde comme il va', may have been suggested by Congreve's *The Way of the World*[10]) appeared in 1748, probably arising out of a visit by Voltaire to Paris in 1739, lasting over two months. He had not set foot in the capital for three years, so he was coming to it with fresh eyes. The conclusion to this story recalls a letter of 1739 where Voltaire compares Paris to Nebuchadnezzar's statue, 'part gold, part muck'. The tale is clearly a parable of the contemporary French capital. However, the *conte* took several years to evolve, as references in it to later events demonstrate.

The tale reads almost like a balance-sheet with 'Assets' and 'Liabilities'. The rather mechanical enumeration makes it structurally less satisfying than some of his other *contes*; but it does testify to an earnest attempt by Voltaire to set a moral valuation upon Paris and, by extension, urban society in general. This enquiry is pursued with the utmost seriousness, for the basic question addressed by Babouc is, quite simply: does Paris deserve to be saved? The subsequent investigation is conducted across a wide range of moral and social issues. Its results are inconclusive, even contradictory. War, for instance, gives rise to appalling horrors; yet it is also the setting for astonishing acts of selfless heroism. The details given are often piquant. A rumour that peace is imminent leads, not as might rationally be expected, to an anticipatory *détente* but only to intensified fighting. (One is reminded of the intense firing on the Western Front as the truce-hour approached on the morning of Armistice Day, 1918.) As in war, so in everything else. Human beings are inexplicable, equally capable of utter baseness and sublime altruism.

In the end, Babouc feels that he must not call down divine thunderbolts upon the human race. One has to be resigned to things as they necessarily are (rather more so than in later years, when Voltaire crusaded against at least some of these abuses). Babouc comes to feel a liking for the city, 'whose inhabitants were civilized, gentle and benevolent, even if they were frivolous, scandal-mongering and full of vanity' (p. 50–51). Evidently, the good qualities just about tip the scales against the bad; worldliness wins out over the temptations of retreat and seclusion. Christian pessimism, incorporating a belief in Original Sin, is irrelevant, as too is the Christian hope of Heaven. Men are, like the world around them, full of contradictions. Irregularity is inherent in our very nature; expecting people to be perfectly wise is as crazy as putting wings on dogs or horns on eagles.[11]

Yet the sense of moral evil cannot be exorcized by this deliberately trite conclusion. War, injustice, oppression are existential realities. Babouc resembles Micromégas in being an observer from afar, of interest only for his reactions to our world. But the awareness of suffering and cruelty is now to the forefront.

Memnon

Written about 1748 (and published in 1750), this story has the same theme as 'Zadig': a naïve protagonist starts out full of confidence that he knows the right way to run his life and becomes disillusioned. In both tales an angel appears and offers advice. But the comparisons serve only to bring out how much darker is the tone of 'Memnon'. 'Zadig' ends ambiguously; the angel may have talked in riddles about Providence, but he is helpful in practical terms and the hero profits from it. In 'Memnon' things are much less ambivalent. Memnon's 'little blueprint of wisdom' (p. 52) is flawed from the outset by his total lack of self-awareness. If he eventually acquires some sort of enlightenment, it is at the irreparable cost of an eye and the loss of happiness which that represents.

The fable carries a classical moral about the folly of aiming at perfect rationality. But any complacent acceptance of that lesson on the reader's part is subverted by the discomfiting manner in which Voltaire narrates it. The angel is no more than a resplendent scarecrow: six fine wings, as tradition dictates, but devoid of head, feet and tail, and he 'resembled nothing at all' (p. 55). The world from which he has come is a weird domain lacking food, sex, money and even corporeal beings. It follows, then, that his message should be a satirical version of the Leibnizian doctrine of Optimism (which in a few years would be receiving its final quietus in 'Candide'), that 'All is well'. If, it appears, a perfect world does exist, that place is totally inaccessible – even to the angel, though his world is far better than our planet.

However, the narration contains humour, even as it tells of Memnon's despair. His downfall is recounted sardonically. He believes, of course, that he is not in the least affected sexually by the beautiful lady ('he was quite sure he was no longer subject to such weakness': p. 53), but only by his finer feelings for her. Be that as it may, the end result is the same. Crossed legs uncross, with devastating consequences. The tone of 'Candide' has entered on the scene, to take up from now on a regular place in Voltaire's stories.

Letter from a Turk

First published in 1750 (and probably written in the same year), this is a work which did not appear in any edition of the stories during Voltaire's lifetime; such is the diverse nature of the genre. In 'Letter from a Turk', Voltaire uses a first-person narration, thereby creating a precedent in his story-telling technique. It may well be that he is recalling his stay in England at the home of his host, Sir Everard Fawkener.[12] At all events, the tale is set in an exotic world of crazy dogmatists, for whom godliness consists of solipsistic self-denial. The author casts a cynical eye over the women who flock to 'consult' the naked Bababec sitting on his bed of nails. Briefly converted to a happier way of life, the fakir discovers that nails in his bottom are preferable to loss of prestige with the opposite sex. The human penchant for masochism, mindless ecstasy and fundamentalist religion is depressing evidence of our readiness to take refuge from facing up to reality.

Although ostensibly about Hinduism, the tale does not simply mock an Eastern religion but is meant also (and mainly) to satirize any cult which puts self-mutilation ahead of social benevolence. Behind the picture of the Indian fakirs, one may glimpse hints of Christian monks or Jansenist purists.

Plato's Dream

Like 'Micromégas', this brief sketch has a cosmic dimension. But it goes somewhat further in its stress upon the question of evil, even though the final conclusion is along Leibnizian lines, that essentially all is well with the universe. It is true, however, that our own world is subject to every sort of physical limitation and peril. Meanwhile, that strange species the human race abuses the faculty of reason with which it has been endowed. Humankind is as much given to murderous aggression as it is vulnerable to plague and pestilence, some of it self-inflicted. Even so, the genie sent by 'the great Demiurge' to create our planet has a good line of defence: have the other genies done any better with their own worlds? It becomes clear that 'the eternal Geometer' alone has the capacity to make perfect things. Final pirouette: Plato awakes; it was nothing but a dream. Voltaire is clearly aware of the miseries of the human lot, but as yet in general terms only. The mood of the tale is speculative, the irony detached. This is not yet the tone of 'Candide'; God is still being cleared of blame for the physical and moral evil in this world. Despite the nominally Platonic base to the narrative, the cosmos outlined here is founded on firm Newtonian principles of order and harmony.

This story was not published till 1756, but there are grounds for thinking that it was at least begun, like 'Micromégas', during Voltaire's years at Cirey.

The History of the Travels of Scarmentado

The pessimism implicit in 'Letter from a Turk' finds its most overt expression in 'Scarmentado' (published in 1756), the most ferociously dark of all Voltaire's *contes*. In part it relates to the author's mood at one of the worst periods of his life, 1753–4, when he was a refugee from Frederick's court in Berlin and at the same time debarred by Louis XV from returning to Paris. This sense of exile was reinforced by Voltaire's historical researches, which confirmed for him that the world is full of unmitigated horrors: 'Candide' without Eldorado or the final garden. Wherever Scarmentado travels, he meets with one disaster after another, cruel absurdities and the total collapse of moral values. Nor is this a fantasy scenario. The events recounted actually occurred around 1615–20 (Voltaire was engrossed in his world history, the *Essai sur les mœurs*, which gives full coverage to this period). In the end, our anti-hero is only too happy to settle for being cuckolded back at home. Derisive bathos is a fitting conclusion to a story that is throughout a series of savage demystifications. The first-person point of view heightens the sense of Voltaire's personal identification with his protagonist. The authorial distancing of, say, 'Memnon' is replaced here by bitter satire.

The Consoler and the Consoled

Also published in 1756, this parody of a classical fable sums up the sad paradox of human bereavement and grief. Philosophical advice to others to show stoical courage proves useless for oneself when one is faced with the existential loss of a loved one. Time alone is a healer; but that is no consolation either. The tale of the unfortunate princess touches on the ridiculous by the sheer plethora of the disasters that befall her, while the notion that hearing such a story can comfort anyone else is comically mistaken. The exercise of pure reason is no answer to suffering.

The Story of a Good Brahmin

Brief though it is, this parable goes to the heart of a paradox fundamental to the period: how, if at all, to combine rational enquiry and happiness? Any complacent views on the matter are quickly swept away by the author. Though the pursuit of earthly happiness is one of the principles of the Enlightenment, the good Brahmin shows that there is a direct correlation between on the one hand intelligence and sensibility and on the other discontent. The only sure guarantor of happiness is imbecility. Thus the thinking person has only one path to take: dignified reason – which is itself a lunatic answer. The tale ends in an impasse.

This story was written probably in 1759, the year when 'Candide' was published, and it springs from the same view, that the world is a mad place, though the conclusions of this story are somewhat different. The Brahmin, elderly like Voltaire (and Pococurante in 'Candide'), lives a civilized life in a fine house and gardens, yet can make no sense of that life. The tale appeared in 1761: the crusading *philosophe* of the 1760s and 1770s had still to make his entry on stage.

Pot-Pourri

This is one of the strangest writings ever to come from Voltaire's pen. The classicist apostle of rational order in aesthetic matters here produces a work of discontinuity as bold as it is bewildering. Its composition over a period of years (1761–4: it was published in 1765) is of a complexity such as to require the use of diagrams for its elucidation.[13] There is no single unifying theme. The nearest approximation to that is furnished by the tale of the marionettes; and yet this stops at Chapter XI (out of fifteen chapters in all). Into this dense fabric are worked a wide range of other topics: *inter alia*, the fate of the Jesuit Order, persecution of the Protestants, the excess of religious festivals.

Not only does the structure defy easy comprehension. The basic gist of the *conte* is not immediately evident either. But Voltaire has left enough clues in his other writings for us to see that the theatre fable is a covert attack upon Jesus Christ and the Catholic Church. Punchinello, who like Christ rejoices in two quite contrary genealogies, is an illiterate whose companions are nomadic beggars. But the Church that he founded grows fat and powerful as the result of a trumped-up miracle of resurrection (Ch. VII); and religious wars follow in its wake. The meaning of this virulent assault upon Christ (the last one by Voltaire – he became more tolerant in this respect in later years) had necessarily to be concealed from the ordinary reader and made understandable only to the cognoscenti, after the manner ascribed to Rabelais in 'Conversation between Lucian, Erasmus and Rabelais'.

Was Voltaire inspired by *Tristram Shandy*? We know that he was acquainted with Sterne's novel from 1760 and owned the first six volumes up to 1762, and also that he took an interest in its bizarre structure of 'preliminaries and digressions'. Voltaire compared it suggestively to Rabelais as 'une espèce de roman bouffon' ('a kind of farcical novel'),[14] and it is possible that he saw a means by which Sterne's grotesque levity could be harnessed to an all-out assault on *l'Infâme*.

An Indian Incident

This brief piece first appeared as the final chapter of a treatise, *Le Philosophe ignorant* (1766), further proof of Voltaire's disregard for genre boundaries. The scene depicted is stark; everything devours everything else. The concluding words 'Sauve qui peut' ('Every man for himself') recur often in Voltaire's writings, consistently signalling a mood of great discouragement. From spiders to human beings, all living things appear to be caught by nature in a web of internecine destruction, while good people like Pythagoras perish. Even so, this despairing picture is painted with brio. The hero, fortunately trained in the universal language of the animal and vegetable domains, learns that to the blade of grass, the sheep is nothing less than a monster. As the cosmic vision expands to embrace ubiquitous horror, the observation by Pythagoras that these barbarous animals are no *philosophes* sounds a note of the blackest humour through its savage understatement.

Lord Chesterfield's Ears

Although Voltaire shared his countrymen's dismay at their defeat by Britain in the Seven Years War, and despite the total hostility he came to show towards Shakespeare as a corrupting influence on French theatre, he retained to the end a benevolent feeling for the land he had visited in his younger days. Even so, England serves here in this late work (published in 1775) only as a background framework. There seems to be no good reason for the title, except perhaps to stimulate curiosity in the reading public. The death in 1773 of Chesterfield, whom Voltaire had known and to whom he had written a friendly letter only two years earlier, may well have triggered his imagination, since the English lord's notorious deafness provided a springboard for the theme of fatality which is announced in the opening sentence.

Structurally, the tale quickly resolves itself into a series of dialogues on topics that deeply interested Voltaire in these final years. The problem of evil has not disappeared from his consciousness, nor will it ever. But here it is simply the stuff of which enlightened men talk around a dinner-table (Ch. V), with the paradoxical result that the very discussion brings them pleasure. Scenes at table are an important element of the narrative, as so often in Voltaire's *contes*. Such conversations testify to the capacity of true *philosophes* for deriving enjoyment from civilized and tolerant discourse that can take in every subject under the sun – unlike the 'parish curates', who are provincial enough to assume that the rest of the universe is just like Exchange Alley in London.

The debate on fatality opens out on to an appreciation of the marvellous way everything in Nature is composed. Chesterfield's surgeon Sidrac, a man of wisdom, argues that Nature is a misnomer; all things in the world have been skilfully created. But we are all, of necessity, what we are. Indeed, even God is bound by the laws of His nature. This provides a certain reassurance on the cosmic level; but it also means that we have to lead our lives in utter ignorance about our own nature, our constitution, our place in the world. Access to the great metaphysical truths is forever denied us. Wherever Sidrac looks, he finds only 'obscurity, contradiction, impossibility, ridiculousness, delusions, extravagance, chimera, absurdity, idiocy, charlatanism' (p. 99). It is not a consoling vision. Human beings are slaves to their intestines: even the most gallant of men, the most coquettish of women (Ch. VII). Henri III became constipated when a north-east wind was blowing, and woe betide anyone, like the duc de Guise, who forgot it. The golden rule is moderation in food and drink; 'and let the rest go its ways' (p. 109).

Tahiti is interwoven as a theme into this context. Both Cook and Bougainville had paid visits there in the 1760s, and they brought back tales of a different moral code, especially in sexual relations, from that followed by European Christians. Poor Dr Goodman wishes he could practise free love on the altar of sacrifice with Miss Fidler, the way the Tahitians do. In the end he wins her, though in a more furtive manner: as an adulterous man of the cloth. But this triumph is no help at all to his vocation, and the story concludes on a derisive resignation to universal fatality. Some people are just plain unlucky, as when Goodman loses his patron just when he needed him; and some are lucky, as when the same Goodman obtains his ecclesiastical living through a brutal exchange of money against married love. So goes the world. The best advice to Goodman, as to all mankind, is: get your bowels in order.

MÉLANGES

Account of the Jesuit Berthier

This is generally considered to be the best of all Voltaire's *facéties* (literally, 'witticisms': a term he applied to brief texts of a polemical nature). In it he exacts his meed of vengeance for the campaign waged by the Jesuits against the *Encyclopédie*, which had resulted in the suspension of the great Dictionary in 1759. In 'Account of the Jesuit Berthier', written as an immediate riposte to that suspension and published that year, the Jesuit menace is conjured by pure ridicule. Berthier, out delivering his *Journal de Trévoux*, succumbs to the noxious airs that this Jesuit periodical emits. Only the *Encyclopédie* might act as an antidote, but it turns out that not even that *philosophe* work can now overturn the fatal effects. Berthier is unluckily handed over to his deadly enemies the Jansenists and is only just saved in the nick of time from dying unconfessed. Thereby Voltaire delights in pouring scorn on both sects through their feuding with each other.

Berthier, a master of casuistry as befits a Jesuit, repeatedly takes refuge in hair-splitting 'distinctions' of nugatory value. While his 'love' of God is unconditional, his 'love' of his neighbour is at best a grudging concession. In the end Berthier gains absolution, but only after he has admitted to a fundamental truth: that his *Journal* is a useless bore. This act of repentance wins him a limited sentence in Purgatory (333,333 years, 3 months and 3 days: Voltaire manifestly delights in exploiting so ridiculously the sacred number three), and, too, because he finally admits to the sin of pride. Father Garassise, to whom he appears in a vision, learns that the *Journal* is harmful as well as absurd and duly renounces it. Game, set and match: the Jesuits go down to defeat through mockery.

Voltaire probably got the idea from Swift, who had in the *Bickerstaff Papers* turned the tables on one John Partridge, an almanach-maker who enjoyed predicting other people's deaths, by foretelling the latter's demise 'upon the 29th of March [1708] next'.[15] The *philosophe* begins with the same sonorous use of the date of Berthier's death. In the event, the latter was to outlive Voltaire, but the fictional death effectively despatched him as a figure of authority. This device is embellished by telling details. We know that the yawning, occasioned at first by the pure boredom emanating from the *Journal de Trévoux*, has turned fatal when Berthier's three writing fingers can no longer clutch a pen. This synecdochic device reduces Berthier to nothing more than a writing hack.

Berthier's penance in Purgatory is exquisite torture, mending Jansenist nuns' smocks and reading aloud from Pascal's hateful polemic against the Jesuits, the *Lettres provinciales*, as though it were a sacred text. As for the reverend Jesuit Fathers, Voltaire reduces them in status to mere 'brothers'. There is in this 'Account of the Jesuit Berthier' a verve of satirical invention that contrasts strongly with the brooding nature of some of the *contes*, though it is also reminiscent of Voltaire's satire of the Jesuits in 'Candide'. The fantastical embroidery of reality demolishes the egregious Berthier; the prestigious editor of the *Journal de Trévoux* is transformed into a ludicrous puppet.

Dialogue between a Savage and a Graduate

These two dialogues (published, along with the 'Dialogue between Ariste and Acrotal', in 1761) differ in tone. In the first Voltaire explodes the primitivist theories of Rousseau (who is never mentioned or even referred to). The name 'Savage' is misleading; he is just as civilized as a European, and much more so than such pseudo-intellectuals as the Graduate, who is forever asking metaphysical questions about mankind to which there can be no answer. But the Graduate does not give up easily; he invites the Savage to dinner.

This turns out to be an unhappy occasion for the latter. Made unwell by the food he has to eat, he is also made to listen to a lecture on the human soul and the external world. A farrago of self-contradictory nonsense about the pineal gland is followed by an equally absurd claim that this is the best of all possible worlds, despite the millions that have been massacred in wars or died from countless maladies, for these tribulations serve only to bring out the best in mankind. After Rousseau, it is now the turn of Descartes and Leibniz to be pilloried. The dinner is no more than a 'dialogue of the deaf' with overtones of Molière and is abruptly terminated by the Savage when he comes to see that further conversation is useless. In brief space Voltaire covers a wide range of philosophical topics: the human condition, society, law. Throughout all this the Savage unfailingly talks good sense, while his interlocutor as consistently spouts nonsense.

Dialogue between Ariste and Acrotal

If the Graduate was absurd, Acrotal (etymologically 'the high-placed') is downright pernicious. He condemns all reasoning people as a danger to the state, since they encourage others to think and to judge independently of authority. Ariste's defence of *philosophes* as peaceable individuals cuts no ice with Acrotal, who sees the spread of philosophy as a straightforward struggle for power. Whereas the doctrinaires of old enjoyed unchallenged supremacy, they are now mocked by the new generation of intellectuals. The key issue here is the appearance of the *Encyclopédie* and the right it claimed to promote independent enquiry. Voltaire captures the odiousness of an attitude that would unhesitatingly drown a Bayle, or burn a Condillac for disseminating Locke's opinions. For his part Ariste, as befits a true *philosophe*, urges an end to disputation and a concentration upon morality through its essential elements of tolerance and pity.

The Education of Daughters

Voltaire does not often dwell on female education. But here he reveals a concern for the independence of young women in their own right. Sophronie has been fortunate in her mother, who did not follow the conventional path of giving her a convent education which teaches girls absolutely nothing about the outside world. Instead she has treated her daughter as a thinking person. This brief piece (probably written in 1761: it appeared in 1765) is a prefiguration of Laclos's *De l'éducation des femmes* (1783), as too of his novel *Les Liaisons dangereuses* (1782) which graphically shows the tragic consequences of a convent upbringing for the ingenuous Cécile, who unlike Sophronie has the misfortune to be the daughter of a totally conformist and stupid mother.

Wives, Submit Yourselves to Your Husbands

We have here a further confirmation of Voltaire's sympathy for women's rights. It fits in nicely, of course, with his detestation of St Paul, and it gives him a marvellous opportunity to point out an area where Islam is more enlightened than Christianity. But Voltaire's attitude goes deeper than that. Men are not accorded superiority in any field. It is even likely that their proclaimed authority derives only from usurpation of rights through brute force. Besides, it is women who suffer the pains and miseries of childbirth and menstruation. As for male sexuality, the experienced Maréchale de Grancey dismisses it as 'of little account' (p. 138). The sexes are equal and interdependent. The Maréchale is the best sort of eighteenth-century woman. But even she was caught up until an advanced age with frivolous entertainments; such is the situation of even the well-placed female in society. Her education in no way had prepared her to be acquainted with great literature. She has had to discover it for herself.

First published in 1765, this piece reflects Voltaire's admiration for Catherine the Great, who had ascended the Russian throne in 1762.

Dialogue between the Cock and the Hen

Voltaire here shows, too, a concern for animals' rights (this work appeared in the same 1765 collection as 'Wives, Submit Yourselves to Your Husbands'). Here is a touching account of two peaceable farm-yard victims, doomed to torture and a cruel death, in order to satisfy human self-indulgence. It allows Voltaire to attack the 'madman they call Descartes', whose thesis that animals are mere machines devoid of thought is cruel as well as absurd, because it provides an excuse for such barbaric acts. In contrast to gluttonous Christians, the author evokes the image of a nobler, vegetarian civilization in India, which followed the precepts of two 'great philosophers of antiquity', Pythagoras and Porphyry (virtuous pagans, who had no need of Christian doctrines to instruct them in morality).

But these animals also serve as an allegory of mankind. Human beings too are abused for others' pleasure: the castration of young boys, or worse yet, the 'roasting' of those who hold the wrong opinions (one is reminded of the auto-da-fé in 'Candide' organized by the Portuguese Inquisition). Cannibalism also exists. In brief, enlightened philosophers are the exception amongst the murderously brutal human race.

One further layer can be seen in this short dialogue. The fate of the condemned fowls conjures up a picture of the general human condition, in which a callous God incomprehensibly inflicts suffering and death. This apprehension of an indifferently cruel deity who punishes us for reasons beyond our understanding is a leitmotif running through Voltaire's work, and suggested here with particular starkness.

Conversation between Lucian, Erasmus and Rabelais

Although this is by no means the last of Voltaire's *Mélanges* (it was published in 1766), one may suitably conclude with this dialogue, since in it the author displays his recipe for handling dangerous material. The contemporary age is just slightly better than the times of Erasmus and Rabelais, though far inferior to second-century AD Greece when Lucian was alive. Erasmus, and even more Rabelais, showed the way of enlightenment; but unlike Lucian they had to present it covertly. By playing the fool and stooping to vulgarity, Rabelais conveyed a satirical view of the fanaticism around him to those readers intellectually equipped to understand. But alas! It is still not possible to reveal the truth to the public at large. So one must be resigned to putting at least one's friends on the right path. In the process of making these points, Voltaire enjoys attributing to the dead, who are beyond the reach of persecution, his contempt for monks and priests and the whole Catholic hierarchy. The legitimate claims of the free mind can be maintained through the medium of laughter. Notwithstanding, the millennium of total enlightenment is not yet in sight.

Haydn Mason

NOTES

1. Roger Pearson, *The Fables of Reason: A Study of Voltaire's Contes philosophiques* (Oxford: Clarendon Press, 1993).
2. To the best of my knowledge, Sylvain Menant was the first to break with this narrow view in his edition: *Contes en vers et en prose*, 2 vols. (Paris: Garnier, 1992–3).
3. René Pomeau, *La Religion de Voltaire*, rev. edn. (Paris: Nizet, 1969), p. 471.
4. *Contes en vers et en prose*, ed. Menant, vol. ii, p. 385.
5. Pomeau, *Religion de Voltaire*, p. 309.
6. S. S. B. Taylor, 'Voltaire's Humour' (*Voltaire and the English*), *Studies on Voltaire and the Eighteenth Century*, 179 (1979), pp. 101–16, remains the most complete short account of Voltaire's comic devices.
7. For a full justification of this claim, see *Contes en vers et en prose*, ed. Menant, vol. i, pp. 57ff.

8. Samuel Beckett, *Waiting for Godot* (London: Faber & Faber, 1956), p. 89.

9. Lucien Febvre, *Le Problème de l'incroyance au XVIe siècle*, rev. edn. (Paris, 1962), p. 209.

10. Voltaire met Congreve while in England, and admired his comedies; see *Lettres philosophiques*, ed. Gustave Lanson, rev. André M. Rousseau, 2 vols. (Paris: Didier, 1964), vol. ii, pp. 108–9.

11. See *Questions sur l'Encyclopédie*, in *Œuvres complètes*, ed. L. Moland (Paris: Garnier, 1877–85), vol. xviii, p. 256. This remark had appeared in a 1742 essay on 'Contradictions'.

12. René Pomeau, *D'Arouet à Voltaire* (Oxford: Voltaire Foundation, 1985), p. 233.

13. A masterly account of the genesis of this story is provided by Frédéric Deloffre and Jacqueline Hellegouarc'h, in *Voltaire: Romans et contes*, ed. Deloffre and Jacques Van den Heuvel (Paris: Gallimard, 1979), pp. 894–925.

14. Ahmad Gunny, *Voltaire and English Literature*, *Studies on Voltaire and the Eighteenth Century*, 177 (Oxford: Voltaire Foundation, 1979), pp. 264–9.

15. Jonathan Swift, *Bickerstaff Papers*, ed. H. Davis (Oxford: Oxford University Press, 1939), p. 145. Voltaire refers to the hoax in two letters: D4815, 5008 (*Correspondence*, ed. Theodore Besterman, Oxford etc.: Voltaire Foundation, 1968–77).

CHRONOLOGY OF VOLTAIRE'S LIFE AND TIMES

1694   Born (probably 20 Feb., at Chatenay, near Paris) François-Marie Arouet, son of a wealthy notary.

1704–11   Educated at the prestigious Jesuit College of Louis-le-Grand, Paris.

1714–16   Active social life in Paris and at various chateaux, including that of the duchesse du Maine at Sceaux. 'Cuckoldage', 'The One-eyed Porter' and 'Cosi-Sancta' all date from this period.

1715   Louis XIV dies; country is governed by the Regent, Philippe duc d'Orléans.

1717–18   Imprisoned in Bastille for 11 months, for scurrilous writings against the Regent.

1718   Adopts name of Voltaire.

1723   Louis XV crowned King.

1726–8   Stay in England, after being obliged to leave Paris following a quarrel with the high-born chevalier de Rohan. Presented at Court of St James's. Meets Pope, Congreve, etc. Corresponds with Swift, and reads admiringly latter's *Gulliver's Travels* (1726). Discovers Newton's works.

1733   *Letters concerning the English Nation* (English version of the *Lettres philosophiques*) published in London.

1734   *Lettres philosophiques* published in France; condemned by the Paris Parlement and publicly burned. A warrant is issued for Voltaire's arrest, but he escapes imprisonment by settling at Cirey in Champagne, home of Mme du Châtelet, who had become his mistress.

1738   Sends Frederick of Prussia the 'Voyage du baron de Gangan' (now lost, but possibly a first working of 'Micromégas'). *Éléments de Newton* (1st edn.) published.

1740	Frederick of Prussia becomes Frederick II.
1745	Voltaire in favour at Louis XV's court at Versailles; appointed Royal Historiographer.
1747	'Zadig', first of Voltaire's *contes* to appear.
1749	Probable composition of 'The World As It Is'. Mme du Châtelet dies.
1750	Voltaire goes to Frederick II's court at Potsdam. 'Memnon' and 'Letter from a Turk' appear.
1751	Publication of vol. I of the *Encyclopédie*. Voltaire will contribute several articles to the early volumes.
1752	'Micromégas' appears.
1753	Voltaire leaves Potsdam after falling out with Frederick. His return to Paris is blocked by Louis XV. A period of wandering ensues.
1755	Settles at Les Délices, on the outskirts of Geneva. Lisbon earthquake (1 Nov.). Voltaire writes his *Poem* on the disaster in a matter of days.
1756	Seven Years War begins. 'Plato's Dream', 'The History of the Travels of Scarmentado', 'The Consoler and the Consoled' published; also *Essai sur les mœurs* (*Essay on the Manners and Spirit of the Nations*), Voltaire's great world history.
1757	*Encyclopédie* suspended by the government, after publication of controversial articles in vol. VII.
1759	'Account of the Jesuit Berthier', 'Candide' published. Voltaire settles at Château de Ferney, just outside Geneva.
1760–67	Sterne's *Tristram Shandy* published.
1761	'The Story of a Good Brahmin', 'Dialogue between a Savage and a Graduate', 'Dialogue between Ariste and Acrotal' published.
1762	Catherine II ascends the throne as Empress of Russia.
1762–5	Voltaire's great campaign, eventually successful, to rehabilitate the posthumous reputation of Jean Calas, Protestant merchant of Toulouse, wrongfully condemned for the murder of his son. This forms part of a general crusade against 'l'Infâme' ('the Infamous one'), i.e. the intolerance and persecution practised by the Catholic Church.

1764   *Dictionnaire philosophique* published.

1765   'Pot-Pourri', 'The Education of Daughters', 'Wives, Submit Yourselves to Your Husbands', 'Dialogue between the Cock and the Hen' published.

1766   'Conversation between Lucian, Erasmus and Rabelais' published.

1767   'L'Ingénu' ('The Naïve One'), the most important *conte* of later years, published.

1774   Louis XV dies; Louis XVI succeeds.

1775   'Lord Chesterfield's Ears' published.

1778   Voltaire leaves Ferney to visit Paris, after an absence of nearly 28 years. The return becomes a glorious triumph; but Voltaire dies there, 30 May.

FURTHER READING

EDITIONS

Frédéric Deloffre and Jacques Van den Heuvel (eds.), *Voltaire: Romans et contes* (Paris: Bibl. de la Pléiade, Gallimard, 1979). The essential work for any study in depth of the prose tales: rigorous scholarship, allied to excellent critical surveys.

Sylvain Menant (ed.), *Voltaire: Contes en vers et en prose*, 2 vols. (Paris: Garnier, 1992–3). Most complete and serviceable of present-day editions; created a precedent by including Voltaire's verse *contes* alongside the prose narratives.

Roger Pearson (trans. and ed.), *Voltaire: Candide and Other Stories* (Oxford: Oxford University Press, 1990). Excellent introduction, translated texts and notes. Limited to five of the major *contes*.

Jacques Van den Heuvel (ed.), *Voltaire: Mélanges* (Paris: Bibl. de la Pléiade, Gallimard, 1961). One of the few collections of the *Mélanges*. Editing apparatus is scholarly and sound, but limited.

STUDIES: GENERAL

René Pomeau, *La Religion de Voltaire*, rev. edn. (Paris: Nizet, 1969). The indispensable intellectual biography of our time.

René Pomeau *et al.*, *Voltaire en son temps*, 5 vols. (Oxford: Voltaire Foundation, 1985–94). Fundamental account of Voltaire's life and times.

Christiane Mervaud, *Voltaire en toutes lettres* (Paris: Bordas, 1991). Brilliantly concise survey.

Haydn Mason, *Voltaire: A Biography* (London: Granada, 1981).

Haydn Mason, *Voltaire* (London: Hutchinson, 1975). A general study of his works.

STUDIES: SPECIFIC

Jacques Van den Heuvel, *Voltaire dans ses contes* (Paris: Colin, 1967). Most thorough investigation of the subject, richly stimulating, but tends to overdo the biographical approach, and concentrates on the major *contes*.

Roger Pearson, *The Fables of Reason: A Study of Voltaire's Contes philosophiques* (Oxford: Clarendon Press, 1993). The most complete coverage, dealing with all twenty-six prose *contes* in a wholly reliable manner.

Robin Howells, *Disabled Powers: A Reading of Voltaire's Contes* (Amsterdam and Atlanta: Rodopi, 1993). An imaginatively fertile study, with reference to the Bakhtinian concept of carnival.

S. S. B. Taylor, 'Voltaire's Humour' (*Voltaire and the English*), *Studies on Voltaire and the Eighteenth Century*, 179 (1979), pp. 101–16. Remains the best succinct account of an essential aspect of Voltaire.

The classic edition of Voltaire is the *Complete Works* (Oxford: Voltaire Foundation, 1968–), with individual editions variously introduced in English and French of Voltaire's original texts.

NOTE ON THE TEXTS

The translations in this volume are based on the texts of the following editions: for the prose *contes*: *Voltaire: Romans et contes*, ed. Frédéric Deloffre and Jacques Van den Heuvel (Paris: Bibl. de la Pléiade, Gallimard, 1979); for 'Cuckoldage': *Voltaire: Contes en vers et en prose*, vol. i, ed. Sylvain Menant (Paris: Garnier, 1992–3); for the *mélanges*: *Voltaire: Mélanges*, ed. Jacques Van den Heuvel (Paris: Bibl. de la Pléiade, Gallimard, 1961).

Grateful thanks are due to Cambridge University Press for permission to reprint 'Dialogue between the Cock and the Hen', translated by Haydn and Adrienne Mason, from *Comparative Criticism*, 20 (1998), copyright Cambridge University Press.

TRANSLATOR'S NOTE

The *allegro con brio* of Voltaire's style is his great achievement. There are dark shadows in the miniature world of these fictions, but at the level of language all is rapidity, transparency, felicity. Put simply, Voltaire's prose may engage with the worst of worlds, but it lives in the best of times. This is what Roland Barthes meant when he described the embattled Voltaire as paradoxically the 'last happy writer', basking in the high noon of expression.

There are many reefs here for the modern translator. First, it has been remarked that the *contes* ('Candide' above all) are written in such a way that the reader has to perform them mentally at a given speed; the translator can only attempt to keep up with the vehicle and its abrupt changes of direction. Secondly, Voltaire's register is chaste, his vocabulary unexceptional, often ironically formulaic – unresonating, unfigurative, functional. It tempts the translator to introduce more specificity – to replace a simple verb with a more interesting verb, a small word with a big word, a colourless epithet with a colourful one. Thirdly, it is a style at once pared down yet full of apparent redundancy: intensifiers which do not intensify, qualifiers which fail to qualify. All of which is essential to Voltaire's foreshortening, to the laconic comedy of his story-telling, its imponderably cool textures, its dozing horrors. The compression is above all syntactical, determined by Voltaire's sentences. It seems equally mistaken for a translator to break these up or run them together. They are rooms, interconnecting via an expressive and rhythmic use of punctuation. Voltaire's paragraphs are chain reactions.

The overall temptation is to render Voltaire's anarchic comedy as merely arch, whereas its elegance is mordant. An unfailingly fluent translation, taking the usual liberties (described above), amounts to a retelling – and it is easy to slip into bowdlerizing Voltaire. His neutrality is deceptive; the prose is abrupt, atavistic, urbane – what it is not is fluent, euphuistic, bland. The danger lies in producing a fat version of a thin work; the tendency of English with its synonyms and its genius for variation is to make Voltaire's words put on weight. Like Mozart, Voltaire composed on a five-octave keyboard, not a concert grand.

I should like to thank Haydn Mason for his many suggestions in helping this translation to lose some weight and gain some precision.

CONTES

Cuckoldage

In times past Jove, jealous of his wife by whose sport he was made a father, brought forth a daughter from his own head, saying: 'Well at least this one is mine.' The good Vulcan likewise, obliged for his pains by the Olympian court to marry Venus, also wished for a little baby of whom he could be sure he alone was the father: for it was beyond him to believe that the lovely Cupid, and the little cupids, those ornaments of Cythera,[1] who, though children, can teach the arts of pleasing, were the offspring of a simple blacksmith like himself. He filled the house with his din; cares and sorrows racked his spirit, jealous suspicions hammered at his brain. A score of times a day he reproached his spouse for her superabundant charms, a dangerous asset. Poor Vulcan made such a commotion that his brain gave birth – to what? to Cuckoldage. This is the god adored in Paris, this the baleful deity, the scourge of husbands. The moment he was born he tried out his infant wrath on his father's head. His novice hands stamped the paternal brow with the first sign of horns,[2] the eternal insult. Hardly had this fledgling's feathers appeared than he made divine war on the gentle Hymen.[3] He could be seen, importuning that god in every place, seizing his possessions before his eyes, going from one household to the next, sometimes bearing flames and destruction, with firebrands in hand lighting up his spoils for all to see; at other times creeping in silent shadow, brow veiled in innocence, the sly one within a husband's home, turning a trick without scandal or sound. Jealousy, with pale and livid flush, and Malice, with false and perfidious gaze, guide his steps to where love leads on, followed uncaringly by Sensuality. His quivers are filled with various shafts, for the conquest of both husbands and their fair wives; arrows are there to pierce reluctant ladies' hearts, horns are there for husbands' brows. Now, a god like this, malicious or not, fully merits that his offices be sung; and, whether from necessity or prudence, we must offer him our devotions, our incense and our candles. Married or unmarried, whether one acts or lives in fear, one must ever court his favours. O Iris,[4] whom I shall always love, when you were still in command of your own wishes, ere a contract upon your affections had yet enslaved your bright days, I invoked only the god of love: but now that Hymen, father of sadness, has placed you beneath his rule, to Cuckoldage must I now turn: he is the only god in whom I can believe.

The One-eyed Porter

Having two eyes does not improve our lot; the one serves to show us the good things in life, the other its evils. Many people have the regrettable habit of closing the first, and too few close the second; which is why there are so many who would prefer to be blind than to see what they do see. Happy the one-eyed, who are deprived only of this bad eye which spoils everything it looks upon! Take Mesrour as an example.

One would have had to be blind not to see that Mesrour was one-eyed. He was thus from birth; but here was a one-eyed man so content with his lot that he had never taken it into his head to wish for a second eye. Nor was it the gifts of fortune that consoled him for the wrongs of nature, for he was a simple porter with no worldly goods except for his strong shoulders; but he was happy, and was proof that more eyes and fewer cares contribute rather little to happiness. Money and appetite always arrived together, in proportion to his exertions; he worked in the mornings, ate and drank in the evenings, slept at night, and looked upon all his days as so many separate lifetimes, so that thoughts of the future never troubled his enjoyment of the present. As you can see, he was at the same time one-eyed, a porter, and a philosopher.

When he chanced one day to see a great princess passing in a brilliant carriage, with one eye more than his, this did not prevent him from finding her very beautiful, and, since the one-eyed differ from other men only in having one eye the less, he fell frantically in love with her. It will perhaps be said that a porter with one eye should at all costs avoid falling in love, particularly with a great princess, and most particularly, a princess with two eyes: I admit there is something to be feared here from not pleasing; however, since there is no love without hope, and our porter was in love, he hoped.

Since he had more legs than eyes, and good ones at that, he kept up with the carriage of his goddess for a distance of four leagues, drawn though it was at a rapid pace by six large white horses. The fashion in those days, among the ladies, was to travel around without lackeys, or coachmen, and to drive oneself: husbands preferred wives to be at all times alone, so as to be more certain of their virtue; which goes directly counter to the view of moralists, who say there is no virtue in solitude.

Mesrour was still running alongside the wheels of the carriage, keeping his good eye on the side of the lady, who was astonished to see a one-eyed man of such agility. While he was proving in this way how indefatigable we are in the service of love, a wild beast pursued by hunters ran across the highway and startled the horses, who, with the bit between their teeth, were now pulling the beauty over a precipice. Her new admirer, more fearful even than herself, though she was very fearful too, uncoupled the traces with admirable dexterity; the six white horses made the perilous leap alone, and the lady, who was no less white, escaped with nothing worse than a scare.

'Whoever you are,' said she, 'I shall never forget that I owe my life to you; ask of me what you will: all I have is yours.'

'Ah, Madame,' said Mesrour, 'I could with much more reason offer you the same; but to offer this, I would be offering you far less: I have but one eye, and you have two; though one eye which looks at you is worth two that cannot see yours.'

The lady smiled: for the gallantries of a one-eyed man are gallantries nevertheless, and gallantries always make a lady smile.

'Would I were able to offer you another eye, but only your mother could have made you such a present; follow me nonetheless.'

So saying she descended from her carriage and continued on foot; her little dog descended too and walked beside her, barking at her strangely visaged equerry. I am wrong to give him the title of equerry, for try as he might to offer his arm, the lady would not accept, on the grounds that he was too dirty; and as we shall see, she was the dupe of her own scruples. She had tiny feet, and her shoes were even tinier than her feet, with the result that she was neither shaped nor shod for a long march.

Pretty feet are a consolation for indifferent legs, when one spends one's days on a chaise longue amidst a crowd of fops; but of what use on a stony path are shoes embroidered with sequins, where they can be admired only by a porter, and a one-eyed porter at that?

Mélinade (the name of the lady, which I had my reasons for withholding, not having thought of it until now) made such progress as she could, cursing her shoemaker, tearing her shoes, grazing her feet, spraining herself at every step. She had been walking for about an hour and a half, at a pace befitting a fine lady, which is to say she had covered about a quarter of a league, when she dropped to the ground exhausted.

Mesrour, whose assistance she had refused while upright, debated whether to offer it now, fearful of dirtying her by his touch; for he was well aware that he was not clean, the lady having given him to understand this quite unequivocally, and the comparisons he had been making along the road between himself and his mistress made him see it even more clearly. She was wearing a silver dress of light fabric, sprinkled with garlands of flowers, which allowed the beauty of her figure to blaze forth; he was wearing a brown smock stained in a hundred places, patched and holed in such fashion that the patches were beside the holes, rather than above them, where they would have been more to the point. He had likewise been comparing his hands, sinewy and callused, with her two tiny hands whiter and more delicate than the lily. Finally, he had seen the beautiful blond hair of Mélinade, which showed through a light gauze veil, some of it held up in tresses and the rest in curls and loops; whereas he sported a black bristling frizzy mane, with only a torn turban for ornament.

Meanwhile Mélinade was trying to get up, but she soon fell back again, and in so revealing a posture as to drive from Mesrour's head what little sense the sight of her face had left him with in the first place. He forgot that he was a porter, that he was one-eyed; he no longer reflected on the distance fate had set between himself and Mélinade; he scarcely remembered that he was a lover, for he lacked that delicacy which is said to be inseparable from true love, and which sometimes constitutes its charm but more frequently its tedium; he made use of the advantages which his condition of porter gave him in the way of brutality; he acted brutally, and was satisfied. At this point the princess no doubt fainted, or else bemoaned her fate; but since she was a just princess, she surely blessed the gods for such consolations as attend all misfortune.

Night had cast its veils over the horizon, and hid in darkness the true fortunes of Mesrour and the apparent misfortunes of Mélinade; Mesrour tasted the joys of consummate lovers, and he tasted them as a porter, which is to say (to humanity's shame) consummately; the faintness of Mélinade returned at each instant, and at each instant her lover's powers returned. 'All-Powerful Mohammed,' he said at one point, as a man transported (but a very poor Catholic), 'all that is lacking to complete my felicity is for it to be shared by her who is its cause. While I am in your paradise, divine prophet, grant me one more favour, which is to appear in Mélinade's eyes as she would appear to my one eye were it now daylight.' He finished praying, and continued enjoying. Aurora, always too diligent as far as lovers are concerned, surprised Mesrour and Mélinade in the position in which she herself might have been surprised with Tithonus[1] a moment earlier. But imagine the astonishment of Mélinade when, opening her eyes to the first rays of daylight, she found herself in an enchanted spot with a young man of noble bearing, whose face resembled the day star for whose return the earth was just now preparing! He had rosy cheeks, and lips of coral; his large eyes, at once tender and piercing, expressed and inspired voluptuousness; a golden quiver, encrusted with precious stones, hung from his shoulders, and pleasure alone made his arrows jingle; his long hair, held back by a diamond fastener, streamed down to his waist, and a transparent gauze, embroidered with pearls, served for clothing and hid nothing of the beauty of his body.

'Where am I, and who are you?' cried out Mélinade in the first flush of surprise.

'You are with the wretch who had the good fortune to save your life, and who has been so well rewarded for his troubles.'

Mélinade, as pleased as she was astonished, regretted only that the metamorphosis of Mesrour had not commenced earlier. She now walked up to a shining palace which dazzled her sight, and read this inscription upon the doors: 'Withdraw, all ye profaners; these gates shall open only for the master of the ring.' Mesrour in turn approached and read the same inscription, but the characters he saw were different, for he read these words: 'Knock without fear.' He knocked, and immediately the doors opened thunderously by themselves. The lovers entered a vestibule of Parian marble, to the accompaniment of a thousand voices and a thousand instruments; from whence they passed into a superb hall, where a delicious feast had been awaiting them for twelve hundred and fifty years without any of the dishes going cold: they sat down to eat, and were each waited on by a thousand slaves of the finest beauty; the meal was punctuated with music and dancing; and when it was finished, all the genies arrived in strictest order, divided into different groups, wearing costumes as magnificent as they were extraordinary, to take an oath of allegiance to the master of the ring, and to kiss the sacred finger that wore it.

Meanwhile back in Baghdad there lived a very devout Muslim who, unable to go and wash in the mosque, used to have the sacred water brought to his house in return for a small consideration paid to the priest. He had just finished his fifth ablution, in preparation for the fifth prayer; his servant, a far from devout young scatterbrain, got rid of the water by throwing it out of the window. It fell on to an unfortunate wretch propped sound asleep against a milestone. He woke up drenched. It was poor Mesrour, who, returning from his enchanted sojourn, had left behind the ring of Solomon in the course of his travels. He had also left behind his magnificent garments, and resumed his smock; his beautiful golden quiver was changed into a wooden porter's hook, and, to crown his misfortunes, he had left the other eye behind. He now remembered that the night before he had drunk a large quantity of *eau de vie*, which had lulled his senses and fired his imagination. Having hitherto enjoyed a taste for this liquor, he now began to entertain an admiring gratitude for it, and returned gaily to work, firmly resolved to use his wages to acquire the means of meeting up again with his precious Mélinade. Another man would have lamented his one wretched eye after having experienced so fine a pair, or have felt the rebuffs of the palace sweepers after having enjoyed the favours of a princess more beautiful than the mistresses of the Caliph; or have resented being at the beck and call of every Baghdad householder after having reigned over the legions of genies – but then Mesrour lacked the eye which looks on the bad side of things.

Cosi-Sancta

A Small Ill for a Greater Good
An African Tale

It is a falsehood universally acknowledged, that we may not commit a small ill in order to secure a greater good. St Augustine was entirely of this opinion, as may be seen from this account of a little episode which occurred in his diocese during the proconsulate of Septimus Acindynus, and described in *The City of God*.[1]

At Hippo[2] there lived an old parish priest, a great promulgator of brotherhoods and confessor to all the young girls of the neighbourhood, and with the reputation of being inspired by God because he dabbled in fortune-telling, an occupation in which he did quite well.

One day they brought him a young girl named Cosi-Sancta, the most beautiful in the whole province. Her father and mother were Jansenists,[3] who had raised her in the strictest virtue; not one of all her suitors had been able to cause her a moment's distraction from her prayers. She had been betrothed a few days earlier to a wizened old creature named Capito, an adviser to the minor appeals court of Hippo. He was a peevish surly little man, not without wit but stiff in conversation, sneering and much given to hoaxes – jealous moreover as a Venetian,[4] whom nothing in the world could induce to be on terms with his future wife's admirers. The poor young creature was doing all she could to love him, because he was to be her husband; she was trying with the best will in the world, but with little success.

She went to consult the parish priest to discover whether her marriage would be happy. The old fellow told her in prophetic tones: 'Daughter, your virtue will cause many misfortunes, but one day you will be canonized for being three times unfaithful to your husband.'

This oracle astounded and cruelly embarrassed the innocent and beautiful girl. She wept; she asked for an explanation, thinking that these words concealed some mystical sense; but the only explanation

11

forthcoming was that the three times were not to be taken to mean three rendezvous with the same lover, but three separate adventures.

Cosi-Sancta protested vehemently; she even directed some imprecations at the priest, and vowed she would never be made a saint. But she was, as we shall see.

Soon afterwards she was married; the wedding was thoroughly romantic; she successfully endured the unpleasant speeches she had to listen to, the insipid innuendoes and ill-disguised vulgarities by which the modesty of young brides is commonly affronted. She danced graciously with a succession of very handsome and well-built young men, but who displayed the worst possible grace in her husband's opinion.

She went to bed beside little Capito with a certain repugnance, spent the greater part of the night asleep and woke up in a rather dreamy state. Her husband was less the subject of her reflections, however, than a young fellow named Ribaldos, who had occupied her mind without her knowing it. This young man seemed moulded by the hands of Love; he had all the requisite charms, audacity and knavishness; he was somewhat indiscreet, but only in the company of those who wished him well, and he was the darling of Hippo. He had set all the women of the town against each other, and all the husbands and mothers against himself. He usually fell in love without thinking, or just out of vanity; but he was in love with Cosi-Sancta by inclination, and he loved her all the more desperately because in this case the conquest was so fraught.

Being a resourceful man, he attempted first to make himself agreeable to the husband, to whom he made a thousand overtures, praising his looks, his easy and gallant wit, losing money to him at cards, and every day finding some little personal confidence or other to share with Capito. Cosi-Sancta thought him the most charming young man. She was already more in love with him than she realized; she did not suspect this, but her husband suspected it for her. Although he had all the vanity of a little man, he did not fail to suspect that Ribaldos's visits were not being paid to him alone. So he found some pretext for a quarrel and forbade Ribaldos the house.

Cosi-Sancta was very vexed by this but dared not say so; and

Ribaldos, rendered more amorous still by these difficulties, spent all his time on the look-out for opportunities to see her. He disguised himself as a monk, as a female pedlar, as a Punch and Judy showman; but not enough to conquer his mistress, and too much not to be recognized by her husband. Had Cosi-Sancta been in league with her lover they would have taken enough precautions for the husband not to suspect a thing; but since she struggled against her inclinations and had nothing to reproach herself with, she saved everything except appearances, and her husband believed the worst of her.

The little fellow, who was given to fits of rage and imagined that his honour depended on his wife's fidelity, insulted her cruelly and punished her for being thought beautiful. She found herself in the most unpleasant situation available to a woman: unjustly accused, maltreated by a husband to whom she was faithful, and racked by a violent passion which she was trying nonetheless to overcome.

She thought that if her lover ceased his pursuit her husband might cease his injustices, and she would be tranquil enough to cure herself of a passion which had nothing further to feed upon. With this in mind, she ventured to write the following letter to Ribaldos:

'If you have any virtuous feelings, desist from making me unhappy: you love me, and your love exposes me to the suspicions and violence of a master to whom I have given myself for the remainder of my life. Would to heaven that this were the only risk I have to run! Pity me and cease your pursuit; I beg you by the love which has created your unhappiness and mine, and which can never bring you happiness.'

Poor Cosi-Sancta had not foreseen that a missive so tender, while at the same time so virtuous, would have an effect exactly contrary to what she hoped for. It inflamed her lover's heart yet further, and he resolved to risk his life to see his mistress.

Capito, who was fool enough to want to know everything, and who had good spies, was tipped off that Ribaldos had disguised himself as a Carmelite friar mendicant come to beg alms of his wife. He now thought himself lost, knowing that a friar's habit is more dangerous than any other to the honour of a husband. He posted his servants to give Brother Ribaldos a thrashing, and in the event was served only too well. When the young man entered the house he was greeted by these gentlemen; in spite of his cries that he was an honest Carmelite and that this was no way to treat poor monks, he was beaten and died a fortnight later from a blow to the head. All the women of the town mourned him; Cosi-Sancta was inconsolable; even Capito was contrite, though for different reasons, since he now found himself with a very unpleasant affair on his hands.

Ribaldos had been a relative of the proconsul Acindynus. This Roman decided to inflict an exemplary punishment for the assassination; and, since he had quarrelled more than once with the appeals court of Hippo, he was not displeased to be in a position to hang one of their number, and decidedly pleased that the punishment should fall upon Capito, who was by far the vainest and most intolerable popinjay of a judge in the province.

So Cosi-Sancta had seen her lover murdered and was about to see her husband hanged, and all because she had remained virtuous; for, as I have said already, had she granted her favours to Ribaldos, the husband would have been far more effectively deceived.

Thus the first part of the priest's prediction was accomplished. Cosi-Sancta now remembered the oracle, and greatly feared she might have to accomplish the rest of it. But, reflecting that no one can escape their destiny, she abandoned herself to Providence, which wound her to its ends by the most honest means possible.

The proconsul Acindynus was a man more debauched than voluptuous, with little time for preliminaries, brutal, over-familiar, a real garrison hero, greatly feared in the province, and with whom all the wives in Hippo had had dealings solely to avoid crossing him.

He sent for Madame Cosi-Sancta: she arrived in tears, which made her seem all the more charming. 'Your husband, madam,' said he, 'is to be hanged, and it's down to you to save him.' 'I would give my life for his,' said the lady. 'That is not what is required of you,' replied the proconsul. 'Then what must I do?' said she. 'I want just one night with you,' replied the proconsul. 'But my nights are not mine to give,' said Cosi-Sancta, 'they belong to my husband. I would give my blood to save him, but not my honour.' 'But suppose your husband consents?' said the proconsul. 'He is my master,' replied the lady, 'and one does as one pleases with one's property. But I know my husband, and he will never consent; he is a stubborn little man, quite capable of letting himself hang rather than let anyone else touch me with the tip of their finger.' 'We shall see about that,' said the judge in a rage.

He had the criminal brought before him immediately: he offered him the choice of being hanged or cuckolded: there was little room for debate. Even so, the little fellow needed a lot of persuading. At last he did what anyone else would have done in his place. His wife charitably saved his life; and this was the first of three.

The same day her son fell ill with a very rare malady unknown to all the doctors of Hippo. There was only one doctor who knew the cure, but he lived in Aquila, several leagues from Hippo. At that time it was forbidden for a doctor established in one town to exercise his profession in another. Cosi-Sancta was herself obliged to go to Aquila with her brother, whom she loved tenderly. On the road they were held up by brigands. The leader of these gentlemen found her very pretty; and, since they were about to kill her brother, he went up to her and suggested that were she to be a little accommodating her brother would be spared, and it would cost her nothing into the bargain. The case was urgent: she had just saved the life of a husband for whom she had little love; she was about to lose a brother whom she loved a great deal; moreover the dangerous condition of her child alarmed her; there was not a moment to lose. She commended herself to God and did all that was required of her; and this was the second of three.

She reached Aquila the same day and alighted at the doctor's house. He was one of those fashionable doctors who are sent for by women who have the vapours, or who have nothing at all. He was the lover of some and the confidant of others; a polite, obliging gentleman, rather out of favour with the Faculty of Medicine, about whom he had been known to make very good jokes.

Cosi-Sancta explained her child's illness and offered a whole sestertium. (You will note that a whole sestertium was worth well over a thousand écus in today's money.) 'It is not in such currency, Madame,' said the gallant doctor, 'that I prefer to be paid. I would for my part offer you all I am worth, were it to your taste to be remunerated for the cures which you alone can effect; only cure me of the malady you have caused, and I shall restore your child to health.'

The lady thought the proposition bizarre; but fate had by now accustomed her to strange things. The doctor was an obstinate gentleman who would take no other price for his services. Cosi-Sancta had no husband at hand to consult; and how could she allow the child she adored to die for lack of the trivial assistance that was hers to give! She was as good a mother as she was a sister. She purchased the cure at the asking price; and this was the last of three.

She returned to Hippo with her brother, who kept thanking her, along the way, for the courage with which she had saved his life.

Thus, Cosi-Sancta through being too virtuous caused her lover to be murdered and her husband condemned to death; and, by being accommodating, saved the lives of brother, son and husband. It was widely considered that such a woman was essential to any family. After her death she was made a saint, because by mortifying herself she had done so much for her nearest and dearest, who had the following motto carved on her tombstone: 'A Small Ill For A Greater Good.'

Micromégas

A Philosophical Story

CHAPTER I

Voyage of an inhabitant of the star Sirius
to the planet Saturn

On one of those planets which orbit the star named Sirius there lived
a young man of great intelligence, whom I had the honour of meeting
during the last visit he made to our little ant hill; he was called
Micromégas, a most suitable name for any man of parts. He was eight
leagues tall: by which I mean twenty-four thousand geometrical paces,
each measuring five feet.

A number of the algebraists, people ever useful to the public,
will now reach for their pens and discover that, since Monsieur
Micromégas, inhabitant of the land of Sirius, measures twenty-four
thousand paces from tip to toe (the equivalent of one hundred and
twenty thousand royal feet), and since we on Earth measure scarcely
five feet and our globe is nine thousand leagues in circumference, they
will find, as I say, that the globe which fostered him must be exactly
twenty-one million, six hundred thousand times greater in circumference than our little Earth.[1] Nothing in nature could be simpler or
more straightforward. To compare the territories of certain German
or Italian sovereigns – which may be toured in half an hour – with
the Turkish or Muscovite or Chinese empires, would be to give but a
feeble idea of the prodigious differences which nature has contrived
between all her creatures.

His Excellency's height being as I have stated, our sculptors and
painters will all readily agree that his waist probably measures fifty
thousand royal feet; which makes for very handsome proportions.

As to his mind, it was among the most cultivated in existence; he knew a great number of things, some of which he worked out for himself: while not yet two hundred and fifty years of age and still a pupil at the Jesuit college of his planet (as was the custom), he independently solved more than fifty of Euclid's Problems. Which is eighteen more than Blaise Pascal, who solved thirty-two of them for his own amusement (or so his sister says), only to develop into a fairly average geometer and a very poor metaphysician.[2] By the age of four hundred and fifty, as childhood was drawing to a close, Micromégas was busy dissecting quantities of those tiny insects which are scarcely a hundred feet in diameter and invisible under ordinary Sirian microscopes. He wrote a most original work on the subject, which nonetheless landed him in trouble. The local Mufti,[3] a celebrated pedant and ignoramus, found some of the arguments in this book to be suspect, offensive, reckless, and unorthodox to the point of heresy. He proceeded against it vigorously. The case turned on whether the substantial form of the fleas on Sirius was of the same nature as that of the snails. Micromégas mounted a spirited defence; he won over all the ladies; the trial lasted two hundred and twenty years. At last the Mufti had the book condemned by jurists who had not opened it, and the author was ordered not to show his face at court for the next eight hundred years.

He was only moderately grieved to be banished from a court so full of squabbling and petty intrigue. He wrote a very amusing song about the Mufti, who was not especially bothered; after which he set out on a voyage from planet to planet to complete his education 'in heart and mind', as the saying goes. Those who travel only by post-chaise or berlin coach will no doubt be amazed at the methods of transport in the world above: down here on our little mud-heap[4] we have no conception of customs other than our own.

Our traveller was wonderfully acquainted with the laws of gravity and with all the forces of attraction and repulsion.[5] These he put to such use that, sometimes with the aid of a sunbeam, at other times through the convenient offices of a comet, he and his retinue went from one globe to the next as a bird hops from branch to branch. He travelled the length of the Milky Way in no time at all, though I am bound to record that not once on his way past the stars with which it is strewn did he glimpse the lovely empyreal heaven which the celebrated Reverend Derham[6] boasts of having seen at the end of his telescope. I do not suggest that the Reverend Derham has poor eyes, Heaven forbid! But Micromégas was there in person, is a good observer, and . . . I have no wish to contradict anyone.

After a lengthy tour, Micromégas arrived on Saturn. Though accustomed to novelties, on seeing the smallness of this globe and its inhabitants he could not at first suppress that smile of superiority which even the wisest of us is occasionally guilty of. Saturn is after all barely nine hundred times the size of the Earth, and its citizens are dwarfs a mere thousand fathoms or so tall. At first he and his retinue amused themselves a little at the expense of their hosts, just as an Italian musician arriving in France invariably laughs at Lully's compositions.[7] However, as the Sirian was not stupid he soon came to appreciate that a thinking being may be far from ridiculous even if he is only six thousand feet tall. He became well acquainted with the Saturnians, after their initial surprise had worn off. He formed a close friendship with the Secretary of the Academy of Saturn,[8] a most intelligent fellow who had not, it is true, made any discoveries of his own, but who could give a very good account of the discoveries of others and was moderately adept at both light verse and heavy computations. I shall here record, for the satisfaction of readers, a singular conversation which Micromégas had one day with Monsieur Secretary.

CHAPTER II

Conversation between the inhabitants of Sirius and Saturn

After His Excellency had gone to bed, and the Secretary had drawn close to his face, the former began:

'One has to admit', he said, 'that nature is full of variety.'

'Why yes,' said the Saturnian, 'nature is like a flower-bed whose blooms –'

'No,' said the other, 'let's not go into your flower-beds.'

'Nature', resumed the Secretary, 'is an assembly of blondes and brunettes, whose costumes –'

'What do I care for your brunettes?' said the other.

'Well, then, nature is like a portrait gallery whose individual features –'

'No!' said the visitor. 'Once and for all, nature is like nature. Why search for comparisons?'

'To please you,' answered the Secretary.

'I don't want to be pleased,' the visitor replied, 'I want to be instructed.[9] You can begin by telling me how many senses the inhabitants of your globe possess.'

'We have seventy-two,' said the Academician; 'and every day we complain at having so few. Our imaginations surpass our needs; with our seventy-two senses, our ring of Saturn and our five moons,[10] we feel too circumscribed; despite all our curiosity, and the profusion of passions arising from our seventy-two senses, we have all the time in the world to be bored.'

'I can well believe it,' said Micromégas. 'We on our globe possess nearly a thousand senses, yet there remains in us some vague unease, some nameless longing[11] which ceaselessly reminds us that we are of little consequence, and that there are beings who enjoy a more perfect state. I have travelled a little. I have seen mortals who are far inferior to us; I have seen others far superior, but I have never seen any who did not have more desires than real needs, and more needs than means to satisfy them. Some day perhaps I shall find the land where nothing is lacking; but so far no one has given me positive news of such a place.'

The Saturnian and the Sirian went on to exhaust themselves in conjecture; but after much ingenious and unsettled argument they were forced to return to facts.

'How long do you live for?' asked the Sirian.

'Ah! All too short a time,' replied the little man from Saturn.

'Just as with us,' said the Sirian. 'We are always lamenting the brevity of life. It must be a universal law of nature.'

'Alas,' said the Saturnian, 'we live for only five hundred entire revolutions of the sun.' (The equivalent, by human reckoning, of fifteen thousand years or thereabouts.) 'Which, as you can see, is to die almost the moment one is born; our existence is a point in time, our span is but an instant, our globe a mere atom. No sooner do we begin to educate ourselves a little than death arrives before we have any experience of life. For myself I do not dare to make plans; I feel like a drop of water in an immense ocean. I am ashamed, particularly in front of you, of the ridiculous figure I cut in this world.'

'Were you not a philosopher,' Micromégas answered, 'I should be afraid of distressing you with the news that our life span is seven hundred times greater than yours; but as you know too well, when the moment comes to return our body to the elements and reanimate nature under another form – what is called dying – when that moment of metamorphosis arrives, to have lived for an eternity or for a single day amounts to precisely the same. I have been in places where they live a thousand times longer than we do, and found that still they grumbled. Yet everywhere there are to be found people of sense, who accept their lot and give thanks to the author of nature. He has distributed through this universe a wealth of varieties with a kind of admirable uniformity. All thinking beings differ, for example, but all are fundamentally alike in sharing the gift of thought and of possessing desires. Matter everywhere has extension, but on each globe it has different properties. On Saturn how many such properties do you recognize in matter?'

'If you mean', replied the Saturnian, 'properties without which we believe this globe could not exist in its present form, then we count three hundred: extension, impenetrability, mobility, gravity, divisibility, and so forth.'

'No doubt so small a number suffices for the ends the Creator had in mind for your little dwelling,' replied the visitor. 'I marvel at His wisdom in all things; everywhere I see difference, but also everywhere proportion. Your globe is small, so too are its inhabitants; you have few sensations; your matter has few properties – all this is the work of Providence. Of what colour is your sun, examined closely?'

'White, tending strongly to yellow,' said the Saturnian. 'And when we separate out one of its rays, we find it to contain seven colours.'[12]

'Ours tends towards red,' said the Sirian, 'and we have thirty-nine primary colours. Of all the suns I have approached not one resembles another, just as on your planet each and every face differs from all the others.'

After several questions of this nature, the Sirian asked how many essentially distinct substances were recognized on Saturn. He learnt that only thirty or so had been identified, such as God, space, matter, beings with extension that are sentient, beings with extension that are sentient and cognizant, beings with cognition but without extension, those which interpenetrate, those which do not interpenetrate, and so forth. The philosopher from Saturn was in turn prodigiously astonished to hear that the Sirian came from a world which recognized three hundred substances, and that he had discovered for himself a further three thousand in the course of his travels. Finally, after acquainting each other with a little of what they knew and a lot of what they did not, and having passed in discussion an entire revolution of the sun, they resolved to make a little philosophical voyage together.

CHAPTER III

The voyage of two inhabitants of Sirius and Saturn

Our two philosophers were ready to launch themselves into the atmosphere of Saturn, with a fine array of mathematical instruments, when the Saturnian's mistress heard the news and arrived in tears to make her reproaches. She was a pretty little brunette, barely six hundred and sixty fathoms tall, but whose many charms made up for her tiny stature.

'Ah, cruel man!' she cried out. 'After resisting you for fifteen hundred years, when at last I was beginning to yield, when I have spent barely two hundred years in your arms, now you leave me to go off on your travels with a giant from another world. Away with you! It was just idle curiosity, you never truly loved me; were you a true

Saturnian you would stay by my side. Where are you going? What are you after? Our five moons are less fickle, our ring of Saturn less changeable than you are. Well, what's done is done, I shall never love another.'

The philosopher embraced her and wept in turn, for all that he was a philosopher; and the lady, having swooned, took her leave and found consolation in the arms of a local dandy.

Meanwhile our two seekers after knowledge departed. They began by leaping on to the ring of Saturn, which they found to be rather flat, as has been independently deduced by an illustrious inhabitant of our own little globe;[13] from here they went without difficulty from moon to moon. A comet happened to be passing close by the last of these, so they leapt on board complete with servants and instruments. After being carried approximately a hundred and fifty million leagues they arrived at the satellites of Jupiter. They continued on to Jupiter itself, where they tarried for a year, during which time they discovered a number of wonderful secrets, which would now be at the printer's were it not that the gentlemen of the Inquisition found some of their propositions a little hard to swallow. I have nevertheless consulted the manuscript of these discoveries in the library of the illustrious Bishop of ——, who, with a kindness and generosity I cannot sufficiently praise, has allowed me to consult his collection.

But let us return to our travellers. After leaving Jupiter they crossed a distance of approximately one hundred million leagues, passing close by the planet Mars, which, as we know, is five times smaller than our little globe; they observed two moons which serve that planet and which have escaped the attention of our astronomers. I am aware that Father Castel[14] will now write (entertainingly, even) against the existence of these two moons; but I take my stand with those who reason by analogy. The good philosophers of that school know how difficult it would be for Mars, so far from the sun, to make do with any less than two moons. Whatever the facts of the case, our friends thought Mars so small that, fearing they would not find room to lay their heads, they continued on their way: like two travellers who scorn a miserable village inn and press on to the next town. But the Sirian and his companion were soon to regret their decision. They carried on for a long time and found nothing. At last they made out a small gleam of light: it was the Earth. A pitiable sight, for people coming from Jupiter. However, fearing they should have cause to repent a second time, they resolved to disembark. They moved along the tail of the comet and, finding an aurora borealis ready and waiting, boarded it and landed on Earth, on the northern shore of the Baltic Sea, on the fifth day of July in the year seventeen hundred and thirty-seven, new style.[15]

CHAPTER IV

What happened to them on planet Earth

After resting for a while, they breakfasted off two mountains, which their servants had prepared for them moderately well. Now they were ready to explore the diminutive place in which they found themselves. First they went from north to south. The average step of the Sirian and his retinue covered about thirty thousand royal feet; the dwarf from Saturn lagged far behind, panting, for he had to take about twelve steps to each of the other's strides: picture to yourself (if the comparison be allowed) a tiny lapdog following a captain in the King of Prussia's guards.

Since these particular visitors move fairly quickly, they had circled the globe within thirty-six hours. It is of course true that the sun, or rather the Earth, makes the same journey in a single day; but you must remember that better progress is made turning on an axis than marching on foot. Here they were, then, back where they started, having seen that pond called the 'Mediterranean' (almost imperceptible to them) and that other pond by the name of the 'Great Ocean', which surrounds our molehill. At no point had the water reached above the dwarf's knee, and his companion scarcely got his heels wet. On their way there and on their way back they had tried their utmost to discover whether this globe was inhabited or not. They stooped, they lay down, they groped in every corner; but, their eyes and hands being out of all proportion to the little creatures crawling about here, they received not the slightest impression which might lead them to suspect that we and our fellow-beings inhabiting this globe have the honour to exist.

The dwarf, who was sometimes a little rash in his judgements, concluded at first that there was no one on Earth. His primary reason was that he had seen no one. Micromégas politely pointed out that this was rather a poor way of reasoning.

'For', said he, 'you with your little eyes cannot see certain stars of the fiftieth magnitude which I can make out quite clearly; do you conclude from this that such stars do not exist?'

'But', said the dwarf, 'I have had a good feel around the whole place.'

'But', replied the other, 'you may have a poor sense of touch.'

'But', said the dwarf, 'look how badly constructed, irregular and ridiculously shaped this globe is! Everything seems to be in a state of chaos: look at these tiny streams, none of which flows in a straight line; these ponds which are neither round, square, oval, nor any other regular form; these little sharp things (he was referring to mountains) which stick up all over the place and have taken the skin off my feet! And look at the overall shape of the globe, how it flattens out at the poles, how it moves round the sun in that awkward way so that the climates at either pole are bound to be hostile to life! But what really makes me think there is no one here is that in my view no one with any sense would want to live here.'

'Very well,' said Micromégas, 'but perhaps the people who live here have no sense. And yet there are signs that all this was not created for nothing. Everything seems irregular, in your words, because everything on Saturn and Jupiter is laid out in straight lines. So, perhaps that is precisely why there is a measure of confusion here. Have I not told you that in my travels I have always met with variety?'

The Saturnian replied to these arguments point by point. The debate might have gone on for ever, had not Micromégas in the heat of argument fortunately chanced to break the string of his diamond necklace. The diamonds dropped; they were pretty little stones, of different sizes, the largest weighing four hundred pounds and the smallest fifty. The dwarf picked up one or two of them and noticed, as he held them to his eye, that from the way they had been cut these diamonds made excellent microscopes. So he took one little microscope, a hundred and sixty feet in diameter, and applied it to his pupil; Micromégas picked another measuring two thousand five hundred feet. Excellent though these were, however, nothing could be seen through them at first: adjustment was needed. At length the Saturnian saw something imperceptible moving about just beneath the surface of the Baltic Sea: it was a whale. He picked it up adroitly with his little finger and, placing it on his thumbnail, he showed it to the Sirian, who for the second time began laughing at the immoderately small size of the inhabitants of our globe. The Saturnian, satisfied by now that our world was inhabited, at once imagined that it must be exclusively so by whales; and, since he was much given to rational analysis, he wanted to work out where so tiny an atom derived its movement, and whether it had ideas, a will and freedom. Micromégas for his part was much perplexed: he examined the creature very patiently, and came to the conclusion that there could be no grounds for believing a soul to be lodged in such a body. The two travellers were thus inclining to the view that there was no intelligent life on Earth, when they saw through their microscopes something larger than a whale floating on the Baltic Sea. It will be recalled that at this moment in time a flock of philosophers was just returning from the Arctic Circle,[16] where they had gone to carry out observations which no one had hitherto taken it into their heads to make. The gazettes merely record that the vessel ran aground on the shores of the Gulf of Bothnia, and that they had a good deal of trouble escaping with their lives; but in this world one never knows what takes place behind the scenes. I shall here relate simply what occurred, and without additions of my own, which is no small effort for a historian.

CHAPTER V

Observations and arguments of the two travellers

Micromégas extended his hand very gently towards the spot where the object had appeared, and stretched out two fingers which he instantly withdrew for fear of making a mistake; then, opening and closing them, he delicately lifted the vessel bearing these gentlemen and placed it on his nail, as before, without squeezing too tightly for fear of crushing it.

'This is a quite different animal from the earlier one,' pronounced the dwarf from Saturn. Micromégas placed the alleged animal in the palm of his hand. The passengers and crew, who thought they had been swept up by a hurricane and now believed they were on some sort of rock, all started to bustle about. The sailors picked up barrels of wine, throwing them on to Micromégas's hand and leaping down after them. The geometers took their quadrants, their sextants, and a few Lapp girls, and climbed down on to the Sirian's fingers. There was so much action that finally he felt something moving and tickling his fingers: the iron tip of an alpenstock was being driven a foot deep into his index finger; from which prickling he concluded that something sharp had projected from the tiny animal he was holding. But at first he suspected nothing more.[17] The microscope, which barely allowed them to see a whale or a ship, had no purchase on a creature as imperceptible as man. I have no wish to offend anyone's vanity, but I must ask those convinced of their own importance to make a preliminary observation with me: if we take the average height of mankind to be approximately five feet, then we cut no more imposing a figure on this Earth than a creature approximately one six-hundred-thousandth of an inch high standing on a ball with a circumference of ten feet. Now imagine a form of matter capable of holding the Earth in its hand, whose organs are in proportion to our own (and there may well exist any number of such forms of matter): then consider, I beg you, what they would make of those battles of ours, where we gain a couple of villages in one skirmish, only to lose them in the next.

I have no doubt that if some captain in the great Grenadiers ever reads this work, he will raise by at least two good feet the height of his company's bearskin bonnets; but I can tell him now that try as he may, he and his men will never be more than infinitesimally small.[18]

What marvellous skill was required, then, for our philosopher from Sirius to spy out the atoms I have just been describing! When Leeuwenhoek and Hartsoeker[19] first saw, or thought they saw, the seed from which we all grow, they were making a far less astonishing discovery. What pleasure Micromégas felt in seeing these tiny machines moving about, in scrutinizing their comings and goings, in following them in all their operations! How he shouted out! With what joy he handed one of his microscopes to his travelling companion!

'I can see them!' they both cried out at once. 'Look at them ferrying their loads, bending down and straightening up again!'

As they spoke their hands trembled with the excitement of seeing such novel objects and with the fear of losing them. The Saturnian, passing from extreme scepticism to extreme credulity, thought he could see some of them engaged in propagating themselves. 'Aha!' he said, 'I have caught nature in the act.' But he was deceived by appearances, which happens all too often, whether one uses microscopes or not.

CHAPTER VI

How they fared in the company of humans

Micromégas, a far better observer of things than his dwarf, could clearly see that the atoms were talking to one other; he drew the attention of his companion who, ashamed at his mistake over pro-creation, was now somewhat reluctant to credit such species with the power to communicate ideas. He had the gift of languages as much as the Sirian; but since he could not hear these human atoms talking, he concluded that they could not talk. Besides, how should such imperceptible beings have speech organs, and what could they possibly have to say to each other? In order to speak one must be able to think, more or less. But if they could think, they must have the equivalent of a soul. Now to attribute the equivalent of a soul to this species seemed to him absurd.

'But', said the Sirian, 'just now you thought they were making love. Do you think one can make love without having thoughts, without uttering the odd word here and there, without at least making oneself understood? Do you further suppose that it is a harder thing to produce an argument than an infant? To my mind how one does either is a great mystery.'

'I no longer dare to believe or disbelieve,' said the dwarf. 'I have no opinions left. We must endeavour to examine these insects, and reason afterwards.'

'Very well said,' Micromégas replied, and he immediately took out a pair of scissors. With these he cut his nails, and with a clipping from his thumbnail he fashioned on the spot a sort of large speaking-trumpet shaped like a vast funnel, the smaller end of which he placed to his ear. The rim of the funnel embraced the ship and its entire company. The faintest voice could be picked up by the circular fibres of the nail; such that, thanks to his industry, the philosopher up above now heard perfectly the buzzing of the human insects down below. Within a few hours he could distinguish words, and succeeded finally in understanding French. The dwarf did likewise, though with greater difficulty. The astonishment of the visitors redoubled by the minute. They were listening to tiny microbes making reasonable sense: this trick on the part of nature seemed wholly unaccountable. You may imagine the impatience with which the Sirian and his dwarf burned to engage these atoms in conversation; but the latter feared that his thunderous voice, not to mention that of Micromégas, would deafen the microbes without being understood by them. They must find a way of diminishing its force. Each therefore placed in his mouth a sort of miniature toothpick, whose finely sharpened end reached down close to the ship. The Sirian held the dwarf on his knee and the ship and company on one nail. He bent his head and began speaking in a low voice. With the aid of these precautions and many more, he addressed them at last:

'Invisible insects, whom the hand of the Creator has been pleased to bring to life in the abyss of the infinitely small, I give thanks to Him for deigning to reveal to me secrets which had seemed impenetrable. Perhaps nobody at my court would deign to look upon you; but I disdain no creature, and I hereby offer you my protection.'

If ever there was astonishment, it was to be found among the company who heard these words, and who could not imagine where they were coming from. The ship's chaplain fell to reciting the prayers for casting out devils; the sailors swore; the philosophers on board invented a system: but whatever the system, they could not explain who was talking to them. The dwarf from Saturn, whose voice was gentler than Micromégas's, informed them briefly as to what manner of beings they were dealing with. He recounted the voyage from Saturn, put them in the picture as to the identity of Monsieur Micromégas, and, after commiserating with them for being so small, enquired whether they had always been in this miserable condition bordering on nothingness and what were they doing on a planet which appeared to be run by whales, whether they were happy, whether they multiplied, whether they had a soul, and a hundred other such questions.

One quibbler on board, bolder than the rest and offended at having doubts cast upon his soul, scrutinized their interlocutor through sights mounted on his quadrant, took two bearings, and on the third said:

'You appear to think, sir, that because you measure a thousand fathoms from head to toe, you are therefore –'

'A thousand fathoms!' exclaimed the dwarf. 'Good heavens! How can he possibly know my height? A thousand fathoms! He is not an inch out in his calculation. What! This atom has actually measured me! He is a geometer, and he knows my size; whereas I, who can only see him through a microscope, have yet to discover his!'

'Yes, I have your measure,' said the physicist, 'and what's more I am now going to measure your big friend.'

This proposal was accepted, and His Excellency stretched out full length on the ground, since had he remained standing his head would have been too far above the clouds. Our philosophers planted a tall tree into him, at a spot which the good Dr Swift would call by its name but which I shall certainly refrain from specifying, out of my great respect for the ladies. Next, by a series of triangulations, they deduced that they were in fact looking at a young man one hundred and twenty thousand royal feet long.

Micromégas now spoke again: 'I see more than ever that one must not judge anything by its apparent size. O God, who has endowed with intelligence forms of matter that seem so contemptible, the infinitely small evidently costs you as little effort as the infinitely great; moreover, if there can possibly exist creatures smaller than these, they may well be of greater intelligence than those superb animals I have seen in the heavens, whose foot alone would cover this globe on which I have landed.'

One of the philosophers replied that he could rest assured; there were indeed intelligent beings far smaller than man. He described for him, not Virgil's fabulations about the bees,[20] but what Swammerdam has discovered and Réaumur[21] dissected. Lastly he informed him that there are creatures which are to bees as bees are to humans, or as the Sirian himself was to those prodigious animals he had mentioned, and as those animals are to yet other forms, beside which they seem but atoms. By degrees the conversation began to flow, and Micromégas spoke as follows.

CHAPTER VII

Conversation with the humans

'O intelligent atoms, in whom the Supreme Being has been pleased to manifest His skill and His might, the joys you experience on your globe must doubtless be extremely pure; for, having so little matter and being apparently all mind, you must pass your lives in thinking and loving – in leading the true life of the spirit. Nowhere have I witnessed real happiness, but surely it is to be found here.'

At this all the philosophers shook their heads, and one of them, more forthright than the rest, owned frankly that, except for a small number of individuals held in low esteem, the rest were a confederacy of the mad, the bad and the miserable.

'We have more than enough matter to do plenty of evil, if evil comes from matter; and too much spirit, if evil comes from the spirit. For instance, do you realize that as I speak a hundred thousand lunatics of our species, wearing hats, are busy killing or being killed by a hundred thousand other animals in turbans,[22] and that almost everywhere on Earth this is how we have carried on since time immemorial?'

The Sirian shuddered and asked what could be the subject of such terrible quarrels between such puny creatures.

'It is all for the sake of a few mud-heaps',[23] replied the philosopher, 'no bigger than your heel. Not that any of the millions who are cutting each other's throats lay claim to the least particle of these heaps. The issue is simply whether it shall belong to one man known as "Sultan" or to another known, for some reason, as "Tsar". Neither man has ever seen or ever will see the little piece of land in question, and almost none of the creatures slaughtering each other has ever seen the animal on whose behalf they are slaughtering.'

'Ah! The devils!' cried the Sirian indignantly. 'Is such fanatical fury conceivable? I am tempted to take three strides and with each stride to trample this whole ant-hill of ridiculous assassins.'

'Spare yourself the trouble,' came the reply. 'They are making a fair job of their own destruction. The truth is that, ten years on, there is never one in a hundred of the wretches left; even those who have not drawn a sword are carried off by hunger, exhaustion or debauchery. Besides, it is not they who should be punished, but the sedentary barbarians holed up in their offices, who command the massacre of a million men while digesting a good meal, and afterwards have a *Te Deum* offered up in thanks to God.'

The traveller felt moved to pity for this tiny species, in whom he was discovering such surprising contradictions.

'Since you are among the few who are enlightened,' he said to these gentlemen, 'and seem not to murder people for a living, tell me, how do you pass your time?'

'We dissect flies,' said the philosopher, 'we measure lines, we combine numbers, we agree upon the two or three things that we do understand, and argue over the two or three thousand that we do not.'

Immediately it occurred to both Sirian and Saturnian to elicit from these thinking atoms what it was that they did agree upon.

'What do you reckon to be the distance', the former asked, 'from the Dog Star to the great star in Gemini?'

'Thirty-two and a half degrees,' they answered in unison.

'And from here to the moon?'

'Sixty times the radius of the Earth, in round numbers.'

'And how heavy is your air?'

He intended to catch them out, but they all replied that air weighs approximately nine hundred times less than the equivalent volume of the lightest water, and nineteen hundred times less than gold for ducats. The little dwarf from Saturn, amazed at their answers, was inclined to take for sorcerers the same people to whom a quarter of an hour earlier he had refused a soul.

Finally Micromégas said to them:

'Since you know so much about what is outside of you, no doubt you know even more about what is within. Tell me what your soul is, and how you form your ideas.'

The philosophers all replied in unison, as before; but now they all gave different answers. The oldest cited Aristotle, another uttered the name of Descartes, another Malebranche, another Leibniz, and yet another Locke.

An aged peripatetic confidently declared in loud tones: 'The soul is an "entelechy",[24] and is the reason by which it has the power to be what it is. So Aristotle specifically states, on page 633 of the Louvre edition: Ἐντελέχεια ἐστι, etc.'

'My Greek is limited,' said the giant.

'Mine too,' said the philosophizing microbe.

'Why, then,' pursued the Sirian, 'do you cite this Aristotle fellow in Greek?'

'Because', replied the scholar, 'one should always cite what one does not understand in the language one least understands.'

The Cartesian now spoke up: 'The soul is pure spirit; it imbibes all metaphysical ideas in the mother's womb, on leaving which it has to go to school, to relearn from scratch what it knew so well and will never know again.'[25]

'So,' replied the animal eight leagues tall, 'there was little point in your soul being so learned inside your mother's womb, if it was to become so ignorant by the time you had some hairs on your chin. And what do you mean by spirit?'

'What a question!' said the theoretician. 'I have no idea. They say it is not the same thing as matter.'

'Do you at least know what matter is?'

'Certainly,' the man replied. 'This stone, for example, is grey and of a certain shape, has three dimensions and weight, and is divisible.'

'So!' said the Sirian. 'This thing which seems to you divisible, weighty and grey – would you mind telling me what it is? You observe some of its attributes, but do you know what it is in itself?'

'No,' said the other.

'Then you have no idea what matter is.'

Monsieur Micromégas now addressed another of the sages perched on his thumb, asking him what his soul was and what it did.

'Not a thing,' replied this disciple of Malebranche.[26] 'It is God who does everything for me. I see everything in Him, I do everything through Him. It is He who arranges everything, without my involvement.'

'One might as well not exist,' countered the sage from Sirius. 'And you, my friend,' he said to a Leibnizian who was present, 'what is your soul?'

'It is the hand that tells the time, just as my body is the clock that chimes; or, if you prefer, it is what chimes while my body tells the time; in other words, my soul is the mirror of the universe and my body the frame on the mirror. That much is clear.'[27]

A tiny partisan of Locke was standing by, who, when spoken to at last, replied: 'I do not know by what means I think, but I know that I have never thought except with the aid of my senses. That there are non-material intelligent substances I don't doubt; but that God should be incapable of bestowing mind on matter I doubt very much. I revere the eternal power, and it is not for me to set bounds to it; I affirm nothing, and am content to believe that more things are possible than we think.'[28]

The animal from Sirius smiled. He found the last speaker by no means the most foolish; and the dwarf from Saturn would have embraced this follower of Locke but for their extreme disparity in size. Unfortunately for everyone, there was present a little animalcule in an academic square cap, who interrupted all the philosopher animalcules. He claimed he had all the answers, and that they were in the Summa of St Thomas Aquinas. He looked the two celestial visitors up and down, then informed them that everything – their persons, their worlds, their suns, their stars – had been created uniquely for Man.[29]

On hearing this speech, our two travellers fell upon each other, choking with that inextinguishable laughter which, according to Homer, is the portion of the gods. Their shoulders and stomachs heaved and fell, and during these convulsions the vessel, which the Sirian had been balancing on his finger-nail, fell into the Saturnian's trouser pocket. These two good people spent a great deal of time searching for it; at last they found both ship and company, and set everything very neatly to rights again. The Sirian picked up the little microbes once more. He still spoke to them with great kindness, despite being privately a little vexed to find that the infinitely small should have a pride almost infinitely large. He promised to write a fine work of philosophy for them, in suitably tiny script, in which they would discover the nature of things. True to his word, he gave them the volume before leaving. It was taken to Paris, to the Academy of Sciences. But when the Secretary opened it, he found nothing but blank pages.

'*Aha*,' said he, '*I suspected as much.*'

The World As It Is

Babouc's Vision

Written by Himself

CHAPTER I

Among the genies who preside over the empires of the world, Ithuriel holds one of the highest posts and has the department of Upper Asia. One morning he descended to the house of Babouc, a Scythian, on the banks of the Oxus, and said to him: 'Babouc, the folly and excesses of the Persians have provoked our displeasure: an assembly of the genies of Upper Asia was held yesterday to decide whether we should punish Persepolis or destroy it. Go into that city and examine everything; then come back and render me an exact account and I shall decide on your report whether the city shall be chastised or exterminated.' 'But, my lord,' said Babouc humbly, 'I have never been to Persia; I don't know anybody there.' 'So much the better,' said the angel, 'you will be quite impartial; Heaven has given you understanding, to which I shall add the gift of inspiring confidence. Walk around, look, listen, observe and fear nothing; you will be well received everywhere.'

Babouc mounted his camel and set out with his servants. After several days he encountered the Persian army near the plains of Sennaar, on its way to engage with the Indian army. He spoke first of all to a straggler, and asked what was the cause of the war. 'By all the gods,' said the soldier, 'I have no idea. It's not my affair: my business is to kill and be killed for a living; it doesn't matter on which side I serve. I may even go over to the Indian camp tomorrow. They are said to give their soldiers nearly half a drachma of copper a day more than we get in this confounded Persian service. If you want to know why we are fighting, ask my captain.'

Babouc handed the soldier a small trifle and entered the camp. He soon made the acquaintance of the captain and asked him what the war was about. 'How do you expect me to know,' said the captain, 'and what does this splendid topic have to do with me? I live two hundred leagues from Persepolis; I hear talk of war being declared; I immediately abandon my family and take off, as is our custom, in search of death or honour, since I have nothing else to do.' 'But surely your fellow-officers must be a little better informed?' said Babouc. 'No,' said the officer; 'scarcely anyone except our chief satraps knows precisely why we are cutting each other's throats.'

Astonished, Babouc gained admittance amongst the generals, and entered into their confidence. Finally one of them explained: 'This war which has devastated Asia for twenty years was originally a quarrel between the eunuch of a wife of the great King of Persia and a clerk in an office of the great King of India. It was over a right worth the thirtieth part of a gold daric. The Indian prime minister and ours supported with dignity the rights of their masters. The quarrel became heated. Each side put a million soldiers into the field; and every year more than four hundred thousand men are needed as recruits. Murders, fires, ruins, devastation multiply apace; the whole world is suffering, and the fury continues. Our respective prime ministers keep protesting that they are only acting for the benefit of mankind; and with each protestation some town is razed and some provinces are ravaged.'

The next day, following a rumour that peace was about to be concluded, the Persian general and the Indian general rushed into battle; there was general carnage. Babouc witnessed all the misdeeds and abominations of war; he saw the machinations of the chief satraps who did what they could to have their own general defeated. He saw officers killed by their own troops; he saw soldiers who finished off their dying comrades in order to rob them of a few bloody, torn, mud-caked rags. He entered the hospitals where the wounded were taken, and where most of them died, owing to the inhuman negligence of the very people who were paid handsomely by the King of Persia to care for them. 'Are these men', cried Babouc, 'or wild beasts? Ah! I can see that Persepolis will indeed be destroyed.'

Occupied with this thought he passed into the Indian camp: he was as well received here as by the Persians, as had been predicted; but he saw exactly the same excesses which had filled him with horror earlier. 'Well!' he said to himself, 'if the angel Ithuriel wants to exterminate the Persians, the angel of India is going to have to destroy the Indians too.' Discovering in more detail what had taken place in both armies, he learnt of acts of generosity, greatness of soul and humanity which astonished and delighted him. 'Inexplicable race of man!' he cried out; 'How can you unite such baseness with such nobility, so many virtues with so many crimes?'

Meanwhile peace was declared. The commanders of the two armies, neither of whom had gained victory but had shed the blood of so many for self-interest, went off to request their reward at their respective courts. Peace was celebrated with public declarations announcing nothing less than the return of the Golden Age on earth. 'The Lord be praised!' said Babouc. 'Persepolis will be the dwelling place of purified innocence; it will not be destroyed, as these wicked genies desired; let me hurry at once to this capital of Asia.'

CHAPTER II

He arrived in this immense city by the ancient entrance,[1] whose vile rusticity was barbarous and offensive to the gaze. This part of the city bore marks everywhere of the age in which it was built: for despite men's obstinacy in praising the ancient at the expense of the modern, it must be admitted that the first attempts in any field are always crude.

Babouc mingled with a crowd composed of the dirtiest and ugliest of either sex. This mob was pressing forward with a vacant air into a vast and gloomy enclosure. From the continuous murmuring and milling around which he observed, and the money which was changing hands for the right to sit down, he imagined he was in a market where rush-bottomed chairs were sold; but very soon, noticing that several women were kneeling and glancing sidelong at the men while pretending to be gazing fixedly ahead, he realized he was in a religious temple. Discordant voices, sharp, raucous and savage, made the vault echo with their obscure chantings,[2] like the cries of asses on the plains of Poitou when they answer to the cowherd's horn. Babouc stopped his ears; but he was tempted likewise to shut his eyes and hold his nose when he saw workmen entering the temple with picks and shovels. They raised a large stone and started digging, throwing up earth to right and left which gave off a foul smell; then they deposited a corpse in the opening and replaced the stone above it.[3]

'What!' exclaimed Babouc; 'this people bury their dead in the very places where they worship the Godhead! Their temples are paved with cadavers! I am not surprised that Persepolis is constantly ravaged by pestilential illnesses. The stench of the dead, combined with that of so many of the living assembled and crowded into one place, is enough to poison the whole world. What a disgusting city! No doubt the angels want to destroy it so as to build a better one in its place, filled with less filthy inhabitants who can sing better. Providence must have its reasons; let us abide them.'

CHAPTER III

Meanwhile the sun was approaching its zenith. Babouc was engaged to dine on the other side of town with a lady to whom he had letters of introduction from her husband, an officer in the army. But first he took a few turns through Persepolis; he saw other temples, better built and ornamented, filled with a civilized congregation and echoing throughout with harmonious music; he noticed public fountains which, though poorly situated, were strikingly beautiful; squares where the greatest kings who had governed Persia seemed to breathe in bronze; other squares where he heard the people crying: 'When shall we see among us the master whom we adore?'[4] He admired the magnificent bridges thrown across the river, the superb and commodious quays, the palaces standing to left and right, and an immense edifice where thousands of old soldiers, wounded but triumphant, gave thanks every day to the god of armies.[5] Finally he reached the lady's house and found her awaiting his arrival, with a respectable company of dinner guests. The house was clean and elegant, the meal delicious, the lady young, beautiful, witty, engaging, and the company worthy of her. Babouc kept saying to himself: 'The angel Ithuriel has some nerve to want to destroy so delightful a city.'

CHAPTER IV

He noticed, however, that the lady, who had begun by asking tenderly for news of her husband, was by the end of the meal conversing even more tenderly with a young mage.[6] Then Babouc noticed a magistrate who despite the presence of his wife was warmly embracing a widow; the indulgent widow had one arm round the magistrate's neck while extending the other to a very handsome and modest young citizen. The magistrate's wife was the first to leave table, so as to converse in an adjoining room with her spiritual director, who had arrived late after being expected for dinner; this director, who was all eloquence, addressed her in this room with such vehemence and suavity that when the lady returned her eyes were swimming, her cheeks inflamed, her walk uncertain, and her speech tremulous.

Babouc began to fear then that Ithuriel might be right after all. His talent for inspiring trust placed him in the confidence of the hostess from that first evening; she confessed the attraction she felt towards the young priest, and assured Babouc that he would find the equivalent of what he had seen in her house in every establishment in Persepolis. Babouc concluded that such a society could not endure; that jealousy, discord and vengeance must devastate all these houses; that tears and bloodshed must flow daily; that husbands were either killing their wives' lovers or being killed by them; and that, in short, Ithuriel was quite right to destroy at a stroke a city given over to constant calamity.

CHAPTER V

He was plunged in these baleful thoughts when there appeared at the door a grave personage in a black cloak, who humbly begged to speak with the young magistrate. Without rising, and without looking at him, the young man haughtily and carelessly handed him some papers and dismissed him. Babouc asked who the visitor was. The hostess whispered: 'He is one of our finest lawyers; he has been studying the law for fifty years. The young gentleman, who is only twenty-five, and has been legal satrap for two days, has just ordered him to make an abstract of a case which he is to judge tomorrow and has not yet looked at.' 'The young scatterbrain acts wisely', said Babouc, 'to ask his elder's advice; but why is the old man not the judge?' 'You jest,' came the reply. 'Those who grow old in laborious and menial posts never attain high office. This young man has an important post because his father is rich and because the right of dispensing justice is purchased here like a smallholding.' 'Oh immoral and unhappy city!' cried Babouc. 'This is the very depth of disorder; doubtless, those who have purchased in this way the right to judge will in turn sell their judgements: I see nothing here but an abyss of iniquity.'[7]

As he was thus giving vent to grief and astonishment, a young warrior who had returned that very day from the army said to him: 'But why do you think legal positions should not be bought and sold? I myself bought the right to face death at the head of two thousand men whom I command; this year it has cost me forty thousand gold darics to sleep on the ground in a red tunic for thirty nights in a row, only to receive two smart arrow wounds which I still feel. If I ruin myself financially to serve the Persian Emperor whom I have never seen, then this legal satrap can surely pay for the pleasure of giving audience to litigants.' Babouc in his indignation could not refrain from mentally condemning a country where the dignities of peace and war were put up for auction; he hastily concluded that the nature of both war and justice must be completely unknown there, and that, even if Ithuriel did not exterminate this nation, it would perish by its own detestable administration.

His poor opinion was confirmed by the arrival of a fat gentleman who, greeting the whole company with great familiarity, approached the young officer and said: 'I can lend you only fifty thousand gold darics, because this year the Customs of the Empire have only brought me in three hundred thousand.' Babouc enquired about this man who complained of earning so little; he learnt that in Persepolis there were forty plebeian magnates who had a lease on the Persian Empire, for which they paid the monarch a cut of their profits.[8]

CHAPTER VI

After dinner he visited one of the most superb temples in the city; he sat among a crowd of men and women who had come there to pass the time. A mage appeared in an elevated machine[9] and spoke for a long time about vice and virtue. He divided into numerous categories what did not need any dividing; he offered methodical proofs of what was quite clear in the first place; he taught what everybody already knew. He worked himself into a passion, methodically, and departed sweating and out of breath. The whole assembly then awoke with the general impression of having received a lesson. Babouc said: 'Now there is a man who has done his best to bore two or three hundred of his fellow-citizens; but his intentions were good; which is not sufficient grounds for destroying Persepolis.'

After leaving the assembly, he was taken to see a public festival which was held every day of the year; it took place in a sort of basilica, at one end of which a palace could be seen.[10] The most beautiful women of Persepolis, and the most important satraps, all ranged in order, made a spectacle so fine that Babouc at first thought this was itself the festival. But two or three persons who seemed to be kings and queens soon appeared in the lobby of this palace; their speech was quite different from that of the people; it was measured, harmonious, sublime. Nobody slept; everyone listened in profound silence, interrupted only by expressions of sensibility and public admiration. The duty of kings, the love of virtue, the pitfalls of the passions, were delineated by strokes so vivid and affecting that Babouc was moved to tears. He had no doubt that these heroes and heroines, these kings and queens he had just heard, must be the appointed preachers of the Empire; he even thought of persuading Ithuriel to come and listen to them, convinced that such a spectacle would forever reconcile him with this city.

As soon as the festival was over, he desired to see the principal queen who had expressed so noble and so chaste a morality in this beautiful palace. He was led to her Majesty, up a small staircase to a poorly furnished apartment on the second floor, where he found an ill-dressed woman, who said to him with a noble and pathetic air: 'This profession does not bring me enough to live on; one of the princes you saw has given me a child; I am expecting the baby soon; I have no money and without money one cannot give birth.' Babouc gave her a hundred pieces of gold, saying: 'Were this the only thing wrong with Persepolis, Ithuriel would be wrong to get angry.'

From there he went and passed the evening with some merchants who traded in useless luxuries. He was taken there by an intelligent man with whom he had become acquainted; he bought what pleased him, and it was politely sold to him for a lot more than its worth. Returning home, his friend pointed out how much he had been swindled. Babouc made a note of the merchant's name in his tablets, so that Ithuriel could single him out on the day the city was punished. While he was writing there was a knock at the door. It was the merchant himself, who had come to return the purse which Babouc had accidentally left behind on his counter. 'How can it be', exclaimed Babouc, 'that you are so honourable and generous, yet you were not ashamed to sell me your trinkets at four times their value?'

'Any merchant of repute in this town', replied the latter, 'would have returned your purse; but you were deceived when you were told that I overcharged you four times for what you bought in my shop: I overcharged you ten times, so much so that if you try to sell these things in a month's time you will not even obtain the tenth of what you paid. But nothing could be fairer: it is men's fantasy which sets the price upon these frivolities; their fantasy in turn provides a living for the hundred workmen I employ; it gives me a beautiful house, a comfortable carriage, horses; it promotes industry, and keeps up taste, the circulation of wealth and affluence. I sell the same baubles to the neighbouring nations more expensively than to you, and in this way I am useful to the Empire.'[11]

Babouc, after reflecting for a moment, struck the merchant's name off his tablets.

CHAPTER VII

Deeply confused as to what he should think of Persepolis, Babouc next resolved to consult the mages and the scholars: for the latter study wisdom and the former study religion; and he flattered himself that they could obtain clemency for the rest of the population. The next morning he repaired to a college of mages. The archimandrite[12] admitted that he had an income of one hundred thousand crowns in return for taking a vow of poverty, and that he enjoyed considerable authority by virtue of his vow of humility; after which he left Babouc in the care of a small friar who did the honours of the place.

While this friar was showing him the splendours of this house of penitence, a rumour spread that Babouc had come on a mission to reform all the religious houses. Immediately he received memoranda from each and every house; the gist of all these reports was: 'Preserve us and destroy all the others.' To listen to their justifications, these institutions were all essential; to listen to their mutual accusations they all deserved to be abolished. He marvelled that none of them wished to edify the universe without ruling it in the process.

There then appeared a little man who was a demi-mage, and who said to Babouc: 'I see that our work is about to be fulfilled, for Zoroaster has returned to the earth, and little girls are prophesying by having themselves pinched and whipped front and rear. We therefore ask your protection against the Great Lama.'[13] 'What!' said Babouc, 'against the Pontiff-King who lives in Tibet?' 'The very same.' 'Are you at war, and raising armies against him?' 'No, but he says that man is free and we believe no such thing; we denounce him in pamphlets which he does not read; he has scarcely even heard of us; he has simply condemned us, as a master orders the destruction of the caterpillars on the trees in his garden.' Babouc shuddered at the madness of these men who made a profession of wisdom, at the intrigues of those who had renounced the world, at the ambition and overweening covetousness of those who preached humility and disinterestedness; he concluded that Ithuriel had good reason to destroy the entire crew.

CHAPTER VIII

Returning home, he sent for some new books to allay his despondency, and invited some men of letters to dinner to restore his spirits. Twice as many came as were invited, like wasps attracted by honey. These parasites were avid for food and talk; they praised two kinds of person, the dead and themselves, but never their contemporaries, with the exception of their host. If one of their number made a witty remark the others lowered their eyes and bit their lips in chagrin for not having thought of it themselves. They dissimulated less than the mages, because the objects of their ambition were so much smaller. Each of them coveted the post of secretary in a great house and the reputation of being a great man; they traded insults openly, which they believed to be shafts of wit. They had heard something of Babouc's mission. One of them privately begged him to exterminate a rival who had not sufficiently praised him five years earlier; another asked him to get rid of a citizen who had never laughed at his comedies; a third asked for the abolition of the Academy because he had never been able to get himself elected to it. When the meal was over each of them left separately, because in the entire tribe there were not two men who could endure or even speak to each other except at the tables of the rich. Babouc concluded that there would be no great harm if all this vermin perished in the general conflagration.

CHAPTER IX

As soon as he had got rid of these men of letters, he began to read some new books. He immediately recognized in them the humour of his departed guests. With indignation he sampled their malicious periodicals, their archives of bad taste dictated by envy, baseness and hunger; their craven satires where the vulture is spared and the dove torn to pieces; their novels devoid of imagination, where one reads so many portraits of women the author has not known.

He threw all these detestable productions on the fire, and went out for an evening stroll. He was introduced to an old scholar who had not come to swell the ranks of the parasites at dinner. This scholar always avoided the crowd; was acquainted with mankind, made use of what he knew, and expressed himself with discretion. Babouc spoke with distress of what he had read and seen.

'You have been reading contemptible dross,' said this wise scholar, 'but in all ages and countries and genres, the bad abounds and the good is rare. You received the dregs of pedantry into your house, because in all professions those who are least worthy to appear thrust themselves forward with the greatest impudence. The truly wise keep their own company, in retired tranquillity; among us there are still men and books worthy of your attention.' While he was speaking, they were joined by another scholar; the conversation was so pleasant and instructive, so elevated above prejudice and so expressive of virtue, that Babouc confessed he had never heard its like. 'Such men', he murmured to himself, 'the angel Ithuriel will not dare to touch, or he lacks all mercy.'

Though reconciled to men of letters, Babouc was still angry with the rest of this nation. 'You are a stranger,' remarked his judicious companion, 'so abuses crowd before your eyes, and the good which is hidden and is sometimes even the fruit of those abuses escapes you.' He then learnt that among men of letters were some who were not envious, and that there were even virtuous men among the mages. He finally understood that these large corporations, which seemed to be preparing a common ruin for themselves by their rivalries, were after all beneficial institutions; that each order of mages acted as a curb on its rivals; that if these rivals differed in some of their opinions they nevertheless all taught the same morality, educated the people and lived in submission to the laws, rather as tutors watch over the son of the house while the master watches over the tutors. Babouc frequented more of them, and discovered marvellous souls. He even learnt that among the lunatics who wanted to make war on the Lama of Tibet there had been some great men. In the end he formed the view that the morals of Persepolis might well resemble its buildings, some of which had seemed pitiful while others had filled him with admiration.

CHAPTER X

He said to his learned friend: 'I can see clearly that these mages, whom I had thought so dangerous, are in fact most useful, especially when a wise government prevents them from becoming too important; but you will at least admit that your young magistrates, who purchase the title of judges as soon as they learn to ride a horse, must parade the most ridiculous impertinence in the courts as well as the grossest injustice. It would surely be better to confer these offices freely upon the elderly jurists who have spent their lives in weighing the scales of the law.'

The man of letters replied: 'You saw our army before you came to Persepolis; you know that our young officers fight very well, despite having purchased their commissions; perhaps you will see that our young magistrates do not judge poorly, despite having purchased the right to judge.'

The next day he brought Babouc to the high court, where an important sentence was to be passed. The case was familiar to everyone. All the elderly lawyers who discussed it vacillated in their opinions; they cited a hundred precedents, not one of which went to the root of the question; they looked at the case from a hundred angles, none of which was the true one. The judges came to a decision in less time than the lawyers spent dithering; their judgement was nearly unanimous; it was a sound judgement because they followed the light of reason, whereas the lawyers pronounced foolishly because they had merely consulted their books.

Babouc concluded that abuses often have their advantages. On the same day he saw how the wealth of financiers, which had so disgusted him, could have excellent effects; for the Emperor needed money, and with their aid he found more in one hour than he could have raised in six months by the usual means. Babouc saw that these fat clouds, swollen with the dew of the earth, gave back in rain what they had received. Moreover, the children of these new men, often better educated than the progeny of older families, were sometimes far more able: for nothing prevents a man from being a good judge, a brave warrior or an adroit statesman, if he has had a clever father.

CHAPTER XI

Little by little Babouc became more forgiving towards the avidity of the financiers, who are at bottom no greedier than other men, and who are necessary to society. He excused the madness of those who ruin themselves to become judges and military officers, a madness which produces great magistrates and heroes. He excused the envy of men of letters, among whose number there were individuals who enlightened the world; he grew reconciled to ambitious and scheming mages, among whom great virtues even outnumbered petty vices; but he still found much to complain of, above all in the intrigues of the ladies. The inevitable miseries consequent upon their behaviour filled him with anxiety and dread.

Since he wished to become familiar with all conditions of men, he called upon a minister of state; but along the way he trembled continually lest some woman should be murdered before his eyes by her husband. Arriving at the statesman's house he waited for two hours in the antechamber before being announced, and two more hours thereafter. During this interval he resolved to recommend this minister and his insolent lackeys to the particular attention of the angel Ithuriel.

The antechamber was filled with ladies of all ranks, mages of all colours, judges, merchants, officers and pedants, all of them complaining about the minister. The miser and the usurer said: 'No doubt, this man is fleecing the provinces.' A capricious character reproached him with being unpredictable. A sybarite said: 'He thinks of nothing but pleasure.' An intriguer flattered himself that he would soon see the minister brought down by a conspiracy; the women were hoping that he would soon be replaced by a younger man.

Babouc listened to their talk; he could not help saying: 'Now here is a fortunate man: he has all his enemies in his antechamber; his power crushes those who envy him; he sees his detesters prostrate at his feet.' At last he entered, and Babouc saw a little old man bowed with the weight of years and business, but still lively and full of intelligence.

He liked Babouc and Babouc thought him a person of worth. The conversation became animated. The minister confessed that he was a very unhappy man; that he was thought to be rich but was in fact poor; that people imagined him all-powerful but he was always being thwarted; that almost everyone to whom he had granted a favour had proved ungrateful, and that during forty years of constant exertion he had scarcely known a moment of consolation. Babouc was moved, and thought that if this man had erred and the angel Ithuriel wished to punish him, the way to do so was not to exterminate him but to leave him in harness.

CHAPTER XII

During their conversation the beautiful lady at whose house Babouc had dined suddenly entered the room. Her eyes and forehead showed signs of pain and anger. She burst into reproaches against the minister; she wept; she complained bitterly that her husband had been refused a position to which by birth he was entitled to aspire, and which his services and his wounds merited; she expressed herself so forcefully, complained so gracefully, countered objections so skilfully, and marshalled her arguments so eloquently, that when she left the room she had made her husband's fortune.

Babouc shook hands with her. 'Is it possible, madame,' he said, 'that you can have given yourself all this trouble for a man whom you do not love, and from whom you have everything to fear?' 'A man I do not love!' she cried. 'My husband is the best friend I have in the world, for whom I would sacrifice everything except my lover; and who would do anything for me, except leave his mistress. I should like you to meet her; she is a charming woman, full of wit, of the most agreeable nature; we are supping together this evening, with my husband and my little mage; come and share our joy.'

The lady took Babouc home with her. The husband, who arrived late and in the depths of despair, greeted his wife with transports of elation and gratitude; he embraced in turn his wife, his mistress, the little mage and Babouc. Concord, gaiety, wit and every social grace suffused the supper. 'Let me explain to you', said the hostess to Babouc, 'that those women who are sometimes referred to as unvirtuous almost always have the merit of possessing a virtuous man. To convince you, come and dine with me tomorrow at the house of the beautiful Teone. She is regularly torn to pieces by a few old vestal virgins but she does more good than all of them put together. She would not commit the smallest injustice to further her interests, however great; she gives her lover nothing but generous advice; she is concerned only for his good name; he would blush before her if he missed any occasion for doing what is right, since nothing encourages virtuous deeds more than to have as witness and judge of one's conduct a mistress whose esteem one wishes to deserve.'

Babouc kept the appointment. What he found was a house in which all the pleasures reigned, and were reigned over by Teone. She knew how to speak to everyone in their own language, and her natural ways put others at ease; she gave pleasure almost inadvertently, was as amiable as she was benevolent, and – which augmented the value of her other qualities – she was beautiful.

Babouc, for all that he was a Scythian and the envoy of a genie, realized that if he remained any longer in Persepolis he would forget Ithuriel for Teone. He had grown attached to this city whose inhabitants were civilized, gentle and benevolent, even if they were frivolous, scandal-mongering and full of vanity. He feared for the destruction of Persepolis; he was even fearful of the account he was going to render.

He gave his account in the following way. He commissioned the best metal-founder in the city to make a statuette composed of every metal, and from clays and stones, both the most precious and the most worthless. He presented it to Ithuriel, saying: 'Will you break this lovely statuette, because it is not all gold and diamonds?' Ithuriel guessed his meaning; he resolved not even to think of destroying Persepolis, and to leave *the world as it is*: '*For if everything is not perfect*,' said he, '*everything is tolerable*.'

So Persepolis was allowed to stand, and Babouc was far from put out – unlike Jonah, who lost his temper when Nineveh was not destroyed. But when a man has spent three days in the belly of a whale he is not as well-disposed as when he has been to the opera, to the theatre, and has dined in excellent company.

Memnon
Or Human Wisdom

One day Memnon conceived the senseless project of becoming perfectly wise. There is hardly a man through whose head such folly has not occasionally passed. Memnon said to himself: 'To be very wise, and consequently very happy, one has only to be without passions; and nothing is easier, as everyone knows. First of all, I shall never fall in love with a woman; when I see a perfect beauty, I shall say to myself: "Some day those cheeks will be wrinkled, those beautiful eyes will be red-rimmed; those round breasts will become flat and drooping, that lovely head will be bald." Thus I have only to see her now with the same eyes as I shall see her then, and assuredly her head will no longer turn mine.

'In the second place, I shall always be sober; however much I may be tempted by good living, delicious wines, and the seductions of society, I have only to picture the consequences of excess – a heavy head, a churning stomach, the loss of faculties, health and time – to remind myself to eat no more than my needs; my health will always be regular, my ideas always clear and luminous. It is all so easy that there is no merit in achieving it.

'Next,' said Memnon, 'I must give some thought to my income; my desires are moderate; my fortune is solidly invested with the Receiver-General of the Finances of Nineveh; I have enough to live independently, and this is the greatest fortune of all. I shall never endure the cruel necessity of paying court to anyone; I shall envy no one and no one will envy me. All this too is very easy. I have friends', he went on, 'whom I shall keep, since they will have no reason to quarrel with me. I shall never be out of temper with them nor they with me; no difficulty there either.'

Having thus made his little blueprint of wisdom in his room, Memnon looked out of the window. He saw two women strolling beneath the plane-trees near his house. One was old and seemed not to be thinking about anything; the other was young and pretty, and seemed to be deep in thought. She sighed, she wept, and was all the more beautiful as a result. Our philosopher was touched, not by the lady's beauty (he was quite sure he was no longer subject to such weakness), but by her affliction. He went down; he approached the young Ninevite with the idea of consoling her with his wisdom. This exquisite creature described to him, in the most artless and touching manner, all the wrongs done to her by an uncle she did not possess, and the artifices by which he had deprived her of a fortune she had never owned, along with all she had to fear from his violence. 'You seem to be a gentleman of such good counsel', she said, 'that if you would be kind enough to come home with me and examine my affairs, I am certain that you would rescue me from these cruel difficulties.' Memnon had no hesitation in following her, to examine her affairs with wisdom and to give her good counsel.

The afflicted lady took him to a perfumed room and politely bade him join her on a large sofa, where they sat facing each other with their legs crossed. The lady spoke with lowered eyes, from which an occasional tear dropped, and when she raised them they always met the gaze of the wise Memnon. Her words were full of a tenderness which redoubled each time they looked at each other. Memnon took her affairs very much to heart, and felt with each passing moment an increasing desire to oblige so virtuous and unfortunate a creature. Little by little, in the warmth of conversation, they ceased to be facing each other. Their legs were no longer crossed. Memnon was advising her so closely, and giving such tender counsels, that neither of them could talk of business and no longer knew where they were.

At this point the uncle arrived, as you might expect: he was armed from head to foot, and the first thing he said, naturally, was that he would kill both his niece and the wise Memnon; and his last word on the subject was that he might be forgiving in return for a large sum of money. Memnon was obliged to hand over all he had with him. In those days a man was lucky to get off so cheaply; America had not yet been discovered, and afflicted ladies were not nearly so dangerous as they are today.[1]

Ashamed and despairing, Memnon returned home; here he found a note inviting him to sup with some intimate friends. 'If I stay at home', he said, 'my mind will dwell upon my unlucky adventure, I shall eat nothing, and I shall fall ill. Better to go and enjoy a frugal meal with my intimate friends. In the pleasure of their company I shall forget the folly of this morning.' So off he went to the gathering. His friends found him a little low in spirits. They made him drink to dispel his sorrow. A little wine taken in moderation is a cure for both body and soul. Thus reflected the wise Memnon; and he got drunk. After dinner a game of cards was proposed. A regular game or two among friends is an honest pastime. He played; he lost the contents of his purse and four times as much against his bond. The game led to a dispute; it grew warm; one of his intimate friends flung a dice-cup at his head and knocked out an eye. The wise Memnon was carried home drunk, moneyless, and short of one eye.

He slept off some of the wine; his head clearer now, he sent his valet for money to the Receiver-General of the Finances of Nineveh, in order to pay off his intimate friends; he was informed that his debtor had that very morning become a defrauding bankrupt, to the distress of a hundred families. Memnon in a rage went to court with a plaster over his eye and a petition in hand, to ask justice of the King against the bankrupt. In the salon he encountered several ladies all wearing, with an air of ease, hoops twenty-four feet in circumference. One of them, knowing Memnon slightly, looked at him askance and remarked: 'Horrors!' Another, who knew him better, said: 'Good evening, Monsieur Memnon, how delightful to see you, but by the way, why have you lost an eye, Monsieur Memnon?' and she passed on without waiting for his reply. Memnon hid himself in a corner and waited for the moment when he could throw himself at the monarch's feet. The moment arrived. He kissed the ground three times and presented his petition. His Most Gracious Majesty received it very favourably and handed it to one of his satraps to give him an account of it. The satrap took Memnon aside and said to him haughtily and with a bitter sneer: 'You are a one-eyed buffoon to address yourself to the King rather than to me, and still more of a buffoon to dare to ask for justice against an honest bankrupt, whom I honour with my protection and who is the nephew of one of the chambermaids of my mistress. Give up this affair, my friend, if you wish to keep your other eye.'

Memnon, having that morning renounced women, the excesses of the table, gambling, all quarrels, and in particular the court, before night had been deceived and robbed by a fair lady, had got drunk, gambled, quarrelled, lost an eye and been to court where he had been laughed at.

Paralysed with astonishment and distracted with grief, he returned home with death in his heart. He tried to enter his house; there he found the bailiffs removing his furniture on behalf of his creditors. He stood under a plane-tree almost in a swoon; here he saw the fair lady of this morning out strolling with her dear uncle, who both burst into laughter at the sight of Memnon with his plaster. Night fell; Memnon lay down on some straw near the wall of his own house. He had an attack of fever, overcome by which he fell asleep, and a celestial spirit appeared to him in a dream.

The spirit was resplendent with light. He had six beautiful wings, but no feet, nor head nor tail, and resembled nothing at all. 'Who are you?' said Memnon. 'Your good angel,' replied the other. 'In which case give me back my eye, my health, my property, my wisdom,' said Memnon, and told him how he had lost them all in one day. 'Adventures like that never happen in the world where I live,' said the spirit. 'And what world do you live in?' said the afflicted man. 'My country', he said, 'is five hundred million leagues from the sun, on a little star near Sirius, which you can see from here.' 'Happy star!' said Memnon; '– You mean to say that where you come from there are no she-devils to deceive a poor man, no intimate friends who win his money and poke out his eye, no bankrupts, no satraps who mock him while refusing him justice?' 'No,' said the inhabitant of the star, 'nothing of the kind. We are never deceived by women, because we have no women; we never over-indulge at table, because we do not eat; we have no bankrupts, because we have neither gold nor silver; we cannot have our eyes poked out, because our bodies are not like yours; and satraps never do us an injustice, because on our little star everyone is equal.'

Then Memnon said to him: 'Your Lordship, without women and without dinner, how do you pass your time?' 'In watching over other worlds which are entrusted to our care,' said the spirit, 'as I am here now to console you.' 'Alas!' replied Memnon, 'why did you not come last night and stop me committing so many follies?' 'I was with Hassan, your elder brother,' said the celestial being. 'He is more to be pitied than you. His Gracious Majesty the King of the Indies, at whose court he has the honour to serve, caused both his eyes to be gouged out on account of a small indiscretion, and at the present moment he is in prison, with irons on his hands and feet.'

'So what is the use of having a good angel in the family,' said Memnon, 'when of two brothers one has lost an eye and the other is blind, one lying on straw and the other in prison?' 'Your lot will change,' said the starry creature. 'It is true that you will always be one-eyed; but aside from that you will be happy enough, provided you never repeat the idiotic project of becoming perfectly wise.' 'Is that then impossible to attain?' cried Memnon with a sigh. 'As impossible', replied the other, 'as being perfectly skilful, perfectly strong, perfectly powerful, perfectly happy. We ourselves are very far from it. There is a world where all that is to be found; but in the hundred thousand millions of worlds scattered through space everything is connected by degrees. There is less wisdom and pleasure in the second than in the first, less still in the third than in the second, and so on down to the last, where everyone is completely mad.' 'I greatly fear', said Memnon, 'that our little terraqueous globe is no other than the bedlam of the universe of which you do me the honour of informing me.' 'Not quite,' said the spirit, 'but close. Everything has to be in its allotted place.' 'But then,' said Memnon, 'certain poets and philosophers[2] must therefore be quite wrong to say that *everything is for the best*?' 'They are quite right', said the philosopher from on high, 'in regard to the arrangement of the universe as a whole.' 'Ah!' replied poor Memnon, 'I shall only believe that when I recover my lost eye.'

Letter from a Turk

Concerning the Fakirs and his Friend Bababec

While I was staying in the town of Benares on the banks of the Ganges, the ancient home of the Brahmins, I made every effort to educate myself. I understood Indian tolerably well; I listened a great deal and observed everything. I was lodging with my correspondent Omri, the worthiest man I have ever known. He was a Brahmin, and I have the honour of being a Muslim: we have never exchanged an angry word on the subject of Mohammed or Brahma. We each performed our ablutions after our own fashion, drank the same lemonade, and ate the same rice, like two brothers.

One day we went together to the pagoda of Gavani. There we saw several groups of fakirs, some of whom were Jangys or contemplative fakirs, while others were disciples of the ancient Gymnosophists,[1] who led an active life. It is well known that they have a learned language, that of the ancient Brahmins, and, in that language, a book which they call the Veda.[2] It is certainly the most ancient book of all Asia, not excluding the Zend-Avesta.[3]

I passed a fakir who was reading this book. 'Ah! wretched infidel!' he cried, 'you have made me lose count of the number of vowels; consequently my soul will enter the body of a hare instead of – as I had every reason to hope – a parrot.' I gave him a rupee to console him. A few paces further on I unfortunately sneezed, and the noise awakened a fakir from his ecstatic trance. 'Where am I?' he said. 'What a dreadful fall! I can no longer see the end of my nose: the celestial light has disappeared.'* 'If I am the cause', said I, 'of your finally seeing beyond the end of your nose, here is a rupee

---

* When fakirs wish to see the celestial light, which is very common amongst them, they fix their eyes upon the end of their nose [Voltaire].

in amends for the ill I have done you; go back to your celestial light.'

Having discreetly extricated myself in this way, I passed on to the other Gymnosophists, several of whom brought me some very pretty little nails to stick in my arms and thighs in honour of Brahma. I bought their nails, and used them to nail down my carpets. Some danced on their hands, or performed acrobatics on a loose rope; and there were others who merely hopped along. Some carried chains, others a pack-saddle, and still others hid their heads under a bushel; despite all of which they were the pleasantest people imaginable. My friend Omri took me into the cell belonging to one of the most famous; he was called Bababec: he was as naked as a monkey and wore round his neck a large chain weighing more than sixty pounds. He was sitting on a wooden chair, suitably furnished with the sharp points of nails, which stuck into his buttocks, yet you would have thought he was on a bed of satin. A stream of women came to consult him; he was the oracle of families, and clearly enjoyed a very great reputation. I was present at a lengthy conversation which Omri held with him.

'Father,' said Omri, 'do you think that after passing through the test of the seven metempsychoses, I shall attain to the dwelling of Brahma?' 'That depends,' said the fakir; 'in what manner do you live?' 'I try', said Omri, 'to be a good citizen, a good husband, a good father, a good friend; I lend money to the rich without interest at times, and I give to the poor; I labour to keep peace among my neighbours.' 'Do you ever stick nails in your bottom?' asked the Brahmin. 'Never, reverend father.' 'I am sorry,' replied the fakir, 'but you will certainly only ever reach the nineteenth Heaven; which is a pity.' 'Well,' said Omri, 'that is good enough; I am very content with my lot; what do I care whether it is the nineteenth or the twentieth Heaven, provided I do my duty during this earthly pilgrimage, and am well received at the final resting-place? Is it not enough to be an honest man in this world, and afterwards to be happy in the country of Brahma? Which Heaven do you yourself propose to enter, Monsieur Bababec, with your nails and your chains?' 'The thirty-fifth,' said Bababec. 'I think it amusing of you', replied Omri, 'to assume you will be placed higher than I; certainly, that can only be the effect of excessive ambition. You condemn those who seek honours in this life, so why do you want such great honours in the next? And what gives you the right to think you will be better treated than I? Let me tell you that I give more in alms in ten days than the cost to you of all the nails you stick into your backside in ten years. Brahma must be mightily pleased that you spend the day completely naked with a chain round your neck; what a service to your country! But I set far more store by the man who sows vegetables, or plants trees, than by all your friends who watch the ends of their noses or carry a pack-saddle from excessive nobility of soul.'

Having spoken thus, Omri quietened down, flattered him, and finally persuaded him to throw away his nails and chain and come and share an honest life. He was scrubbed down, anointed with perfumed essences, and properly dressed. He lived thus for a fortnight very soberly, and admitted he was a hundred times happier than he had been before. But he had lost his influence with the people; the women no longer came to consult him; so he left Omri and returned to his nails in order to regain esteem.

Plato's Dream

Plato dreamt a great deal, and men have not been dreaming any the less ever since. He dreamt for example that human nature was formerly double, and that in punishment for its faults it was separated into male and female.[1]

He had proved that there can only exist five perfect worlds, since there are only five regular bodies in mathematics.[2] His *Republic* was another great dream. He had also dreamt that sleeping comes from waking, and waking from sleeping, and that we must undoubtedly lose our sight if we look at an eclipse of the sun other than reflected in a pond.[3] Great reputations used to be made by dreams.

Here is one of Plato's dreams, by no means one of the least interesting. He dreamt that the great Demiurge, the eternal Geometer, having peopled infinite space with innumerable globes, decided to test the scientific ability of the genies who had witnessed these works. He gave each of them a little piece of matter to work with, rather as Phidias and Zeuxis[4] are said to have given their disciples statues and paintings to make, if one may compare little things with great.

So Demogorgon was allotted the piece of mud which is known as *the Earth*[5] and, after arranging it in the fashion we still see around us today, claimed he had created a masterpiece. He thought he had silenced envy, and stood waiting for praises, even from his fellow-artists. He was deeply surprised to be greeted by them with derision.

One of these, a rather unpleasant ironist, said: 'Yes, you've done a grand job. You've divided your world in two, and put a vast body of water between your hemispheres so that there can be no contact between them. Anyone living at your two poles will die of cold, or die of heat on your equinoctial line. You have prudently laid out great deserts of sand, so that travellers can die of hunger and thirst. I don't mind your sheep and your cows and hens, but frankly, why the snakes and reptiles? Your onions and artichokes are fine, but what is the idea of covering the earth with so many poisonous plants, unless you plan to kill off all its inhabitants? Moreover, you seem to have created thirty or more species of monkey, many more species of dog, but only four or five species of man. It is true that you have endowed this latter creature with what you call *reason*, but in all honesty it is a quite ridiculous faculty, far too close to lunacy. It strikes me moreover that you set little store by this two-legged animal, since you have given him so many enemies and so few defences, so many illnesses and so few cures, so many passions and so little wisdom. You seem not to want very many of these humans to survive: not counting the dangers to which you expose them, you have calculated things so nicely that one day the smallpox will wipe out a tenth of the entire species every year, while her sister the pox will poison the sources of life for the remaining nine-tenths. Were this not enough, you have disposed matters so that half of the survivors will spend their time in litigation while the other half murder each other. No doubt they will all feel greatly obliged to you, and you must indeed be complimented on fashioning a masterpiece.'

Demogorgon blushed; he felt keenly that there were both moral and physical defects in his work, but he maintained that there was more good than ill. 'It is easy to criticize,' he said, 'but do you think it is easy to create an animal who always acts according to reason, who is free, and who never abuses his freedom? Do you think that, when there are nine or ten thousand plants to take root, it is easy to stop some of them developing harmful qualities? Do you imagine that, with a given quantity of water, sand, mud and fire, you can avoid having deserts or oceans? Well, Sir Irony, you have just finished fashioning Mars; let us see how you have fared with your two great rings,[6] and what pretty effects your nights will make with no moon. Let's see if there isn't any madness or illness among your inhabitants.'

So the genies conducted an examination of Mars, and came down very harshly on its ironical artificer. Nor was the painstaking genie who moulded Saturn spared; and his fellow-artists who fashioned Jupiter, Mercury and Venus had all to endure their share of criticism.

Which led to a flurry of long books and short pamphlets being written on all sides; witticisms were exchanged, songs composed, insults traded, and the opposing parties became embittered. Finally the eternal Demiurge imposed silence on all of them: 'You have done well,' he said, 'and you have done ill – because you have plenty of intelligence, and because you are imperfect; your works will last for only a few hundred million years;[7] after which, being better educated, you will do better: it belongs to me alone to make perfect and immortal things.'

So Plato taught his disciples. When he had stopped speaking, one of them said to him: '*And then you woke up.*'

The History of the Travels
of Scarmentado

Written by Himself

I was born in the city of Candia[1] in 1600. My father was the Governor, and I remember that a mediocre poet named Iro,[2] whose harshness was anything but mediocre, wrote some bad verses in my praise to the effect that I was directly descended from Minos; but my father subsequently falling into disgrace, he wrote other verses in which I was traced back only to Pasiphaë and her lover.[3] This Iro was a wicked creature, and the most tedious rogue on the whole island.

At the age of fifteen my father sent me to study in Rome. I arrived hoping to learn every truth: for until then I had been taught just the contrary, after the fashion of this evil world from China to the Alps. Monsignor Profundo, to whom I was recommended, was a peculiar man and one of the most redoubted scholars in the world. He would have taught me the Aristotelian Categories, and was on the point of placing me in the category of his catamites: I had a narrow escape. I saw processions, exorcisms, and a few acts of plunder. It was said, though quite falsely, that Signora Olympia,[4] a person of great prudence, used to sell numerous things which should not be sold. I was at an age when all this seemed highly amusing. A young lady of very tender morals, named Signora Fatelo,[5] took it into her head to fall in love with me. She was being courted by the reverend Father Poignardini and by the reverend Father Aconiti,[6] both of them young professed monks of an order which no longer exists. She reconciled them by bestowing her favours on me, but at the same time I ran the risk of being excommunicated and poisoned. I left, delighted by the architecture of St Peter's.

I travelled in France; it was during the reign of Louis the Just.[7] The first question I was asked was if I should like for my lunch a small portion of the maréchal d'Ancre, whose flesh had been roasted by the populace and was being distributed very cheaply to whoever wanted it.[8]

This state was continually in the grip of civil wars, sometimes over a place in the Cabinet, sometimes over a couple of controversial pages. For more than sixty years this fire, at times smothered and at other times violently fanned, had been ravaging these beautiful climes. Such were the liberties of the Gallican church. 'Alas,' I said, 'this people was nevertheless born gentle; what can have diverted them thus from their innate character? They make jokes, and then they organize the St Bartholomew Massacres.[9] Happy the times when they are only joking!'

I crossed over to England: there the same quarrels excited the same fury. Devout Catholics had resolved, for the good of the Church, to blow up with gunpowder the King, the Royal Family and the entire Parliament, and to rid England of these heretics.[10] I was shown the square where the blessed Queen Mary,[11] daughter of Henry VIII, had burned more than five hundred of her subjects. An Irish priest assured me that this was a very good thing: first, because those who were burned were English; second, because they never used holy water and did not believe in St Patrick's well.[12] He was particularly astonished that Queen Mary had not yet been canonized; but he hoped she soon would be, when the Cardinal Nephew[13] had a little more leisure.

I went to Holland, where I hoped to find more tranquillity among a more phlegmatic people. When I arrived in The Hague they were just cutting off the head of a venerable old gentleman. It was the bald head of Barneveldt,[14] the Prime Minister, who had deserved the most from the republic. Moved to pity, I enquired as to his crime and whether he had betrayed the state. 'He's done far worse than that,' replied a black-cloaked preacher;[15] 'he believes that we can be saved by good works as well as by faith. You must realize that if such opinions become established, the republic could not endure and that severe laws are needed to repress such scandalous horrors.'

A learned politician of the country told me with a sigh: 'Alas, Monsieur, these good times will not last for ever; it is no accident that this people is so zealous; fundamentally their character leans towards the abominable dogma of toleration. One day things will come to that: it makes one shudder.' For myself, awaiting that dark day of moderation and lenience, I rapidly took leave of a country where severity was not softened by any amenity, and I embarked for Spain.

The court was at Seville, the galleons had returned safely,[16] everything breathed abundance and joy at the loveliest season of the year. At the end of an avenue of orange- and lemon-trees I saw an immense arena surrounded by tiered seats covered with precious draperies. The King, the Queen, the infantes, the infantas, were all present under a superb canopy. Opposite this august family was another, more elevated throne. I said to one of my travelling companions: 'Unless that throne is reserved for God, I do not see what purpose it can serve.' These indiscreet words were overheard by a grave Spaniard and were to cost me dear. Meanwhile I imagined we were going to witness some tournament or bullfight, when the Grand Inquisitor appeared on this throne, from which he blessed the King and the people.

Then came an army of monks in procession, two-by-two, white, black, grey, with and without sandals; with and without beards; with and without pointed cowls; then came the executioner; then, surrounded by alguazils and grandees, came forty individuals covered with sacks on which were painted devils and flames.[17] These were Jews who had preferred not to renounce Moses totally, and Christians who had either married their godmothers, or failed to worship Our Lady of Atocha, or been unwilling to part with their cash in favour of the Order of St Jerome. Some very beautiful prayers were devoutly chanted, after which all of the guilty were slowly burned; which seemed to give the royal family much edification.

That evening, as I was going to bed, there arrived two familiars of the Inquisition, accompanied by the Holy Hermandad:[18] they embraced me tenderly and led me, without a word being spoken, to a very cool cell furnished with a straw bed and a fine crucifix. I remained there for six weeks, at the end of which the reverend Father Inquisitor sent to request that I would come and speak with him: he folded me in his arms for a while with fatherly affection, told me he was sincerely distressed to hear that I had been so badly accommodated, but that all the rooms in the house were full, and how he hoped on another occasion I should be more comfortable. He then asked cordially if I did not know why I was there. I replied to the reverend Father that apparently it was on account of my sins. 'Well, my dear child, and for which sin in particular? You may tell me in confidence.' Try as I might I could not guess; he kindly put me on the right track.

At last I remembered my indiscreet words. I was let off with a scourging and a fine of thirty thousand reals. I was taken to pay my respects to the Grand Inquisitor: he was a polite man who asked me what I had thought of his little entertainment. I told him it was delightful, and then went to urge my travelling companions to quit this country straightaway, beautiful as it was. They had had time to discover all the great things the Spaniards had done for religion. They had read the memoirs of the famous Bishop of Chiapa,[19] from which it appears that ten million infidels in the Americas had been slaughtered or burned to death or drowned in order to convert them. I thought the Bishop was exaggerating, but even if the number of sacrifices were reduced to five million victims it would remain impressive.

The desire to travel still urged me on. I had thought of finishing my tour of Europe in Turkey, so we headed in that direction. I firmly resolved not to offer any more opinions about the spectacles I might witness. 'These Turks', I told my companions, 'are miscreants who have not been baptized, and are consequently bound to be far crueller than the reverend Father Inquisitors. Let us keep silent when we are among the Muslims.'

I went among them. I was strangely surprised to find many more Christian churches in Turkey than there had been in Candia. I even saw numerous troops of monks who were allowed to pray openly to the Virgin Mary and to curse Mohammed, some in Greek, some in Latin, and others in Armenian. 'What excellent people are these Turks!' I exclaimed. But the Greek Christians and the Latin Christians in Constantinople were mortal enemies; these slaves persecuted one another like dogs which bite each other in the street and have to be separated with sticks by their masters. At that time the Grand Vizier was protecting the Greeks. The Greek Patriarch accused me of having supped with the Latin Patriarch, and I was condemned in a session of the Divan[20] to a hundred strokes of the bastinado on the soles of my feet, redeemable against a fine of five hundred sequins. The next day the Grand Vizier was strangled; the following day his successor, who was for the Latin party and was strangled only a month later, condemned me to the same fine for having supped with the Greek Patriarch. I found myself under the sad necessity of attending no more either the Greek or the Latin church. To console myself I hired a very beautiful Circassian girl, who was in private the tenderest of companions, and the most devout of worshippers at the mosque. One night, in the soft transports of love, she exclaimed in my embraces: 'Allah, Illah, Allah!'[21] These are the sacramental words of the Turks; I thought they must be words of love, so I cried out just as tenderly: 'Allah, Illah, Allah!' 'Ah!' she said, 'praise be to God the merciful! You are a Turk.' I told her that I blessed Him for giving me my prowess, and thought myself only too happy. The next morning the Imam came to circumcise me; and, as I made some objection, the Cadi[22] of the quarter, a forthright fellow, offered to impale me; I saved my foreskin and my backside with a thousand gold sequins, and immediately fled into Persia, resolved never to attend another mass, Greek or Latin, in Turkey, and never again to cry out 'Allah, Illah, Allah!' in the midst of a love-tryst.

Arriving in Ispahan, I was asked if I were for the black sheep or the white sheep. I replied that it was a matter of indifference to me, so long as they were tender. You must understand that the Persians were divided at this time between the White Sheep and Black Sheep factions. They thought I was mocking both parties; so at the gates of the city I found myself embroiled in a violent quarrel: it cost me a further fortune in gold sequins to shake off these sheep.

I pressed on as far as China with an interpreter, who assured me that here was a country where everyone lived freely and happily. The Tartars had made themselves its masters, after spreading devastation and bloodshed; and the reverend Father Jesuits on the one side, like the reverend Father Dominicans on the other, claimed they were garnering souls for God, without anyone knowing anything about it. Never have there been such zealous missionaries: for they persecuted each other freely, sent back volumes of calumnies to Rome, and treated each other as infidels and corrupt officials. Above all there was a dreadful quarrel going on between them over the method of bowing. The Jesuits wanted the Chinese to salute their fathers and mothers after the Chinese custom, and the Dominicans wanted them to salute after the manner of Rome. It so happened that the Jesuits took me for a Dominican. I was presented to His Tartar Majesty as a Papal spy. The supreme council ordered a first mandarin, who in turn ordered a sergeant, who commanded four local policemen to arrest and ceremonially bind me. After one hundred and forty genuflections I was taken before His Majesty. He asked me if I was the Pope's spy, and if it were true that this prince was coming in person to dethrone him. I replied that the Pope was a seventy-year-old priest; that he lived four thousand leagues away from His Sacred Majesty of Tartar-China; that he had about two thousand soldiers who mounted guard under parasols; that he was not given to dethroning anybody, and that His Majesty could sleep in peace. This was the least disastrous adventure of my life. I was sent to Macao, from where I embarked for Europe.

My vessel needed to be refitted off the coast of Golconda, so I took the opportunity to visit the court of the great Aureng-Zebe,[23] about whom such incredible things were said around the world; he was at that time resident in Delhi. I had the consolation of seeing him on the day of a pompous ceremony when he received the celestial present sent to him by the Sherif of Mecca. This was a broom which had been used to sweep out the holy house, the Kaaba or Beth Alla. This broom is the symbol of the divine broom which sweeps out all the filth of the soul. Aureng-Zebe did not seem to have much need of it, being the most pious man in all Hindustan. It is true that he had cut the throat of one of his brothers and poisoned his father, and that twenty Rajahs and as many Omras had been tortured and put to death. But this counted for nothing, and only his piety was spoken of. He was compared to no less than His Sacred Majesty and Most Serene Emperor of Morocco, Muley Ismaël,[24] who chopped off heads every Friday after prayer.

I said nothing; travel had educated me, and I felt that it was not my place to decide between two such august sovereigns. A young Frenchman with whom I was lodging was lacking, I confess, in respect towards the Emperors of the Indies and of Morocco. He took it into his head to say most indiscreetly that in Europe there were to be found pious sovereigns who governed their states well and even frequented churches, without however killing their fathers and brothers, and without cutting off the heads of their subjects. Our interpreter translated this impious speech into Hindu. Instructed by past events, I quickly had my camels saddled and the Frenchman and I took off. I learned afterwards that the officers of the great Aureng-Zebe came for us that very night, but found only the interpreter. He was executed in the public square, and all the courtiers confessed without flattery that his death was richly deserved.

I still had to see Africa, so as to enjoy all the pleasures of our Continent. And see it I did. My ship was captured by negro pirates. Our captain protested loudly and asked them why they were violating international law in this manner. The negro captain replied: 'Your nose is long, and ours is flat; your hair is straight and ours is frizzy; your skin is the colour of ashes, ours the colour of ebony; consequently by the sacred laws of nature we must always be enemies. You purchase us in markets on the coast of Guinea, like beasts of burden, to make us work at occupations as painful as they are ridiculous. You beat us with whips made from a bull's pizzle to make us dig in the mountains for a kind of yellow earth which in itself is good for nothing and not nearly as valuable as a good Egyptian onion. So, when our paths cross, and we happen to be the stronger, we make slaves of you and make you labour in our fields, or we cut off your noses and ears.'

There was nothing to be said in answer to so wise a speech. I went to work the fields belonging to an old negress, in order to keep my nose and ears. I was ransomed at the end of a year. I had seen all that is beautiful, good and admirable on earth: I resolved henceforth to see nothing but my household gods. I married in my own country. I was cuckolded, and I came to see that this was the most agreeable condition life has to offer.

The Consoler and
the Consoled

One day the great philosopher Citophilus said to a grief-stricken lady, who moreover had good reason to grieve: 'Dear lady, once upon a time the Queen of England, daughter of the great Henri IV,[1] was as unhappy as you. She had been exiled from her kingdoms; she had come close to perishing on the seas amid tempests, and she had seen her royal husband die on the scaffold.'

'I feel sorry for her,' said the lady, and began to weep over her own misfortunes.

'And then,' continued Citophilus, 'remember Mary Stuart: she was deeply in love with a gallant musician endowed with a very fine bass-baritone. Her husband killed her musician in front of her eyes. Then her good friend and cousin Elizabeth, who called herself the Virgin Queen, had her beheaded on a scaffold draped in black, after keeping her in prison for eighteen years.'[2]

'That was very cruel,' said the lady, and fell back into her melancholy.

'Perhaps', said her consoler, 'you have heard of the beautiful Queen of Naples, who was seized and strangled?'[3]

'I vaguely remember,' said the sufferer.

'After dinner', said the other, 'I must tell you about a sovereign queen who was dethroned in my own lifetime, and perished on a desert island.'

'I know all about her,' replied the lady.

'Very well, then, I shall tell you what happened to another great princess, whom I introduced to the study of philosophy. She had a lover, as do all great and beautiful princesses. Her father entered her chamber and surprised the lover, whose face was on fire and his eyes glittering like carbuncles, the lady likewise extremely flushed. The

70

young man's visage so displeased the father that he gave it the most resounding slap that had ever been heard throughout the province. At which the young man took a pair of fire-tongs and cracked the skull of the father, who has never fully recovered, and still bears the scars. The distracted lady leapt from the window and dislocated her foot; to this day she limps visibly though otherwise she has an admirable figure. The lover was condemned to death for fracturing the skull of a great prince. You may imagine the princess's state of mind while he was being led off to be hanged. I visited her at length in prison; she only ever spoke about her misfortunes.'

'Why then do you insist on relieving me of mine?' asked the lady.

'Because', replied the philosopher, 'you must not dwell on them, and because so many great ladies have been so unfortunate, that it ill becomes you to despair. Think of Hecuba,[4] think of Niobe.'[5]

'Ah!' said the lady, 'had I lived in their time, or the time of all those great princesses, and you were to describe my misfortunes to them by way of consolation, do you think they would have listened?'

The next day the philosopher lost his only son, and was close to dying of grief. The lady drew up a list of all the kings who had lost their children, and brought it to him. He read it, found it very accurate, and continued to weep nonetheless. Three months later they met again, and were astonished to find each other in very good spirits. They had a handsome statue erected, which they dedicated to Time, with the inscription: TO THE ONE WHO CONSOLES.

The Story of a Good Brahmin

During my travels I met an old Brahmin, a very wise man of lively intellect and great learning; who was moreover wealthy and, consequently, all the wiser: for, lacking nothing, he had no need to deceive anyone. His household was well managed by three beautiful wives who strove to please him. When he was not enjoying himself with his wives, he passed the time in philosophizing.

Near his house, which was beautifully decorated with charming gardens, there lived an old Indian woman, bigoted, imbecilic and impoverished.

One day the Brahmin said to me: 'I wish I had never been born.' On my asking him why, he replied: 'I have been studying for forty years, which is to say forty wasted years; I teach others yet am ignorant of everything; this state of affairs fills my soul with so much humiliation and disgust that my life is intolerable. I was born into Time, I live in Time, and I do not know what Time is. I find myself at a point between two eternities, as our wise men say, yet I have no conception of eternity. I am composed of matter, I think, but have never been able to discover what produces thought. I do not know whether or not my understanding is a simple faculty within me, such as walking or digesting, and whether or not I think with my head in the same way that I hold things with my hands. Not only is the origin of my thought unknown to me, but the origin of my movements is equally hidden: I do not know why I exist. Yet every day people ask me questions on all these issues. I must give answers, yet have nothing worth saying, so I talk a great deal, and am confused and ashamed of myself afterwards for having spoken.

'It is worse still when I am asked if Brahma was born of Vishnu or if they are both eternal.[1] God is my witness I have not the remotest idea, and my ignorance is clear from my replies. "Ah, Holy One!" they say to me, "tell us why evil swamps the earth." I am as perplexed as those who ask me this question. Sometimes I tell them that everything is for the best; but those who are tormented by the gravel, or who have been ruined and mutilated in the wars, do not believe a word of it, and nor do I. I return home overwhelmed both by my own curiosity and my ignorance. I read our ancient books, and they only increase my darkness. I ask my companions; some reply that we must enjoy life and make a sport of mankind; others think they know something, and lose themselves in extravagant speculation. Everything increases the anguish I feel. I am ready sometimes to despair when I think that after all my seeking I neither know where I come from, nor where I am going, nor who I am, nor what I shall become.'

The state of this good man was truly painful to me: nobody was more rational or more sincere than he. I perceived that his unhappiness increased in proportion as his understanding developed and his sensitivity deepened.

The same day I saw the old woman who lived near him. I asked her if she had ever been afflicted by the thought that she was ignorant of the nature of her soul. She did not even understand my question. Never in her life had she reflected for a single moment on any of the problems which tormented the Brahmin; she believed with all her heart in the metamorphoses of Vishnu and, provided she could occasionally obtain a little Ganges water to perform her ablutions, thought herself the happiest of women.

Struck by the contentment of this poor creature, I returned to my philosopher: 'Are you not ashamed to be unhappy,' I said, 'when outside your gates there is an old automaton who thinks about nothing and yet lives happily?' 'You are right,' he replied; 'I have told myself a hundred times that I would be happy were I as brainless as my neighbour, and yet I would not want such happiness.'

This answer from my Brahmin impressed me more than all the rest. I set to examining myself, and saw that in truth I would not care to be happy at the price of being an imbecile.

I put the matter before some philosophers, and they were of my opinion. 'Nevertheless', I said, 'there is a furious contradiction in this way of thinking: for what is at issue after all is – how to be happy. What does it matter whether one has brains or not? Moreover, those who are happy in their existence are certain of their happiness, whereas those who reason are not certain that they reason well. It is clear, therefore,' I continued, 'that one must elect not to have common sense, however little common sense contributes to our discomfort.' Everyone agreed, and yet I found nobody who was willing to accept the bargain of becoming an imbecile in exchange for happiness. From which I conclude that, if we attach importance to happiness, we attach even greater importance to reason.

But on reflection, to prefer reason to felicity would seem to be highly irrational. How can this contradiction be explained? Like all other contradictions: it is matter for much talk.

Pot-Pourri

Brioché[1] was the father of Punchinello;[2] not his real father but his
tutelary father. Brioché's actual father was Guillot Gorju, who was the
son of Gilles, who was the son of Fat-René,[3] who in turn drew his
origins from the Prince of Fools and from Mother Fool; such is the
account given in the *Almanac of the Fairground*.[4] Monsieur Parfaict,[5]
an equally trustworthy source, claims Tabarin as Brioché's sire, out of
Big-William, out of John-the-Sausage,[6] but traced back nonetheless to
the Prince of Fools. If these two historians contradict one another, that
is proof of the pudding as far as Father Daniel[7] is concerned, who
reconciles the two accounts with admirable sagacity, and in so doing
makes short work of the Pyrrhonism of history.

CHAPTER II

As I was finishing this opening paragraph of the notebooks of Merry
Hissing in my study, whose window gives on to the rue Saint-Antoine,
I saw the syndics of the society of apothecaries passing by, on their
way to seize contraband drugs and verdigris which the Jesuits of the
rue Saint-Antoine were selling; my cousin Monsieur Husson, who is
a level-headed fellow, came to visit me and said: 'My friend, you laugh
to see the Jesuits vilified; you are delighted to learn that they are
convicted of parricide in Portugal,[8] and of fomenting a rebellion in
Paraguay;[9] the public outcry which has been raised against them in
France,[10] the hatred borne them, the increasing opprobrium heaped

upon them, all this seems to console you. But you must realize that if they are ruined, as all honest folk desire, you will gain nothing by it: you will be overwhelmed instead by the Jansenist faction.[11] These are rabid enthusiasts, with souls of bronze, worse than the Presbyterians who overthrew Charles I. Remember that fanatics are more dangerous than crooks. One can never talk reason to a firebrand, whereas crooks will listen.

I argued at length with Monsieur Husson; finally I said: 'Console yourself, sir; perhaps the Jansenists will one day be as clever as the Jesuits.' I tried to mollify him; but you can never bend the opinions of a head made of iron.

CHAPTER III

Brioché, seeing that Punchinello was humped front and rear, wanted to teach him to read and write. After two years Punchinello's spelling was adequate, but he never mastered the use of a pen.[12] One of his biographers notes that he tried one day to write his name, but that nobody could read it.[13]

Brioché was very poor; he and his wife could not feed Punchinello, still less apprentice him to a trade. Punchinello said to them: 'Father and mother, I am a hunchback, and I have a good memory; together with three or four of my friends I can set up a puppet theatre: I shall make a little money; people have always liked marionettes. There are sometimes losses in setting up from scratch, but also great profits to be made.'

Monsieur and Madame Brioché admired the good sense of the young man; the theatrical company was formed, and went to set up its small stage in a Swiss village on the road from Appenzel to Milan.

This happened to be just the village in which the mountebanks of Orvieto had set up a shop for their orvietan.[14] They noticed that little by little the rabble started going to the puppet theatre, and that local sales of their patent toilet soap and ointments against burns were down by half. They accused Punchinello of various bad business practices, and brought their accusations before the magistrate.[15] The petition stated that Punch was a dangerous drunk, and that one day in the middle of the market-place he had administered a hundred kicks in the stomach to some peasants who were selling trinkets.

It was also claimed that he had molested a tradesman selling turkey-cocks; finally, they accused him of being a sorcerer.[16] Monsieur Parfaict, in his History of the Theatre, claims that he was eventually swallowed by a toad; but Father Daniel thinks or at least says otherwise. We do not know what happened to Brioché.[17] Since he was only the putative father of Punchinello, the historians have not seen fit to tell us his fate.

CHAPTER IV

The late Monsieur Dumarsais[18] contended that the greatest of abuses was the sale of offices. 'It is a great misfortune for the state', he said, 'that a man of merit, without fortune, cannot succeed at anything. How many buried talents, how many fools in posts! What a detestable policy, to stifle the spirit of competition!' Monsieur Dumarsais, without realizing, was speaking in his own defence; for he was reduced to teaching Latin, who would have done the state great services had he been employed. I know hack writers who would have enriched an entire province had they been in the place of those who ruined it. But to have such a position you must be the son of a rich man who leaves you the wherewithal to purchase an office, a post, or what is termed *a dignity*.

Dumarsais contended that, had they wielded power, a Montaigne, a Charron, a Descartes, a Gassendi, a Bayle would neither have sent schoolboys to the galleys for arguing the case against Aristotle's philosophy, nor ordered to be burned alive the priest Urbain Grandier[19] or the priest Gaufredi,[20] nor would they have, etc., etc.

CHAPTER V

Not long ago, the knight Roginante, a gentleman of Ferrara, who wished to make a collection of paintings of the Flemish school, went on a shopping expedition to Amsterdam. He bargained with the dealer Vandergru for a rather handsome Christ. 'Is it possible', said the Ferraran to the Batavian, 'that you who are not a Christian (since you are a Dutchman[21]) can be in possession of a Christ?' 'I am both Christian and Catholic,' replied Vandergru, keeping his temper, and he sold his painting for a good price. 'Do you believe, then, that Jesus Christ is God?' asked Roginante. 'Certainly,' said Vandergru.

Another collector of curios inhabited the adjoining house: a Socinian,[22] who sold him a Holy Family. 'What is your view of the Christ child?' asked the Ferraran. 'I think that he was the most perfect creature that God ever placed on earth.'

From here the Ferraran went to see Moses Mansebo,[23] who merely had some fine landscapes for sale, and no Holy Family. Roginante asked why such subjects were not to be found in his gallery. 'That is because we hold that Family in abomination,' he replied.

Roginante passed on to the house of a well-known Anabaptist, who had the prettiest children in the world, and he asked them in which church they had been baptized. 'What a question, Monsieur!' they replied, 'we are not yet baptized, thank God.'

Before he was half-way down the street Roginante had already encountered a dozen sects each wholly opposed to the others. His travelling companion, Monsieur Sacrito, said to him: 'Let us get out of here at once – this is the hour when the Bourse opens, and all these people will doubtless be at each other's throats, according to ancient custom, since they all think differently; and the mob will beat us up for being the Pope's subjects.'

They were both astonished to see all these good people leave their houses with their clerks, greet each other civilly, and go together to the Bourse. On this particular day, there were all told fifty-three different religions present, including Armenians and Jansenists. Fifty-three million francs' worth of trading was done in the most peaceful manner imaginable, and the Ferraran returned to his country where he found more *Agnus Dei* wax medals than bills of exchange.[24]

Every day the same spectacle is seen in London, Hamburg, Danzig, even Venice, etc. But the most edifying sight I have encountered was in Constantinople.

I had the honour, fifty years ago, of attending the inauguration of a Greek Patriarch by the Sultan Ahmed III,[25] may God receive his soul. He presented this Christian priest with a ring, and a staff in the form of a crutch. There followed a procession of Christians in Cleobula Street, headed by two janissaries.[26] I had the pleasure of publicly receiving communion in the patriarchal church, and I could obtain a canonry if I wanted.

I confess that on my return to Marseilles I was greatly astonished to find no mosque there. I expressed my surprise to the Intendant and to the Bishop. I told them that it was highly uncivil, and that if Christians had churches in Muslim countries we might at least pay the resident Turks the courtesy of a few chapels. They both promised that they would write in favour of it, but there the matter rested, thanks to the edict *Unigenitus*.[27]

Oh my brother Jesuits! You have not been tolerant, and no one is tolerant of you. Console yourselves: others will in turn become persecutors, and will in turn become as loathsome.

CHAPTER VI

I was relating these matters, a few days ago, to Monsieur de Boucacous, a passionate native of Languedoc and a zealous Huguenot. '*Cavalisque!*' he exclaimed, 'so they treat us in France as they treat the Turks: they are refused mosques, and we are refused churches!' 'As to mosques,' said I, 'the Turks have not yet asked for any; and I dare to cherish the hope that they will obtain them when they wish, because they are our staunch allies; but I doubt very much that your churches will be re-established, in spite of all the courtesy on which we pride ourselves; the reason being that you are, so to speak, our enemies.' 'Your enemies!'

cried Monsieur de Boucacous, 'we who are the most ardent supporters of the King!' 'You are indeed very ardent,' I replied, 'so ardent that you have set off nine civil wars, not counting the Cévennes Massacres.'[28] 'But if we have started civil wars,' said he, 'that is because you were roasting us alive in the public squares; in the long run one gets tired of being burned alive, and not even the patience of a saint can endure it: so long as we are left in peace I swear that we shall be the most faithful of subjects.'

'That is precisely what we are doing,' I said; 'we close our eyes to your existence, we let you go about your business, and you have a pretty reasonable amount of freedom.' 'Some freedom!' replied Monsieur de Boucacous; 'it only takes four or five thousand of us to assemble in the middle of the countryside to sing four-part psalms, for a regiment of dragoons immediately to show up to make each and every one of us return to our homes. Is that a way to live? Is that freedom?'

So then I said: 'There is no country in the world where one can assemble without permission of the sovereign; all assemblies are against the law. Worship God in your own homes after your fashion; stop deafening people with the bellowing which you call *music*. Do you really think God is well pleased with you when you sing his command-ments to the tune of "*Wake up, sleeping beauty*"?[29] Or when you say, like the Jews, about a neighbouring people: "Happy shall he be, who destroys thee forever, who, tearing children from the breast, will crush their infidel heads!"[30] Does God categorically want us to dash out the brains of little children? Is that human? Furthermore, does God like bad poetry and bad music?'

Monsieur de Boucacous interrupted me, and asked me if the dog Latin of our own Psalter was preferable. 'Doubtless not,' I replied; 'I even admit that there is some sterility of imagination in praying to God only in a viciously corrupt translation of the ancient canticles of a people whom we abhor; we are all Jews at vespers, as we are all pagans at the Opera.

'What irritates me most is that Ovid's *Metamorphoses* are, by the mischief of the devil, far better written and more pleasing than the Jewish Psalter: for it must be admitted that the Hill of Sion, and those basilisk mouths, and those other hills that skip like rams,[31] and all those tedious repetitions, do not stand up well against either Greek or Latin or French poetry. Whatever chilly little Racine junior[32] may do, this unnatural child will not prevent his father from remaining – to speak profanely – a better poet than King David.

'Be that as it may, at the end of the day we are the official religion in this land; you are not allowed public assemblies in England, so why do you expect such a liberty in France? Do what you please in your own homes, and I have the assurance of both the Governor and the Intendant that by behaving yourselves you will be left in peace: only foolhardiness leads to and will lead to persecutions. I find it very bad that your civil marriages, the status of your children, and your rights of inheritance should suffer the slightest interference.[33] It is unjust to bleed and purge you because your fathers were fools. But what do you expect? This world is a great Bedlam where lunatics put other lunatics in chains.'

CHAPTER VII

Reduced to beggary, which was their natural state, Punchinello's companions joined forces with other bohemians, and went from village to village.[34] They arrived in a small town, and found a fourth-floor room where they set about making drugs, the sale of which helped them for a while to survive. They even cured of its scabies a spaniel belonging to a lady of quality; the neighbours proclaimed a miracle, but despite all their ingenuity the troupe made no money.

They were lamenting their obscurity and misery, when one day they heard a noise over their heads, like a wheelbarrow being rolled along the floor. They went up to the fifth floor, where they found a little man making puppets on his own account; he was called Sir Good-Deed, and he had just the gifts necessary for the exercise of his art.

Nobody understood a word he said; but he spoke a most agreeable gibberish, and his life-sized puppets were not badly put together. One of the company, who also excelled in gibberish, spoke to him thus:

'We believe you are destined to set our puppets back on their feet; for we have read in Nostradamus[35] these apt and prophetic words: *olle ni hcnup kcab gnirb lliw deed-do og*, which read backwards clearly says: *Good-Deed will bring back Punchinello*. Our Punch was swallowed by a toad, but we have recovered his hat, his hump and his squeaker. You will provide the vital brass wire to operate him. I also believe you might be able to give him a moustache just like the one he had; and when we join forces, we are bound to be a great success. Punchinello will be fulfilled by Nostradamus, and Nostradamus by Punchinello.'

Sir Good-Deed accepted the proposition. He was asked what he would like in return for his trouble. 'I want great honours and a lot of money,' he replied. 'We have neither,' said the spokesman for the troupe, 'but in time we shall have both.' So Sir Good-Deed joined forces with the bohemians, and they all went to Milan to set up their theatre under the protection of Madame Carminetta.[36] Notices were put up to the effect that Punchinello himself, who had been swallowed by a toad in a village in the canton of Appenzel, would reappear on the boards of Milan, and would dance with Madame Gigogne.[37] Every pedlar of orvietan[38] might vainly oppose it for all he was worth, Sir Good-Deed also knew the secret recipe of orvietan, and maintained that his was superior: he sold a lot of it to the ladies, who were all crazy about Punchinello, and he became so rich that he elected himself leader of the troupe.[39]

As soon as he had what he wanted and what everyone wants – honours and riches – he became very ungrateful towards Madame Carminetta. He bought a fine house opposite his benefactress, and found a way of having it paid for by his companions. He was no longer seen paying court to Madame Carminetta; on the contrary, having invited her to dine at his house, when finally she deigned one day to come, he had the door shut firmly in her face.[40]

CHAPTER VIII

Not having understood a word of Merry Hissing's preceding chapter, I repaired to my friend Monsieur Husson's house for an explanation. He told me that it was a dark allegory about Father La Valette,[41] a bankrupt American merchant; but that it was a long time since he had ceased to trouble himself with such idiocies, and he no longer went to puppet shows; moreover that *Polyeucte*[42] was playing that day at the theatre, and he wanted to see it. So I accompanied him.

Throughout the first act Monsieur Husson kept shaking his head. In the interval I asked him why his head was shaking so much. 'I must admit', said he, 'that this fool Polyeucte, and the brazen Nearchus, irritate me to death. What would you say of the son-in-law of the Governor of Paris – supposing him to be a Huguenot – who, accompanying his father-in-law on Easter Day to Notre-Dame, went and smashed to pieces the ciborium and chalice, and then kicked the archbishop and his canons in the stomach? Would his actions be perfectly justified on the grounds that we are idolaters, and that he heard as much from Sire Lubolier, an Amsterdam preacher, and also from Sire Morfyré, a Berlin chronicler and compiler of the *Germanic Library*, who in turn had it from a preacher by the name of Urieju?[43] Well, that is an exact description of how Polyeucte behaves. How can one take any interest in this dull fanatic, seduced by the equally fanatical Nearchus?'

Monsieur Husson amicably offered me these opinions during the intervals. He began laughing when Polyeucte had to relinquish his wife to his rival; and he found it rather bourgeois of her when she tells her lover that she is going to her room rather than accompanying him to church:

> *Adieu, trop vertueux objet, et trop charmant;*
> *Adieu, trop généreux et trop parfait amant;*
> *Je vais seule en ma chambre enfermer mes regrets.*

> Farewell, too virtuous, too charming object;
> Farewell, too generous, too noble lover;
> I go alone to my chamber to bury my sadness.

But he admired the scene in which she asks her lover for clemency towards her husband.[44] 'Here', he said, 'we have a Governor of Armenia who is clearly the most craven and base of men; this father of Pauline even admits that he has the morals of a rogue:

> Polyeucte est ici l'appui de ma famille;
> Mais si par son trépas l'autre épousait ma fille,
> J'acquerrais bien par là de plus puissants appuis,
> Qui me mettraient plus haut cent fois que je ne suis.

> Polyeucte is here the support of my family;
> But if through his death the other were to marry my daughter,
> I should through that obtain more powerful support,
> Which would elevate me far higher than I now am.[45]

A public prosecutor at the Châtelet would hardly think or express the thing any differently. Yet there are honest souls who swallow this stuff. Well, I am not of their number. If such wretched sentiments can figure in a tragedy in the land of the Gauls, then we may as well burn the *Oedipus* of the Greeks.'

Monsieur Husson is a tough man. I did what I could to soften his opinions, but I was unable to get very far. He persisted in his views, and I in mine.

CHAPTER IX

We left Sir Good-Deed very rich and very insolent. He got on so well with his intrigues that his reputation grew as an agent for large numbers of puppets. As soon as he acquired this rank he paraded Punchinello in every town, and posted bills to the effect that everyone must address him as *Monsieur*, or there would be no performances. Which is why, in all puppet shows, Punch never replies to his partner unless the latter calls him Mr Punchinello. Little by little Punchinello became so important that no performances were given without his being paid a percentage, just as provincial opera houses pay a percentage to the Paris Opera.[46]

One day, a servant who acted as both ticket collector and theatre-box usher rebelled against Good-Deed after being dismissed, and set up a competing puppet troupe who denounced all the dances of Madame Gigogne and all the sleights of hand of Good-Deed.[47] Moreover, he omitted more than fifty of the ingredients which go to make up orvietan, and made his own with just five or six drugs; he sold it much cheaper, taking a huge number of customers away from Good-Deed, thereby provoking a furious legal row and protracted battles in the courtyard of the puppet fair.

CHAPTER X

Monsieur Husson spoke to me yesterday about his travels: having spent several years in the Ports of the Levant, he visited Persia, stayed for a long period in India, and saw the whole of Europe. 'I noticed', he said, 'that a prodigious number of Jews are waiting for the Messiah, who would let themselves be impaled sooner than admit that he has already come. I have met a thousand Turks who are convinced that Mohammed had hidden the other half of the moon up his sleeve. Ordinary people, the world over, believe the most extraordinary things. However, were a philosopher to divide an écu with the most imbecilic of these unfortunates, in whom the light of human reason is so dreadfully dimmed, it follows that if there is a sou to be won then the imbecile will get the upper hand of the philosopher. How comes it that moles, so blind to the larger interests, are so lynx-eyed about the smaller? Why is the same Jew who cuts your throat on Friday so loath to steal a farthing from you on the Sabbath? This contrariness of our species merits examination.'

'Is it not simply the case', I replied, 'that men are superstitious by custom, but wicked by instinct?'

'I shall think about that,' said Monsieur Husson; 'but it seems a reasonable explanation.'

CHAPTER XI

After the episode of the theatre-box usher, Punchinello suffered many disgraces. The English, who are disputatious and gloomy, have persisted in preferring their Shakespeare over him;[48] but elsewhere his farces have been very fashionable, and, aside from the Opéra-Comique, his was the leading theatre. He had great quarrels with Scaramouche and Harlequin, and the outcome has still to be decided. However . . .

CHAPTER XII

'In which case, Monsieur,' I went on, 'how is it possible to be at the same time so barbarous and so entertaining? Why, in the history of a people, does one find on the one hand the St Bartholomew's Day Massacre and on the other the tales of La Fontaine, etc.? Is it the effect of climate? Or of the laws?'

'The human species', replied Monsieur Husson, 'is capable of anything. Nero wept when he had to sign the death warrant of a common criminal, he acted in farces, and he assassinated his mother. Monkeys perform extremely funny capers, but they also smother their little ones. Nothing is more gentle, more timid than a greyhound bitch; but she will tear to pieces a hare, and steep her long muzzle in its blood.'

'You should write a fine book for us', I said to him, 'which would develop all these contradictions.'

'That book exists already: you have only to observe a weathervane; it turns sometimes to the gentle breath of Zephyrus, sometimes to the violent North wind: such is man.'

CHAPTER XIII

Often nothing is more convenient than to fall in love with one's cousin. Or one's niece; but it costs eighteen thousand livres, payable to Rome, to marry a cousin, and eighty thousand livres to sleep with a niece in the legitimacy of the marriage bed.

I calculate that forty nieces per year marry their uncles, and two hundred cousins are joined together in wedlock, which makes six million eight hundred thousand livres lost to the realm annually in marriage ceremonies. Add to this approximately six hundred thousand livres for what are termed the *papal revenues on French lands*, which the French King accords his subjects in the form of benefices; add minor expenses on top, and this makes about eight million four hundred thousand livres which we pay without demur to the Holy Father every year. Perhaps I exaggerate a little; but it will be agreed that if there is a glut of pretty cousins and nieces, and if the mortality rate affects the beneficiaries, then the figure could double. The burden would be heavy, given that we also have ships to build and armies and investors to pay.

It astonishes me that, among the enormous quantity of books by authors who have governed this state for the past twenty years, none has thought to reform these abuses. I asked a friend of mine who is a Doctor of the Sorbonne to show me the place in the Scriptures which says that France must pay Rome the aforesaid sums: he could not find it. I spoke of the matter to a Jesuit; he replied that this tax was imposed on the Gauls by St Peter, from the first year he came to Rome. As I doubted that St Peter had ever made that journey, he convinced me by telling me that the keys to Paradise which Peter always carried around on his belt are still to be seen in Rome. 'It is true', added this Jesuit, 'that no canonical author speaks of the journey of this Simon Bar-jona;[49] but we have a fine letter of St Peter, dated from Babylon. Now assuredly Babylon means Rome, and therefore you Frenchmen owe the Pope money whenever you marry your cousins.' I admit that I was struck by the force of this argument.

CHAPTER XIV

I have an aged relative who served the King for fifty-two years. He retired to the Haute-Alsace, where he has a small estate which he cultivates, in the diocese of Porentru.[50] One day he wanted to have his fields given their final ploughing – the season was advanced and time was short. His farmhands refused, on the grounds that it was the Feast of St Barbara, the most celebrated saint in Porentru. 'Well! my friends,' said this relative, 'you have already been to mass in honour of Barbara, and have rendered to Barbara what is Barbara's; now render to me what is mine: go and till my field instead of taking off to the tavern. Does St Barbara order you to get drunk in her honour, while I remain without wheat this year?' The head farmhand replied: 'Monsieur, you can see that I should be damned in hell if I worked on such a holy day. St Barbara is the highest saint in Heaven; she once traced the sign of the cross on a marble column with the tip of her finger; and with the same finger, and the same sign, she made all the teeth fall out of a dog that had bitten her on the buttocks. I'll not work on St Barbara's Day, and that's that.'

My relative sent off for some Lutheran farmhands, and his field was tilled. The Bishop of Porentru excommunicated him. My relative appealed against this as excessive; the case has yet to be tried. Nobody believes more firmly than my relative that we must honour the saints, but he also claims that we must till the soil.

I estimate that there are approximately five million workers in France, whether labourers or artisans, who earn on average twenty sous per day, and who are piously constrained to earn nothing on thirty days of the year, not including Sundays: which makes a hundred and fifty million less in money circulation, and a hundred and fifty million less in manpower. What a prodigious advantage our neighbouring countries must have over us, who have neither a St Barbara nor a Bishop of Porentru! The reply to these objections was that the taverns, open on feast days, contribute a great deal to the state coffers. My relative agreed; but he maintained that this was a minor compensation; and that besides, if one can go to work after mass one can go to the tavern after work. He maintains that it is all a civic matter, and nothing to do with the episcopate; moreover, that it is better to work in the fields than it is to get drunk. I greatly fear that he will lose his lawsuit.

CHAPTER XV

A few years ago, travelling through Burgundy with Monsieur Evrard, who is known to you all, we saw a vast palace under construction. I enquired as to which prince owned it. A mason replied that it was Monsignor the Abbot of Cîteaux; that the deal had been struck at seventeen hundred thousand livres, but that it would probably cost a lot more than that yet.

I thanked God for placing his faithful servant in a position to raise such a handsome edifice, and lavish so much money upon the region. 'You jest, surely?' said Monsieur Evrard. 'Is it not rather an abomination that idleness should be rewarded by an income of two hundred and fifty thousand livres, when the vigilance of a poor country priest is punished by a "due portion", amounting to a hundred écus? Is this inequality not the most unjust and odious thing in the world? Of what benefit is it to the state that a monk is lodged in a palace worth two million? Twenty families of impoverished officers, if they shared this two million, would each have an honest fortune, and would produce more officers for the king. Petty monks, who are today the useless subjects of one elected from their own number, would become members of the state instead of being merely a canker which gnaws away at it.'

I replied to Monsieur Evrard: 'There you go too far, and too fast; what you suggest will certainly come to pass in two or three hundred years; have patience.' 'But it is precisely because it will come to pass only in the course of two or three centuries that I lose all patience,' he replied; 'I am tired of all the abuses I see: it seems to me that I am walking in the Libyan desert, and our blood is being sucked by insects when we are not being devoured by lions.'

'I had a sister,' he continued, 'sufficiently imbecilic as to be a Jansenist in good faith rather than out of political faction. The noble episode concerning the bills of confession[51] caused her to die of despair. My brother had a lawsuit in which he had won the first round; his fortune depended on it. For some reason I do not understand the judges stopped dispensing justice, and my brother was ruined. I have an old uncle riddled with wounds who was having his furniture and plate transported from one province to the next; some nimble clerks seized everything on the pretext of a minor infringement; my uncle was unable to pay the fine, and died in prison.'

Monsieur Evrard told me stories of this nature for two whole hours. I said to him: 'My dear sir, I have endured even more than you; mankind is the same the world over: we imagine that abuses reign only in our own countries; you and I are both like La Fontaine's Astolphe and Joconde, who started by thinking that only their wives were unfaithful; but everywhere on their travels they found men belonging to the same brotherhood.'

'Yes,' replied Monsieur Evrard, 'but they had the pleasure everywhere they went of giving back what had been so obligingly lent to them at home.'

'Just try for three years being director of this, that or the other,' I suggested, 'and you will avenge yourself with interest.'

Monsieur Evrard took me at my word: in the whole of France today he is the man who robs both king, state and his fellow-men in the most nobly disinterested fashion; he enjoys the best fare, and nobody appreciates a new play with greater zest.

An Indian Incident

Translated by an Ignoramus

As everyone knows, Pythagoras,[1] during his sojourn in India, learnt from Gymnosophists the languages of animals and plants. Strolling one day in a meadow quite close to the seashore, he heard these words: 'How miserable I am to have been born grass! Hardly have I grown two inches high than a ravaging monster appears, a hideous creature who tramples me under his huge feet, whose jaws are armed with a row of scythes with which to cut me down, tear me to pieces and swallow me. And men call these monsters *sheep*. I do not believe there is in this world a more abominable animal.'

Pythagoras advanced a few steps further; he found an oyster lying half-open on a little rock; Pythagoras had not as yet embraced that admirable law according to which it is forbidden to eat our fellow-creatures. He was about to swallow the oyster when it spoke these touching words: 'O Nature! How happy to be grass, which like me is one of your works; when it is cut down it is reborn, for it is immortal; but in vain are we poor oysters protected by our double armour; blackguards eat us by the dozen for dinner, and that is the end of us for ever. What a dreadful fate to be an oyster, and what a barbarian is man!'

Pythagoras shuddered; he felt the enormity of the crime that he was about to commit: he begged forgiveness of the oyster with tears in his eyes, and placed it carefully back on its rock.

Pondering this incident deeply on his way back to town, he saw spiders eating flies, swallows eating spiders, and sparrow-hawks eating swallows. 'None of this lot', he said to himself, 'is a philosopher.'

Entering the city, Pythagoras was jostled, crushed and knocked down by a crowd of ruffians and their womenfolk, who ran along shouting: 'Well done, well done, they had it coming to them!' 'Who?

What?' said Pythagoras, getting to his feet; but they continued running past and shouting: 'What a pleasure it will be to watch them cook!'

Pythagoras thought they must be talking about lentils or some other vegetables. Not at all; they were discussing two poor Indians. 'Ah,' said Pythagoras, 'doubtless these are two great philosophers who are tired of life; they are looking forward to being reborn in another form; it is pleasant to change house, even though one is always poorly housed; there is no disputing about tastes.'

He advanced with the crowd to the public square, where he saw a great pyre burning, and facing it a bench named a *tribunal*, and on this bench a row of judges, each of whom was holding a cow's tail in his hand, and on his head a bonnet exactly like the ears of the animal which carried Silenus in former times, when he came to this country with Bacchus, having crossed the Red Sea without getting his feet wet, and after stopping in their tracks the sun and the moon, as is faithfully recorded in the *Orphic Poems*.

Among the judges was an honest man well known to Pythagoras. This Indian sage explained to the sage from Samos the meaning of the festival about to be performed for the populace.

'These two Indians', he said, 'have no desire whatever to be burned alive. My solemn colleagues have condemned them to this torture; the first for saying that the substance of Xaca is not the same substance as that of Brahma; and the other, for offering the view that one can please the Supreme Being through being virtuous, without needing to hold a cow by the tail when at the point of death, since, he claimed, one can be virtuous at all times, but one cannot always get hold of a cow at the right moment. The good women of the city have been so shocked by these two heretical propositions that they have given the judges no respite until they ordered the execution of these two unfortunates.'

Pythagoras concluded that, from the blade of grass to man himself, there is no lack of distressing subjects. Nonetheless he managed to make the judges, and even the believers, hear reason – though it is the only recorded occasion on which this has ever happened.

He then went to Croton and preached tolerance, where a fanatic set fire to his house and he who had saved two Indians from the flames was himself burned to death. *Sauve qui peut!*

Lord Chesterfield's Ears

and Parson Goodman

Ah! Fate governs irremissibly everything in this world. I judge, as is natural, from my own experience.

Lord Chesterfield, who was very fond of me, had promised to be of assistance. A good 'preferment' in his nomination fell vacant. I hurried up to London from the depths of the country; I presented myself before his Lordship; I reminded him of his promises; he shook me warmly by the hand and said that indeed I did look ill. I replied that my greatest ill was poverty. He answered that he wished to cure me and gave me a letter on the spot for Mr Sidrac, near the Guildhall.

I had no doubt that Mr Sidrac was the man to expedite my nomination to a living. I rushed to his house. Mr Sidrac, who was his Lordship's surgeon, began to examine me forthwith, and assured me that if I had the stone he would happily open me up.

You must understand that his Lordship had heard I was suffering great pain in the bladder, and with his usual generosity intended I should be operated upon at his expense. He had gone deaf, just like his brother, and I had not been informed of it.

While I was wasting time defending my bladder against Mr Sidrac, who wanted to examine me at all costs, one of the fifty-two competitors who were after the same living arrived at his Lordship's, asked for my living, and obtained it.

I was in love with Miss Fidler, whom I was to marry as soon as I became a vicar; my rival took my place and my mistress.

His Lordship, learning of my disaster and his error, promised to set everything right; but he died two days afterwards.

Mr Sidrac made me see, as clear as daylight, that my good patron could not have lived a minute longer, owing to the state of his internal organs, and proved to me that his deafness came only from the extreme dryness of the tympanic cord and drum of his ear. He even offered to harden up my two ears with spirits of wine, such as to make me deafer than any peer of the realm.

I realized that Mr Sidrac was a very learned man. He inspired me with a taste for the science of nature. Moreover, I saw that he was a charitable man, who would operate upon me for nothing if necessary, and would aid me in whatever accident might arise in the neck of my bladder.

So I began to study nature under his direction, to console myself for the loss of my vicarage and my mistress.

CHAPTER II

After much observation of nature through my five senses plus telescopes and microscopes, I said to Mr Sidrac one day: 'We are dupes. There is no such thing as nature; everything is art. It is by the most admirable art that all the planets dance regularly around the sun, while the sun turns round upon himself. Evidently someone as learned as the members of the Royal Society of London must have arranged things in such a way that the square of the revolutions of each planet is always proportionate to the cube root of their distance from their centre; and a man must be a sorcerer to guess it.

'The ebb and flow of our Thames seem to me the constant result of an art no less profound and not any the less difficult to understand.

'Animals, vegetables, minerals, all seem to me arranged with weight, measure, number and movement. Everything that exists is a spring, a lever, a pulley, a hydraulic machine, a chemical laboratory – from the blade of grass to the oak-tree, from the flea to the man, from a grain of sand to our clouds.

'Surely there is nothing but art, and nature is but a delusion.'

'You are right,' said Mr Sidrac, 'but you are not the first in the field; this has already been stated by a dreamy fellow on the other side of the English Channel,[1] though nobody has paid any attention to him.'

'What astonishes me and delights me most,' said I, 'is that by means of this incomprehensible art, two machines always produce a third; I am very sorry not to have done likewise with Miss Fidler, but I see that it was arranged from all eternity that Miss Fidler should make use of a machine other than myself.'

'What you say', replied Mr Sidrac, 'has been said before and said better: which probably means that you are thinking correctly. Yes, it is most amusing that two beings should produce a third; but that is not true of all beings. Two roses do not produce a third by exchanging kisses; two stones, two metals, do not produce a third; and yet a metal and a stone are things which all human industry could not make. The great, the beautiful and constant miracle is that a boy and girl should make a child together, that a nightingale should make a little nightingale with his nightingale mate, and not with a warbler. We ought to spend half our lives in imitating them, and the other half in blessing Him who invented this procedure. Reproduction harbours a thousand strange secrets. Newton says that Nature is everywhere like herself: *Natura est ubique sibi consona*. This is not true of Love: fish, reptiles, birds, do not make love as we do – there is infinite variety. The workings of acting and sentient beings delight me. Vegetables also have their value. I am always amazed that a grain of wheat cast on the ground should produce several others like it.'

'Ah!' said I, like the fool I then was, 'that is because the wheat must die to be born again, as they say in the Schools.'[2]

Mr Sidrac laughed circumspectly and replied: 'That was true in the time of the Schools, but the meanest labourer today knows that the thing is ridiculous.'

'Ah, Mr Sidrac, I beg your pardon. I have been a theologian, and a man cannot shake off old habits immediately.'

CHAPTER III

Some time after these conversations between poor Parson Goodman and the excellent anatomist Sidrac, the latter ran into him in St James's Park looking pensive and preoccupied, with an air more embarrassed than a mathematician who has just made an error of calculation. 'What is the matter?' said Sidrac. 'Have you pains in your bladder or colon?' 'No,' said Goodman, 'only in my gall-bladder. I have just seen the Bishop of Gloucester[3] ride by in a fine carriage; he is an insolent and whiffling pedant. Meanwhile I was on foot, and it irritated me. I remembered that, if I wanted to have a bishopric in this realm, ten thousand chances to one I should fail, since there are ten thousand parsons in England. Since the death of Lord Chesterfield (who was deaf) I have had no patron. Let us suppose that the ten thousand Anglican parsons each have two patrons; the odds are then twenty thousand to one against my obtaining a bishopric. That is annoying, when one thinks of it.

'I remembered that long ago it was suggested I go to India as a cabin-boy; I was assured I should make a great fortune there, but I did not feel cut out to become an admiral. So, having considered all the professions I have remained a parson, without being good for anything.'

'Give up being a priest,' said Sidrac, 'and turn yourself into a philosopher. It is an occupation which neither demands nor bestows wealth. What is your income?' 'I have only thirty guineas a year, and after the death of my old aunt I shall have fifty.' 'My dear Goodman, that is enough to live in freedom and to think. Thirty guineas makes six hundred and thirty shillings – nearly two shillings a day. Philips[4] only needed one. With that amount of guaranteed income a man may say whatever he thinks about the East India Company, Parliament, the Colonies, the King, life in general, Man and God – all of which is a great source of amusement. Come and dine with me, which will save you money. We shall talk, and your thinking faculty will have the pleasure of communicating with mine by means of speech, which is a marvellous thing insufficiently admired by men.'

CHAPTER IV

Conversation between Dr Goodman and Sidrac the Anatomist, concerning the soul and other matters

GOODMAN: But, my dear Sidrac, why do you always speak of *my thinking faculty*? Why not just say *my soul*? It is easier to say, and I should understand you just as well.

SIDRAC: But I should not understand myself. I feel, I know, even, that God has given me the faculty of thinking and speaking; but I neither feel nor know that he has given me an entity called a soul.

GOODMAN: Really, when I think about it, I see that I know nothing more than you about the matter, and that I have long been rash enough to think I did know. I have noticed that the oriental peoples call the soul by a name which means Life. Following their example, the Romans first used the word *anima* to mean the life of an animal. The Greeks used to speak of the respiration of the soul. This respiration is a breath, and the Latins translated the word *breath* by *spiritus*; whence the word equivalent to *spirit* among nearly all modern nations. Since nobody has ever seen this breath, this spirit, it has been made into an entity which no one can see or touch. It has been said to reside in our body without occupying any place there, and to move our organs without touching them. What has not been said? It seems to me that all our talk is founded on ambiguities. I see the wise Locke felt that these ambiguities in all languages had plunged human reason into chaos. He includes no chapter on the soul in his book, the only sensible work of metaphysics ever written.[5] And if he chances to use the word in certain passages, he only uses it to mean our intelligence.

Indeed, everyone clearly feels he has an intelligence, that he receives ideas, which he associates and dissociates; but nobody feels that he has within him another entity which gives him movement, sensations and thoughts. It is ridiculous to use words we do not understand and to admit entities of which we cannot have the slightest idea.

SIDRAC: We are agreed then about a matter which has been the subject of dispute for so many centuries.

GOODMAN: And I marvel that we are in agreement.

SIDRAC: It is not so surprising; we are honestly searching for the truth. If we were on the benches of the Schools, we should be arguing like Rabelais's characters.[6] If we lived in the terrible dark ages which for so long engulfed England, one of us would probably have the other burned. But we live in an age of reason; we easily find what seems to us to be the truth, and we dare to express it.

GOODMAN: Yes, but I fear this truth is a very paltry affair. In mathematics we have achieved prodigies which would astonish Apollonius and Archimedes,[7] and would make them our pupils. But what have we discovered in metaphysics? Our own ignorance.

SIDRAC: And is that nothing? You admit that the great Being has given you the faculty of feeling and thinking, as he has given your feet the faculty of walking, your hands the power of doing a thousand things, your intestines the power of digesting, your heart the power of pumping blood along your arteries. We hold everything from Him; we could not do anything for ourselves, and we shall always remain ignorant of the manner in which the Master of the universe manages to guide us. For my part, I give thanks to him for having taught me that I know nothing of first principles.

Men have always enquired how the soul acts upon the body. They ought first of all to have established whether we have a soul. Either God has bestowed this gift on us, or He has imparted something to us which is its equivalent. However He went about it, we are under His hand. He is our master, and this is all I know.

GOODMAN: But tell me at least what you suspect to be the case. You have dissected brains, you have looked upon embryos and foetuses; have you discovered any sign of a soul in them?

SIDRAC: Not in the least, and I have never been able to understand how an immortal, immaterial entity can spend nine months uselessly hidden in an evil-smelling membrane between urine and excrement. I have found it difficult to conceive that this so-called simple soul could exist prior to the formation of its body. For what can it have been doing down the centuries before being a human soul? And how are we to imagine a simple entity, a metaphysical entity, which waits for an eternity for its turn to animate a piece of matter for a few minutes? What becomes of this unknown entity, if the foetus it is meant to animate dies in the womb?

It seems to me still more ridiculous that God should create a soul at the moment a man lies with a woman, and blasphemous that He should await the consummation of an adultery, or an incest, to reward such turpitudes by creating souls in their image. It is worse still when I am told that God conjures immortal souls out of nothingness to make them suffer incredible tortures for all eternity. What! Burn simple entities, which have nothing burnable about them! How should we go about burning the sound of a voice, or a wind which has just passed? Even so, this sound and this wind were material for the brief moment of their passage; but what of a pure spirit, a thought, a doubt? I am at sea here. Whichever way I turn, I find nothing but obscurity, contradiction, impossibility, ridiculousness, delusions, extravagance, chimera, absurdity, idiocy, charlatanism.

But I am perfectly at ease when I say to myself: God is the master. He who causes stars without number to gravitate towards each other, He who made the light, is certainly powerful enough to give us feelings and notions without our needing a small, foreign, invisible atom called a *soul*.

God has certainly given feeling, memory and activity to all animals. He has given them life, and it is as noble to give life as to give a soul. It is generally agreed that animals are alive; it is proved that they have feeling, since they have organs of feeling. And if they have all that without a soul, why should we wish to have one at all costs?

GOODMAN: Perhaps from vanity. I am convinced that if a peacock could speak, he would boast of having a soul and would say his soul is in his tail. I am much inclined to suspect with you that God made us to eat, to drink, to walk, to sleep, to feel, to think, to be full of passions, pride and misery, without telling us one word of His secret. We do not know any more on this subject than the peacock I mentioned; and he who said that we are born, live and die without knowing how, expressed a great truth.

Likewise he[8] who calls us the puppets of Providence seems to me to have defined us well. After all, for us to exist there needs must be an infinity of movements. But we did not create movement; we did not establish its laws. There is someone who, having made the light, makes it travel from the sun to our eyes in seven minutes. It is only through movement that my five senses are stirred; it is only through my five senses that I have ideas: therefore it is the Author of movement who gives me my ideas. And when He tells me how He does this, I shall render Him my humblest thanks. Already I give Him great thanks for allowing me to contemplate for a few years the magnificent spectacle of this world, as Epictetus[9] says. It is true that He could make me happier and let me have a good ecclesiastical living and my mistress, Miss Fidler; but even as I am, with my income of six hundred and thirty shillings, I am still greatly indebted to Him.

SIDRAC: You say that God might have given you a good living and that he could make you happier than you are. There are some people who would not allow you to get away with such an assertion. Do you not remember how you yourself complained of Fate? A man who intended to be a parson is not allowed to contradict himself. Do you not see that, had you obtained the parsonage and the woman you asked for, it would have been you and not your rival who gave Miss Fidler a child? This child might have been a cabin-boy, become an admiral, won a naval battle at the mouth of the Ganges, and completed the dethronement of the Great Mogul. That alone would have changed the make-up of the universe. A world entirely different from ours would need to have been created in order that your competitor should not have the living, should not marry Miss Fidler, and that you should not have been reduced to six hundred and thirty shillings while awaiting the death of your aunt. Everything is linked, and God will not break the eternal chain for the sake of my friend Goodman.

GOODMAN: I did not expect this line of reasoning when I spoke of Fate; but after all, if things are thus, God is as much a slave as I am?

SIDRAC: He is the slave of His will, of His wisdom, of the laws He himself made, of His necessary nature. He cannot infringe all this, because He cannot be weak, inconstant and fickle as we are; the necessarily Eternal Being cannot behave like a weathercock.

GOODMAN: Mr Sidrac, what you are saying leads straight to irreligion. For if God can change nothing in the affairs of this world, what is the use of singing His praises and addressing prayers to Him?

SIDRAC: And who told you to pray to God, and praise Him? Much does He care about your praise and petitions! We praise a man because we think him vain; we pray to him when we think him weak and hope to make him change his mind. Let us do our duty to God, adore Him, act justly; that is true praise and true prayer.

GOODMAN: Mr Sidrac, we have covered a lot of ground; for, without counting Miss Fidler, we have discussed whether we have a soul, whether there is a God, whether He can change, whether we are destined to two lives, whether . . . these are profound reflections and perhaps I should never have thought about them if I had been a parson. I must go deeper into these necessary and sublime matters, since I have nothing else to do.

SIDRAC: Well, Dr Grou is coming to dine with me tomorrow: he is a very well-informed doctor; he went round the world with Banks and Solander;[10] he must certainly understand God and the soul, the true and the false, the just and the unjust, far better than those who have never left Covent Garden. Moreover, Dr Grou saw almost the whole of Europe in his youth; he witnessed five or six revolutions in Russia; he visited the pasha comte de Bonneval,[11] who, as you know, became a confirmed Muslim in Constantinople. He was intimate with the Irish papist priest MacCarthy[12] who had his foreskin cut off in honour of the Prophet, and with our Scottish Presbyterian Ramsay,[13] who did the same, and afterwards served in Russia and was killed in a battle against the Swedes in Finland. Dr Grou has moreover conversed with the reverend Father Malagrida,[14] who has since been burned at Lisbon because the Holy Virgin revealed to him everything she did when she was in the womb of her mother, St Anne. So you can see that a man like Dr Grou, who has seen so much, must be the greatest metaphysician in the world. Tomorrow, then, at my house for dinner.

GOODMAN: And again the day after tomorrow, my dear Sidrac, for more than one dinner is needed to become a man of learning.

CHAPTER V

The next day the three thinkers dined together; and, as they became a little merrier towards the end of the meal, which is the custom of philosophers at dinner, they amused themselves by talking of all the miseries, the follies, the horrors which afflict the animal kind from Australia to the Arctic Pole, and from Lima to Macao. The variety of human abominations is nevertheless very diverting. It is a pleasure unknown to stay-at-home citizens and parish curates, who know nothing beyond their own church spire and who think that the rest of the universe is like Exchange Alley in London, or the Rue de la Huchette in Paris.

'I have noticed', said Dr Grou, 'that in spite of the infinite variety of this globe, all the men I have seen – whether blacks with woolly hair, blacks with straight hair, browns, reds, greyish-browns who are called whites – all of them have two legs, two eyes and a head on their shoulders, despite St Augustine who asserts in his thirty-seventh sermon that he had seen acephalous, in other words headless, men or monoculous men with only one eye, and monopeds who have only one leg. As to cannibals, I admit there are swarms of these, and that everyone was a cannibal once.

'I have often been asked if the inhabitants of the immense country called New Zealand, who are today the most barbarous of all barbarians, were baptized. I have always replied that I did not know, but that it might be so; that the Jews, who were yet more barbarous, had two baptisms instead of one, the baptism of justice and the baptism of domicile.'[15]

'I am well acquainted with both,' said Mr Goodman, 'and have had long disputes with those who think that we Christians invented baptism. No, gentlemen, we have invented nothing; we have only patched things up. But pray tell me, Dr Grou, among the eighty or hundred religions you have seen in your travels, which seemed the most pleasant? That of the New Zealanders, perhaps, or of the Hottentots?'

DR GROU: That of the island of Tahiti, without any doubt. I have travelled through both hemispheres, and I never saw anything like Tahiti and its religious Queen. It is in Tahiti that Nature dwells.

Elsewhere I have seen nothing but masks, scoundrels deceiving fools, charlatans cheating others of their money to gain authority, and cheating authority so as to have money with impunity; who sell you spiders' webs in order to eat your partridges, and promise you riches and pleasures when we are all dead, so that you will turn the spit for them while they are alive.

By heavens! It is not like that in the Isle of Tahiti. This island is much more civilized than New Zealand or the country of the Kaffirs, or, dare I say it, than our own England, because Nature has granted it a more fertile soil; she has given it the bread-fruit tree, a gift as wonderful as it is useful, which she has bestowed only upon a few islands in the South Seas. Moreover, Tahiti possesses numerous edible birds, vegetables and fruits. In such a country it is not necessary to eat one's neighbour; there is a gentler, more natural, more universal necessity which the religion of Tahiti commands shall be satisfied in public. It is certainly the most respectable of all religious ceremonies; I have been an eye-witness, together with the whole crew of our ship. This is no missionary fable, such as are to be found in the *Edifying and Curious Letters* of the reverend Jesuit Fathers.[16] Dr John Hawkesworth[17] is as we speak completing the publication of our discoveries in the southern hemisphere. I have frequently accompanied that worthy young man, Banks, who has devoted his time and money to the observation of Nature in the regions of the Antarctic Pole, while Dawkins and Wood[18] were returning from the ruins of Palmyra and Baalbek where they had been excavating the most ancient monuments of the arts, and while Hamilton was teaching amazed Neapolitans the natural history of their own Mount Vesuvius.[19] With Banks, Solander, Cook and a hundred others, I have seen what I am about to describe to you.

'The Princess Obeira, Queen of the Island of Tahiti . . .' – at that moment coffee was served; and as soon as it was taken, Dr Grou went on with his story as follows:

CHAPTER VI

'The Princess Obeira, as I was saying, after heaping us with presents, with a politeness worthy of a Queen of England, was curious to be present one morning at our Anglican service. We celebrated it with as much pomp as we could. In the afternoon she invited us to her service: this was on 14 May 1769. We found her surrounded by about one thousand persons of both sexes arranged in a semi-circle and respectfully silent. A very pretty girl, simply decked out in a garment of amorous transparency, was lying on a platform which served as an altar. Queen Obeira ordered a fine young man of about twenty to make the sacrifice. He repeated a sort of prayer and climbed on to the altar. The two sacrificers were half-naked. The Queen, with a majestic air, instructed the young victim in the most suitable method of consummating the sacrifice. All the Tahitians watched so attentively and respectfully that not one of our sailors dared to interrupt the ceremony with an indecent laugh. That is what I have seen, I tell you; that is what our whole crew saw; it is for you to draw your own conclusions.'

'This sacred festival does not surprise me,' said Dr Goodman. 'I am convinced that it was the first festival ever celebrated by man; and I do not see why we should not pray to God when we are about to make a being in His image, as we pray to Him before the meals which sustain our bodies. To labour to bring into being a creature of reason is the most noble and sacred of acts. Thus thought the early Indians, who revered the Lingam, the symbol of generation; or the ancient Egyptians, who carried the Phallus in procession; or the Greeks, who erected temples to Priapus. If one may quote the miserable little Jewish nation, clumsy imitator of all its neighbours, its holy books say that this nation too adored Priapus and that the queen mother of the Jewish king Asa was high priestess of Priapus.*

'However this may be, it is very probable that no race ever established or could establish a cult from libertinism. Debauchery sometimes

---

* 1 Kings 13, 2 Chronicles 15 [Voltaire's note].

crept in over the course of time, but the institution as such is always innocent and pure. Our earliest love-feasts, where boy and girl kissed each other innocently on the mouth, did not degenerate into assignations and infidelities until much later; and would to God that I might sacrifice with Miss Fidler with no ulterior motives before Queen Obeira. That would assuredly be the finest day and the finest action of my life.'

Mr Sidrac, who had hitherto kept silent because Goodman and Grou were still talking, at last abandoned his reserve and said: 'What I have just heard ravishes me with admiration. Queen Obeira seems to me the greatest queen of the southern hemisphere (I dare not say both hemispheres). But amidst such majesty and felicity, there is one thing which makes me tremble and which Mr Goodman raised without your replying. Is it true, Dr Grou, that Captain Wallis,[20] who anchored off that fortunate isle before you, brought the two most dreadful scourges on earth, the pox and the smallpox?'

'Alas!' replied Dr Grou, 'the French accuse the English and the English accuse the French. Bougainville[21] says that the cursed English gave the pox to Queen Obeira; Captain Cook asserts that the Queen contracted it only from Bougainville himself. However this may be, the pox is like the fine arts, nobody knows who invented them, but eventually they run through Europe, Asia, Africa and America.'

'I have been a surgeon for a long time,' said Sidrac, 'and I confess I owe the greater part of my fortune to this malady; yet I do not detest it any the less. Mrs Sidrac communicated it to me on the first night of our wedding; and, as she is an excessively delicate woman in all matters touching her honour, she published in all the London newspapers the statement that she was indeed prey to an infamous disease, but that she had contracted it in her mother's womb, and that it was an old family habit.

'What was *Nature* (as we call her) thinking of, when she poured this poison into the very wellsprings of life? It has been said,[22] and I repeat, that this is the most fundamental and detestable of all contradictions. Man, they say, was after all created in God's image! *Finxit in effigiem moderantum cuncta deorum*,[23] and yet it is in the spermatic vessels of this image that pain, infection and death are to be found! What then becomes of Lord Rochester's noble verse: *Love, in a land of atheists, would lead to God?*'[24]

'Alas!' said the excellent Goodman, 'Perhaps I have to thank Providence that I did not marry my dear Miss Fidler; for who knows what might have happened? We are never sure of anything in this world. At any rate, Mr Sidrac, you have promised me your help in everything to do with my bladder.' 'I am entirely at your service,' replied Sidrac, 'but you must banish these gloomy thoughts.' Goodman, speaking in this way, seemed as if to foresee his fate.

CHAPTER VII

The next day the three philosophers debated the great question: what is the primary motivation behind all the actions of man? Goodman, whose loss of his living and his beloved was always on his mind, said that the universal principle was love and ambition. Grou, who had seen more of the world, said that it was money; and the great anatomist Sidrac insisted that it was the commode. His two companions were taken aback with astonishment; but here is how the scholarly Sidrac proved his thesis:

'I have always remarked that the affairs of this world depend in every case upon the opinions and wishes of a principal actor, whether king, prime minister or senior civil servant. Now these opinions and wishes are the immediate consequence of the manner in which the animal spirits filter through the cerebellum, and from there into the spinal cord. These animal spirits depend upon the circulation of the blood; the blood is dependent on the formation of chyle; chyle is formed in the mesentery network of the stomach; this mesentery is attached to the intestines by means of very slender threads; and the intestines are, if I may speak frankly, full of shit. Now in spite of the three strong tunics with which each of the intestines is clothed, they are riddled with holes: for everything in nature is open-work, and there is not a grain of sand so small that does not have less than five hundred pores. You could thread a thousand needles through a cannonball if you could find needles fine enough and strong enough.

'What occurs therefore in the case of the constipated man? The finest and most delicate particles of his excreta mix with the chyle in the Azellian veins, travel to the portal vein and into the Pecquet's reservoir;[25] they pass into the sub-clavicle; and they enter the heart of even the most courteous of men, even the most charming of women. It is an essence of dried turd that penetrates the whole body. If this essence saturates the parenchyma, vessels and glands of a bilious subject, his ill-humour turns to ferocity; the whites of his eyes become a smouldering gloom; his lips are stuck together; his complexion turns muddy. He would seem to threaten you; do not approach, and, if he is a senior minister, refrain from presenting him with a petition. He looks upon every piece of paper as an aid which he would dearly like to employ after the abominable manner of Europeans from time immemorial. Find out discreetly from his favourite manservant whether he was at stool that morning.

'This is more important than you think. Constipation has been responsible for some of the bloodiest episodes of history. My grandfather, who died a centenarian, was Cromwell's apothecary. He often told me how Cromwell had not been to the toilet for a week at the time he ordered the King's head to be cut off.

'Anyone at all familiar with European affairs knows that the scarface duc de Guise was often warned not to cross Henri III in winter when a north-east wind was blowing. At such times the king went to the toilet only with extreme difficulty. His faecal matter mounted to his head at such times, and he was capable of extremes of violence. The duc de Guise paid no attention to these counsels of wisdom. And what happened? He was murdered together with his brother.[26]

'Charles IX, Henri's predecessor, was the most constipated man in his kingdom. The passages of his colon and rectum were so blocked that in the end the blood spouted through the pores of his skin. We know only too well how this dried-up humour was one of the principal causes of the St Bartholomew's Day Massacre.[27]

'On the other hand, stout persons with well-lined intestines, a flowing bile duct, an easy and regular peristaltic movement which is discharged every morning as soon as they have breakfasted, with a well-rounded stool as easily passed as one spits . . . such individuals favoured by nature are gentle, affable, gracious, attentive, sympathetic, obliging. A *no* uttered by them has more grace than a *yes* in the mouth of the constipated.

'The toilet exercises such an influence that having the runs, on the other hand, often makes a man pusillanimous. Dysentery drains courage. Don't ask a man weakened by lack of sleep, by a lingering fever, and by fifty putrid evacuations, to go attacking a demi-lune[28] in the middle of the day. Which is why I cannot believe that our entire English army had dysentery during the battle of Agincourt, as is claimed, and that they carried the day with their pants down. A few soldiers may have had the runs after gorging themselves on bad grapes while on the march. Yet historians will claim that an entire sick army fought bare-bottomed, and that, so as not to show this to the French dandies, they beat them hollow, according to the expression of the Jesuit historian Father Daniel. *"Now there's a fine example of how to write history."*[29]

'In the same way French historians all repeat, one after another, that our great Edward III had six burghers of Calais presented with a rope around their necks,[30] intending to hang them for their courage in daring to withstand the siege, and that his wife finally obtained their pardon with her tears. These writers of fiction are unaware that it was the custom in those barbarous times for burghers to offer themselves up before their conqueror with a rope around their neck, when they had delayed him for too long in front of some ill-fortified hovel. But certainly the generous Edward had no intention of squeezing the breath out of these six hostages, whom he in fact showered with presents and honours. I am tired of all the trifles with which so many so-called historians have larded their chronicles, and all the battles they have so poorly described. I should as soon choose to believe the story that Gideon carried off his victory with the signal to break three hundred pitchers.[31]

'I only read natural history now, thank God, and only so long as a Burnet, a Whiston or a Woodward[32] do not bore me with their confounded systems; and that a Maillet[33] no longer tells me that the Irish Sea produced the Caucasus mountain, or that our globe is made of glass; and so long as nobody tries to persuade me that little aquatic bulrushes are man-eating animals, or that corals are insects; or so long as charlatans do not insolently palm off on me their day-dreams as verities. I set more store by a good diet which maintains my humours in equilibrium, and procures me a decent digestion and a sound sleep. Drink hot drinks when the weather freezes, and cold drinks in the dog days; neither too much nor too little of anything; digest, repose, enjoy yourself, and let the rest go its ways.'

CHAPTER VIII

As Mr Sidrac was proffering these words of wisdom a servant came in to inform Mr Goodman that Lord Chesterfield's steward was at the door, in his carriage, and wished to speak with him on urgent business. Goodman ran out to hear what he had to say, and was invited into the steward's carriage.

'No doubt you know, sir, what happened to Mr Sidrac on his wedding night?' asked the steward.

'Yes, sir, he told me the story of that little adventure just now.'

'Very well! The same thing occurred between the fair Miss Fidler and her parson husband. The next morning they fought; the day after that they separated, and the parson has now been deprived of his living. I am in love with Miss Fidler, I know that she loves you, but nor does she hate me. I can rise above the unimportant disgrace which was the cause of her divorce. I am in love and I am without fear. Give up Miss Fidler to me and I shall see to it that you get the living, which is worth over a hundred and fifty guineas a year. You have ten minutes to make up your mind.'

'This is a delicate proposition, sir. I must consult my philosophers Sidrac and Grou; I shall return to you forthwith.'

He ran back to his two advisers. 'I see', he said, 'that the affairs of this world are not decided by digestion alone, and that love, ambition and money play a large part.' He laid before them his situation, and begged them to decide for him at once. They both concluded that with an income of a hundred and fifty guineas he could have all the girls in his parish and Miss Fidler into the bargain.

Goodman saw the wisdom of this decision; he took the parsonage, had Miss Fidler in secret, which was far more agreeable than having her for a wife. Mr Sidrac was prodigal with his good offices where they were needed. Goodman became one of the most terrible priests in England, and remains more convinced than ever that fate governs everything in this world.

MÉLANGES

Account of the Illness, Confession, Death and Apparition of the Jesuit Berthier

It was on 12 October 1759 that, unluckily for him, Brother Berthier[1] travelled from Paris to Versailles with Brother Coutu,[2] his usual companion. Berthier had put a few copies of the *Journal de Trévoux* into the carriage, to present them to his various protectors: the chambermaid to Madame the wet-nurse, one of the palace cooks, an apprentice apothecary to the King, and several other noblemen who appreciate talent. On the way, Berthier started to feel nauseous; his head grew heavy, he yawned repeatedly. 'I don't know what's the matter with me,' he said to Coutu, 'I have never yawned so much.' Brother Coutu replied: 'Reverend Father, it's only to be expected.' 'What do you mean, only to be expected?' said Brother Berthier. 'Look,' said Brother Coutu, 'I'm yawning too, and I don't know why, because I haven't read a thing all day, and you haven't said a word to me since we set off.' As he said this, Brother Coutu yawned more than ever. Berthier replied with a yawn which continued as if he would never stop. The coachman turned round, and seeing them, began to yawn too; the malady spread to all the passers-by, and to all the neighbouring houses. Such an effect upon others does the very presence of a learned man sometimes have!

Meanwhile Berthier was breaking out in a cold sweat. 'I don't know what's wrong with me,' he said, 'I feel like ice.' 'I know what you mean,' said his companion. 'You know what I mean?' said Berthier, 'what do you mean by that?' 'Well, I'm frozen too,' said Coutu. 'And I'm almost asleep,' said Berthier. 'I'm not surprised,' said the other. 'How's that?' said Berthier. 'Well, I'm falling asleep too,' said his companion. So there they both were, in the grip of a soporific, lethargic malady, and in this state they arrived at the coach entry to Versailles. When the coachman opened the door of the carriage, he tried to rouse them from their profound slumber, but he failed. He called for help. At last the companion brother, who was more robust than Brother Berthier, gave some signs of life; but Berthier was colder than ever. Some of the court doctors, returning from dinner, passed by the carriage. They were asked to cast an eye on the sick man. One of them took his pulse, then went off saying that he had nothing more to do with medicine now that he was at court. Another, having examined Berthier more carefully, declared that the sickness proceeded from the gall-bladder, which was too full; a third maintained that it came from the brain, which was too empty.

While they were arguing, the patient's condition worsened. His convulsions began to look fatal, and the three fingers with which one holds a quill were already quite rigid, when a principal doctor, who had studied under Mead and Boerhaave[3] and knew rather more than the others, opened Berthier's mouth with a feeding-bottle, and, having carefully considered the odour of his breath, pronounced that he had been poisoned.

At this word, everyone cried out. 'Yes, gentlemen,' he went on, 'he has been poisoned; just touch his skin, and you can see the exhalations of a cold poison seeping through the pores; in my view a poison worse than hemlock, black hellebore, opium, nightshade and henbane combined. Coachman, have you by chance brought some parcel for our apothecaries in your coach?' 'No, sir,' replied the coachman; 'the only package is the one the reverend Father ordered me to bring.' At which he rummaged in the trunk and pulled out two dozen copies of the *Journal de Trévoux*. 'Well, gentlemen, was I wrong?' asked the great doctor.

Everyone present admired his prodigious sagacity: they all acknowledged the source of the evil, and the pernicious packet was immediately burned under the nose of the patient. The action of the fire lessened the weight of the particles, and Berthier's condition was slightly relieved; but as the sickness had made great progress, and his head was affected, he was still in danger. The doctor proposed that he be made to swallow a page of the *Encyclopédie*, in some white wine, to revivify the humours of his clotted bile; this resulted in a copious evacuation, but his head was still dreadfully heavy, the vertigo con-

tinued, and the few words he could utter made no sense; he remained
in this state for two hours, after which it was found necessary to hear
his confession.

At that moment, two priests were walking along the rue des
Récollets. They were approached. The first refused: 'I shall not be
responsible for the soul of a Jesuit, it's too risky: I shall have nothing
to do with that lot, either for the affairs of this world or the next.
Whoever wants to can shrive a Jesuit, but it won't be me.' The second
priest was not so difficult. 'I'll undertake it,' he said, 'one can turn
anything to good account.'

He was led immediately to the room where the sick man had
been carried; as Berthier still could not speak distinctly, the confessor
decided to resort to questions. 'Reverend Father,' he began, 'do you
believe in God?' – 'That's a strange question,' said Berthier. 'Not so
strange,' said the other; 'there's believing and believing: to be certain
that one believes in the correct way, one must love God and one's
neighbour – do you love them sincerely?' – 'I would make a distinction
there,' said Berthier. 'No distinctions, please,' replied the confessor;
'and no absolution, if you do not accept these two duties from the
start.' 'All right, then,' said Berthier, 'since you insist, yes, I love God,
and my neighbour as well as I can.'

'Have you not often read wicked books?' asked the confessor. 'What
do you mean by wicked books?' asked the other. 'I don't mean books
which are simply tedious,' said the confessor, 'like the *Roman History*
by Fathers Catrou and Rouillé, and your college tragedies, and your
collections of "great literature", and Lemoine's *Louisiade*,[4] and Ducerceau's verses about salad dressing,[5] and his noble stanzas on the
messenger from Le Mans, and his expression of thanks for pâtés to
the duc du Maine, and your books of *Reflections*,[6] and all your fine
flowers of the monastic spirit. But what I do mean is those fantasies by
Father Bougeant,[7] condemned by the Parlement and the Archbishop
of Paris; I mean those sweet nothings by Father Berruyer, who has
reduced the Old and the New Testament to a kind of gutter romance
in the style of *Clélie*, so justly scorned both in Rome and in France;[8] I
mean the theology of Brother Busenbaum and Brother Lacroix,[9] who
have gone to further extremes than anything penned by Brothers

Guignard, Guéret,[10] Garnet, Oldcorn,[11] and all the others; I mean
Brother Jouvency,[12] who with such discrimination compares President
de Harlay[13] to Pontius Pilate, the Parliament to the Jews, and Brother
Guignard to Jesus Christ, all because an over-angry citizen, but one
suffused with righteous anger against an advocate of parricide, took it
into his head to spit in the face of Brother Guignard, assassin of Henri
IV, when that impenitent monster refused to demand pardon of the
King and the judiciary; finally I mean that interminable crowd of
casuists, towards whom Pascal's eloquence was too merciful,[14] and
above all your Sanchez, who in his volume *De Matrimonio* has made
a collection of all those things that Aretino and the Carthusian Porter
would never have dared to say.[15] In so far as you have read any works
of this kind, your eternal salvation is in danger.'

'I would make a distinction,' said Berthier. 'No distinctions!'
repeated the confessor. 'Have you read all these books, yes or no?' –
'Sir,' said Berthier, 'I have a right to read what I choose, given my
eminent position in the Society.' – 'And what might that great position
be?' asked the confessor. 'Well, since you must know, it is I who am
the editor of the *Journal de Trévoux.*'

'What! You the editor of this work which sends so many to their
damnation?' – 'But my good sir, my work damns nobody; what sin
could it possibly cause the reader?' – 'Ah, Brother!' said the confessor,
'do you not know that whoever calls his brother *Raca* is in danger of
hell fire?[16] And it is your misfortune to bring whoever reads you into
the immediate temptation of calling you Raca: how many honest
people have I seen who, after reading just two or three pages of
your periodical, throw it on the fire in a transport of rage! "What
impertinence!" they say. "What an ignoramus, a boor, a pedant, a
donkey!" They could not stop: the spirit of charity was completely
extinguished in them, and their eternal salvation clearly imperilled.
Judge for yourself how many evils you have caused! There are perhaps
nearly fifty people who read you, fifty souls which you place in
peril each month. What excites anger above all in the faithful is the
confidence with which you rule on all matters which surpass your
understanding. This vice clearly derives from two mortal sins: pride
and avarice. Is it not the case that you write your periodical for money,

and that you are drunk with arrogance when you so inopportunely criticize Abbé Velly,[17] and Abbé Coyer,[18] and Abbé d'Olivet,[19] and all our good authors? I cannot give you absolution, without the firm promise that you will not write for the *Journal de Trévoux* for the rest of your days.'

Father Berthier did not know what to say; his head was not clear, and he was furiously attached to his two favourite sins. 'And yet you hesitate!' his confessor continued; 'Consider that in a few hours it will all be over for you: can one still harbour passions when they must be given up for ever? Will you be asked on Judgement Day whether you did or did not write for the *Journal de Trévoux*? Was it for this that you were born? Was it so as to bore us to death that you took vows of chastity, humility and obedience? You desiccated tree, you shrivelled tree which will be burnt to a cinder – make the most of your remaining moments; bear yet some of the fruits of penitence; renounce above all the spirit of calumny which has possessed you until now; try to have as much religion as those you accuse of having none. Know this, Brother Berthier, that piety and virtue do not consist in believing that your Francis Xavier,* after dropping his crucifix in the sea, had it humbly retrieved for him by a crab.[20] One can be an honest man, and doubt that the same St Francis can have been in two places at one time;[21] your books may say so, but we are permitted to believe not a word of what is in your books, dear Brother.

'Concerning which, Brother, were you not in communication with Brother Malagrida and his accomplices?[22] I had in fact forgotten this little peccadillo: do you think that because the attempt on his life once cost Henri IV a mere tooth, and because today it costs the King of Portugal a mere arm, that you can save yourself through the argument of intentionality?[23] You think these are venial sins, and that so long as the *Journal de Trévoux* keeps being churned out you need care little for the rest.'

'I would make a distinction, sir,' said Berthier. 'More distinctions!' said the confessor. 'Well! I make no distinctions, and I shall not give you absolution.'

---

* Miracle reported in *The Life of St Francis Xavier* [Voltaire's note].

As he was speaking, Brother Coutu arrived hastily, running, breath-less, sweating, panting, stinking; he had made enquiries about the priest who had the honour of confessing the reverend Father. 'Stop, stop,' he cried, 'no sacraments, no sacraments, reverend Father, I beg of you, my dear reverend Father Berthier, die without the sacraments; this fellow is the author of the *Nouvelles ecclésiastiques*,[24] and you're the fox confessing to the wolf:[25] if you've told the truth, you're lost.'

Amazement, shame, pain, anger, rage enlivened, for a moment, the spirit of the sick man. 'You are the author of the *Nouvelles ecclési-astiques*!' he exclaimed. 'And now you've caught a Jesuit!' – 'Yes, my friend,' replied the confessor with a bitter smile. 'Give me my con-fession back, scoundrel,' said Berthier; 'give me my confession back at once! God's enemy that you are, the enemy of kings, even of the Jesuits; it's you who have taken advantage of my condition: you traitor – if only you had an apoplexy, and I were administering you extreme unction! So you think yourself less tedious, less of a fanatic than me? Yes, I've written stupid things, I agree; I've made myself despicable and hateful, I allow; but you, are you not the lowest, vilest scribbler upon whom lunacy ever bestowed a pen? Admit it: isn't your *History of Convulsions* equal to our *Lettres édifiantes et curieuses?*[26] We want to dominate everywhere, I admit; but you want only to sow discord. We would seduce those in authority; you would rather raise sedition against them. The courts have had our books burned, I agree; but have they not burned yours as well? We are all imprisoned in Portugal, I agree; but have you and your accomplices not been pursued by the police a hundred times over? If I have been foolish enough to criticize enlightened men, who until then had disdained to crush me, have you not been equally impertinent? Are we not both, therefore, equally ridiculous? Should we not admit that in this century, the sewer of the ages, we are, the pair of us, the vilest of all the insects buzzing round the mire of this dungheap?' The force of truth tore these words from Berthier's mouth. He spoke like one inspired; his eyes, filled with a sombre flame, rolled distractedly; his lips were twisted, covered in spittle, his body tensed, his heart palpitating. Soon these convulsions were succeeded by a general collapse, and in his weakness he tenderly clasped Brother Coutu's hand. 'I admit', he said, 'that there are many failures in my *Journal de Trévoux*; but one must excuse human weakness.' – 'Ah! Reverend Father, you are a saint,' said Brother Coutu; 'you are the first author ever to admit that he is a bore; go now, die in peace; you may mock at the *Nouvelles ecclésiastiques*; die now, reverend Father, and be sure that you will work miracles.'

So passed Brother Berthier from this life to the next, on 12 October, at half past five in the evening.

Apparition of Brother Berthier to Brother Garassise, his Successor on the Journal de Trévoux

'On 14 October, I, Brother Ignatius Garassise, grand-nephew of Brother Garasse,[27] at two hours after midnight, being awake, had a vision, in which the ghost of Brother Berthier came towards me, the sight of which gave me the longest and most terrible yawning fit I have ever experienced. "Are you dead, then, reverend Father?" I asked. Yawning at me, he nodded to signify "Yes." – "That is good," I said to him, "since Your Reverence must doubtless be among the saints; you must hold one of the most important places. What a pleasure to know you are in Heaven with all our Brothers, past, present and to come! It is true, isn't it, that there are now some four million haloed heads, since the founding of our Society until today? I don't think there can be as many from the ranks of the Oratorians. Speak to me, reverend Father, stop yawning, and describe your happiness."

'"Oh, my son!" said Brother Berthier in a mournful voice, "How wrong you are! Alas! the *Paradise Open to Philagie*[28] is closed to the Fathers!" – "Is it possible?" I exclaimed. – "Yes," he said, "shun the pernicious vices which have damned us; and above all, when you write for the *Journal de Trévoux*, do not imitate me; do not calumniate, nor reason falsely, and above all do not be a bore, as I had the misfortune to be, and which is, of all sins, the most unforgivable."

'I was gripped with holy terror at Brother Berthier's dreadful words. "So you're damned?" I exclaimed. "No," he replied; "happily, I repented at the last moment. I am in Purgatory for three hundred and thirty-three thousand, three hundred and thirty-three years, three months, three weeks and three days, and I shall not be released unless one of our Brothers can be discovered who is humble, peaceful, has no desire to live at court, will not slander others in front of princes, will not interfere in the affairs of the world; and who, when he writes books, will make nobody yawn, and will transmit all these merits to me."

'"Ah, Brother," I said to him, "Purgatory will last a long time for you. Tell me then, I beg you, what is your penance down there?" – "I am obliged", he replied, "to prepare chocolate for a Jansenist every morning; at dinner I have to read one of the *Provincial Letters*[29] aloud, and for the rest of the time I am kept busy mending the smocks of the nuns at Port-Royal."[30] – "You make me tremble!" I replied. "What has happened in that case to all our Fathers, for whom I had such veneration? Where is the reverend Father Le Tellier,[31] the leader, the apostle of the Gallican Church?" – "Damned without mercy," replied Brother Berthier, "and he deserved it fully: he had deceived his King, lit the flame of discord, forged letters from bishops, and in the most cowardly and intemperate fashion persecuted the worthiest Archbishop ever to have been appointed to the capital of France;[32] he has been irrevocably condemned as a forger, calumniator, and disturber of the public peace: above all it is he who betrayed us all, he who doubled our madness, which now sends us to Hell by the hundreds and thousands. We believed, since Brother Le Tellier was respected, that we should all be respected; we imagined, since he had deceived his royal penitent, that we should all deceive ours; we believed, since one of his books had been condemned in Rome,[33] that we too must only write books which invited condemnation; and, to make matters even worse, we produced the *Journal de Trévoux*."

'As he spoke to me, I tossed on my left side, then on my right, then I sat up in bed, and cried out: "Oh, dear friend in Purgatory, what must we do to avoid the state you are in? Which sin is the most to be feared?"

'Berthier opened his mouth, and replied: "As I passed by Hell on my way to Purgatory, I was taken into the cavern of the seven capital sins, which is on the left-hand side of the entrance; first I addressed Lust: she was a great lump of a girl, fresh and appetizing, reclining on a bed of rose-leaves, with Sanchez' book at her feet and a young abbé at her side. I said to her: 'Madame, you, it would seem, are the one who damns all us Jesuits?' – 'No,' she replied, 'I do not have that honour; I have, it is true, a younger brother who corrupted Abbé Desfontaines[34] and a few others of his type, while they wore your habits; but for the most part I do not get involved in your affairs; sensual pleasures are not for everyone.'

'"Avarice sat in a corner, weighing Paraguay grass[35] in one scale against gold in the other. 'Is it you, Madame, who have the most credit with us?' – 'No, reverend Father, I ruin only a very few of your bursars.' – 'Might it be you?' I said to Wrath. 'No; ask the others; I am a transient, I enter all hearts, but I do not stay; my sisters soon take over.' Then I turned to Gluttony, who was at table. 'As for you, Madame, I'm well aware, thanks to our Brother the cook, that it's not you who have lost us our souls.' Her mouth was full, so she could not reply; but she made a sign, shaking her head, that we weren't worthy of her attention.

'"Sloth was resting on a couch, half asleep; I did not wish to waken her: I could guess the aversion she would have for people like us who spend our time rushing all over the world.

'"Then I noticed Envy in a corner, gnawing at the hearts of three or four poets, a handful of preachers, and a hundred-odd pamphleteers. 'You look just the one' – I said to her – 'to have a hand in our sins.' – 'Ah, reverend Father,' she replied, 'you are too kind; how could people who have such a high opinion of themselves possibly depend on a poor wretch like me? You should talk to my father.'

'"In fact, her father was beside her, seated in an armchair, in a coat trimmed with ermine, his head held high, with a disdainful look, and red, full, hanging cheeks. I knew this to be Pride: I prostrated myself, for he was the only figure present to whom I might pay such tribute. 'Forgive me, Father,' I said, 'that I did not approach you first of all; I have always worn you in my heart of hearts: yes, it is you who rule us all. The most trivial of writers, even the author of the *Année littéraire*,[36] is inspired by you. Most magnificent devil! You reign over mandarin and hawker, over grand lama and capucin, over sultana and city wife; but our Society are your chief favourites: your divinity shines out in us, through the many veils of policy; I have always been the proudest of your disciples, and I cannot but feel that I love you still.' He replied to my hymn of praise with a protective smile, and I was conveyed at once to Purgatory."'

Here ends the vision of Brother Garassise; he resigned from the *Journal de Trévoux*, and moved to Lisbon, where he had long sessions with Brother Malagrida, and at last went off to Paraguay.

Dialogue between a Savage and a Graduate

First Dialogue

One day the Governor of Cayenne brought a savage from Guyana, who showed plenty of innate good sense and spoke fairly good French. A graduate of Paris had the honour of engaging him in conversation.

THE GRADUATE: Sir, you have no doubt witnessed many of your fellows pass their entire existence in solitude; for is it not said that such is the true life of man, and that human society is but an artificial deviation?

THE SAVAGE: I have never seen the people you mention. Man seems to me to be born for society, like many species of animal; each species follows its instinct; where we come from everyone lives in society.

THE GRADUATE: What! In society? So you have beautiful walled cities, kings and courtiers, entertainments, monasteries, universities, libraries, taverns?

THE SAVAGE: No; but have I not heard it said that on your continent there are Arabs, Scythians, peoples who have never had any of these things, and who are nevertheless sizeable nations? Well, we live like them. Neighbouring families lend each other help; we inhabit a hot country, where we have few needs; we procure food with ease; we marry, make children, raise them, and die. Just like you, give or take a few ceremonies.

THE GRADUATE: But, my dear Sir, you are therefore not a savage after all?

THE SAVAGE: I do not know what you mean by that word.

THE GRADUATE: In truth, neither do I. I must be dreaming. We call 'savage' a man of ill temper who flees company.

THE SAVAGE: I have already told you that we live together amidst our families.

THE GRADUATE: We also call 'savage' those animals which are not tame, and which disappear into the forests; from whence we have given the name savage to men who live in the woods.

THE SAVAGE: I frequent the woods, as you do, when you hunt.

THE GRADUATE: Do you have thoughts from time to time?

THE SAVAGE: One cannot avoid having some ideas.

THE GRADUATE: I should be curious to know about yours; what do you think of man?

THE SAVAGE: I think that he is a two-footed animal who has the faculties of reason, speech and laughter, and who uses his hands a lot more skilfully than monkeys. I have seen several species of man, whites like you, redskins like me, blacks like those to be found at the Governor of Guyana's. You have a beard, we have none; negroes have woolly heads, we have hair. It is said that in your North everyone has blond hair; in our Americas everyone is dark; that is all I know.

THE GRADUATE: But your soul, sir, what of your soul? What notion do you entertain of it? Where does it come from? What is it? What does it do? How does it act and where does it go to?

THE SAVAGE: I have no idea; I have never seen it.

THE GRADUATE: Incidentally, do you believe animals are machines?

THE SAVAGE: They seem to me to be machines with organs, possessed of feelings and memory.

THE GRADUATE: And what about you yourself, what do you think you possess, that is superior to the beasts?

THE SAVAGE: An infinitely superior memory, many more ideas, and, as I have already said, a tongue which forms incomparably more sounds than those of animals; more versatile hands, and the faculty of laughter with which an all-powerful rational Being has endowed me.

THE GRADUATE: And, may I ask, how do you come to have all this? And of what nature is your mind? How does your soul animate your body? Do you think all of the time? Do you have free will?

THE SAVAGE: All these questions! You ask me how I come to possess what God has deigned to give to man: it's as if you asked me how I was born. It must follow that, since I was born a man, I have those attributes which constitute man, as a tree has a bark, roots and leaves. You would have me know what is the nature of my mind: I have not taken it upon myself to know this. How my soul animates my body? I am no better instructed in that respect. It seems to me that one needs to see the workings of a watch to decide how it tells the time. You ask me if I think continually. No; sometimes I have half-thoughts, as when I make out objects vaguely from a distance; sometimes I have clearer ideas, as when I see an object from close up and distinguish it better; sometimes I have no thoughts at all, as when I close my eyes and see nothing. Then you ask me if my will is free. I do not understand you at all; these are things which you know, doubtless; you will do me the honour of explaining them to me.

THE GRADUATE: Ah! Indeed, yes, I have studied all these matters; I could speak of them to you for a month without drawing breath, and you would understand nothing. Tell me a little more: do you know the difference between good and evil, between justice and injustice? Do you know what is the best form of government, or the best religion? Are you familiar with the rights of man, with public law, or civil law, or canon law? Or the names of the first man and woman who populated America? Do you know why it rains on the sea, and why you have no beard?

THE SAVAGE: Truly, sir, you take advantage of the admission I have made to possessing a better memory than the animals; I have trouble even in remembering your questions. You speak about good and evil, justice and injustice; it seems to me that whatever gives us pleasure without doing harm to others is both very good and perfectly just; that what does harm to others without giving us pleasure is abominable; and that what gives us pleasure while harming others is good for us at the time, but highly dangerous for ourselves and very bad for others.

THE GRADUATE: And it is with these maxims that you live together in society?

THE SAVAGE: Yes, with our relatives and our neighbours. Without a great deal of effort and troubles, we persist calmly to a hundred years of age; some of us even reach one hundred and twenty; after which our bodies fertilize the earth which has nourished them.

THE GRADUATE: You seem to me to have a good head; I should like to turn it around. Let us dine together; after which we shall begin to philosophize with method.

Second Dialogue

THE SAVAGE: I have now swallowed food which disagrees with me, although I have a strong stomach; you have made me eat when I was no longer hungry, and drink when I was no longer thirsty; my legs are not as firm under me as they were before dinner, my head feels heavier, my ideas are no longer so clear. Never in my own country have I felt this diminution of myself. Here the more one puts into one's body, the more one loses one's being. Please tell me, what is the cause of this nuisance?

THE GRADUATE: I shall explain. First of all, I know nothing as to what is happening with your legs; but the doctors know, and you can address yourself to them. As to what is happening to your head, I know very well. Listen: the soul, occupying no place, is seated in the pineal gland, or in the *corpus callosum*, in the centre of the head. The animal spirits which begin in the stomach rise up to the soul, which they cannot touch because they are matter and it is not. Now, since they cannot act one upon the other, this means that the soul receives their impression; and since it is a simple substance, and consequently cannot feel any change, this means that it changes, becomes heavy and sluggish, when one has over-eaten; which explains the fact that many a great man sleeps after dinner.

THE SAVAGE: What you say seems very ingenious and profound; but do me the honour of giving me an explanation within my reach.

THE GRADUATE: I have told you all that can be said on this important subject, but to accommodate you I shall enlarge a little; let us proceed by degrees; are you aware that this is the best of all possible worlds?

THE SAVAGE: What! Is it impossible for the Infinite Being to create something better than what we see before us?

THE GRADUATE: Certainly, and what we see before us happens to be the best there is. It is perfectly true that human beings pillage and slaughter one another; but always while praising equity and gentleness. In times past twelve million or so of you Americans were massacred: but only to make the rest of you see reason. A mathematician has calculated that since a certain Trojan War, of which you are ignorant, up to the War of Acadia, which you do know about,[1] there have been killed in pitched battle at least five hundred and fifty-five million six hundred and fifty thousand men, not counting the women and little children crushed to death in cities reduced to ashes. But this was all for the public good. The four or five thousand cruel illnesses to which mankind is prey make one realize the price of health; and the crimes which cover the earth set off wonderfully the merit of devout men, among whose number I count myself. You can see that all this works for the best, at least as far as I am concerned.

Now everything could not exist in such perfection were the soul not located in the pineal gland; because, well . . . But let's proceed step by step: what notion do you have of the law, of justice and injustice, of the beautiful, of Plato's τὸ καλὸν?

THE SAVAGE: But, sir, going step by step you speak to me of a hundred things at once.

THE GRADUATE: Such is the way of conversation. Tell me, then, who made the laws of your country?

THE SAVAGE: Public interest.

THE GRADUATE: Those are eloquent words. For us there are none which carry greater force; but what do you mean by them, tell me?

THE SAVAGE: I mean, that those who had coconut trees and corn forbade others to touch them, and those who had none were obliged to work for the right to eat of them. Everything I have learned in my country and in yours has taught me that there is no other meaning to 'the spirit of laws'.

THE GRADUATE: But women, Monsieur Savage, what about women?

THE SAVAGE: Women? Ah! They please me greatly when they are

beautiful and gentle. They are far superior to coconut trees; they are a fruit which we allow no one else to touch: no one has any more right to take my wife from me than to take my child. There are, it is said, people who find such practices acceptable – but they are their own masters, and everyone must do with his possessions as he sees fit.

THE GRADUATE: But what of inheritances, partitions, heirs, collaterals?

THE SAVAGE: There has to be inheritance. I can no longer own my field when I am buried in it: I leave it to my son; and if I have two sons, they share it. I understand that among your people, in many places, the laws leave everything to the eldest, and nothing to the younger sons: it is self-interest which has dictated such a bizarre law; presumably the elder sons created it for themselves, or else the fathers wanted the elder sons to be dominant.

THE GRADUATE: What, in your opinion, are the best laws?

THE SAVAGE: Those where the interests of my fellow-men have been consulted.

THE GRADUATE: And where does one find such laws in practice?

THE SAVAGE: Nowhere, from what I hear.

THE GRADUATE: Tell me, where do your people think they came from? Who does one think populated America?

THE SAVAGE: We believe that God did.

THE GRADUATE: That is not an answer. I ask you where did your first ancestors come from?

THE SAVAGE: From the land where our first trees came from. It seems to me a quaint jest on the part of you Europeans to claim that we can have nothing without you: we have just as much right to think of ourselves as your ancestors as you to think of yourselves as ours.

THE GRADUATE: What an obstinate savage you are!

THE SAVAGE: And what a prattling graduate!

THE GRADUATE: Hold on there, my dear savage! One more question: in Guyana do you believe that one must kill those who are not of the same opinion as yourself?

THE SAVAGE: Yes; as long as you eat them afterwards.

THE GRADUATE: It is you who are the jester. And the papal bull *Unigenitus*,[2] what do you make of that?

THE SAVAGE: I'm making off.

Dialogue between Ariste
and Acrotal

ACROTAL:[1] Oh for the good old days, when students at the university, bearded to the last man, battered to death the mathematician Ramus[2] and dragged his body naked and bleeding to make honourable amends before the door of each and every college!

ARISTE: So this Ramus must have been an abominable person? He committed enormities?

ACROTAL: Most certainly. He wrote against Aristotle, and was suspected of even worse. It is a shame they didn't batter Charron[3] to death while they were about it, who took upon himself to write about wisdom; or your Montaigne,[4] who dared to reason and make jests. All those who reason are a plague on the state.

ARISTE: People who reason badly can be unbearable; however, I do not see that one should hang a fellow for a few false syllogisms; and it seems to me that the men whom you mention reasoned fairly well.

ACROTAL: So much the worse. That's what makes them the most pernicious.

ARISTE: In what respect, pray? Have you ever seen a philosopher bring war or plague or famine to a country? Bayle, for example, whom you abuse so virulently – has he ever undermined the Dutch dikes in order to drown the inhabitants,[5] as it is said one of our great ministers, who was no philosopher, contemplated doing?[6]

ACROTAL: Would to God this Bayle had been drowned, along with his Dutch heretics! Has there ever been a more abominable creature? He expounds things with such obnoxious accuracy; he places before our eyes both sides of a question with such craven impartiality; he writes with such intolerable clarity that he enables people who have only common sense to judge and even to doubt for themselves. This cannot be borne, and for my part I admit that I go into a holy rage when anyone speaks of this man and his like.

ARISTE: I don't think they ever intended to anger you . . . But where are you off to now in such a hurry?

ACROTAL: To Monsignor Bardo-Bardi. I have been requesting an audience for the past two days; but he is always either dallying with his page-boy or with the Signora Buona-Roba; I have so far been unable to have the honour of speaking with him.

ARISTE: He is at this moment at the opera. What have you to tell him that is so pressing?

ACROTAL: I wanted to ask him to bring his influence to bear in the burning of a little priest[7] who has been insinuating the ideas of Locke amongst us – an English philosopher, if you please! Can you imagine a worse horror?

ARISTE: Well! And what, pray, are the horrific notions of this Englishman?

ACROTAL: How do I know! That our ideas do not come from us, for example; that God, who is master of everything, can bestow ideas and sensations upon whomever he chooses; that we know neither the essence nor the elements of matter; that men do not think all the time; that a completely drunk man who falls asleep does not have clear ideas in his sleep; and a hundred other such impertinences.

ARISTE: Well! If your little priest, the disciple of Locke, is so ill-advised as not to believe that a sleeping drunk can have thought processes – is that a reason to persecute him? What evil has he done? Has he conspired against the state? Has he preached theft, calumny or homicide from the pulpit? Tell me, between the two of us, has a philosopher ever caused the slightest trouble to society?

ACROTAL: Never, I admit.

ARISTE: Are they not for the most part solitary people? Are they not poor, without patronage, without support? And is it not partly for these reasons that you persecute them, because you know you can oppress them so easily?

ACROTAL: It is true that formerly there were hardly any to be found among this sect except citizens without any credit, such as Socrates, Pomponazzi, Erasmus, Bayle, Descartes. But now philosophy has risen into the courts and even ascended the throne; everyone prides themselves on their reason (except in certain countries where we have managed to restore order). That is what is truly baneful, and that is why we exert ourselves to exterminate at least those philosophers who have neither fortune, influence, nor honours in this world, since we cannot avenge ourselves on those who do.

ARISTE: Avenge yourselves? For what, may I ask? Have these poor creatures ever coveted your posts, your prerogatives, your fortunes?

ACROTAL: No; but they despise us, if the truth be known; and they mock us from time to time, which we can never forgive.

ARISTE: That is of course bad, to mock you: one must never mock anyone; but pray tell me, why has no one ever scoffed at the laws and magistrature in any country, whereas you are scoffed at so mercilessly, according to what you tell me?

ACROTAL: That is precisely what makes our blood boil; for we are well above the laws.

ARISTE: Which is precisely why so many honest men have turned you to ridicule. You would have those laws founded on universal reason – which the Greeks named the Daughters of Heaven – give way to all kinds of opinions which caprice both creates and destroys. Can you not see that what is just, clear and self-evident is universally respected for all time, and that wild fancies cannot always secure the same veneration?

ACROTAL: Let us leave aside laws and judges, and concentrate on philosophers: there can be no doubt that formerly they uttered just as many idiocies as we do; therefore we must rise up against them, if only for reasons of professional rivalry.

ARISTE: Several of them have undoubtedly uttered idiotic remarks, because philosophers are only men; but their fancies have never kindled civil war, such as yours have triggered more than once.

ACROTAL: Which is what is admirable about us. Is there anything finer than to shake the world by means of a few arguments? Do we not resemble the ancient sorcerers who summoned up tempests with words? We should be masters of the world were it not for these rascally intellectuals.

ARISTE: Well, tell them, if you like, that they have no intellect; show them that their reason is corrupt; if they ridicule you, why not ridicule them back? But I beg you to spare this poor disciple of Locke whom you wanted to burn alive; do you not see, dear Doctor, that burning is no longer the fashion?

ACROTAL: You are right; we must find a new way of silencing these petty philosophers.

ARISTE: Believe me, keep silent yourselves; have nothing more to do with argufying; become honest men; exercise compassion; stop looking for evil where it does not exist, and it will no longer be found where it does exist.

The Education of Daughters

MÉLINDE: Eraste has departed, and I see you are plunged into deep reverie. He is young, handsome, witty, rich and amiable, so I forgive you your daydreaming.

SOPHRONIE: He is everything you say, I admit.

MÉLINDE: And what's more, he loves you.

SOPHRONIE: I admit that too.

MÉLINDE: I think you are not insensible to his charms.

SOPHRONIE: That is the third admission, which my friendship for you has no fear of conceding.

MÉLINDE: Let us add a fourth; I can see that you will soon be married to Eraste.

SOPHRONIE: I can tell you, in the same confidence, that I shall never marry him.

MÉLINDE: What! Can your mother oppose so presentable a match?

SOPHRONIE: No, she allows me the freedom to choose; I love Eraste, but I shall never marry him.

MÉLINDE: And what reason can you have for this tyranny over yourself?

SOPHRONIE: The fear of being tyrannized. Eraste is a man of intelligence, but he is imperious and caustic; he has graces, but soon he will set them to work on others than myself: I have no wish to become the rival of one of those women who sell their charms, who cast a glow upon the purchaser, who outrage half the town by their splendour and ruin the other half by their example, and who triumph in public at the expense of an honest woman reduced to weeping in solitude. I have a strong inclination for Eraste, but I have studied his character; he goes too much against my inclination. I want to be happy; I shall not be so with Eraste. I shall marry Ariste, whom I esteem, and whom I hope one day to love.

MÉLINDE: You are remarkably sensible for your age. There are few girls whom the fear of a troubled future prevents from embracing an agreeable present. How can you have such self-command?

SOPHRONIE: The little sense I have I owe to the education given me by my mother. She did not raise me in a convent, for it was not in a convent that I was destined to spend my life. I pity those girls whose mothers entrust their early youth to nuns, just as they have entrusted the care of their early infancy to unrelated wet-nurses. I hear that in these convents, as in most institutions where the young are raised, one learns scarcely anything except what one needs to forget for the rest of one's life; our early prime is buried beneath stupidities. You leave your prison, only to be promised to a stranger who comes to spy at you through the grille; whoever he is, you regard him as your liberator and, if he be a monkey, you think yourself all too fortunate; you give yourself to him without knowing him; you live with him without loving him. It is a transaction to which you are not party, and soon afterwards both parties repent.

My mother thought me capable of thinking for myself, and of choosing a spouse for myself when the time comes. Had I been born to earn my own livelihood, she would have taught me to succeed in those occupations appropriate to my sex; however, born to live in society, she instructed me early on in everything that concerns society; she formed my mind by making me fear the pitfalls of pure wit; she took me to all those choice theatrical spectacles which are capable of forming taste without corrupting morals, where the dangers of passion are displayed even more than its charms, where propriety reigns, where one learns to think and to express oneself. Tragedy has often seemed to me the school of the soul, comedy the school of the proprieties. I would go so far as to say that these lessons, which are regarded as mere amusements, have been more useful to me than books. Finally, my mother always treated me as a thinking being whose spirit needed to be cultivated, not as a puppet to be fitted out, shown off, and put back in its box immediately afterwards.

Wives, Submit Yourselves to Your Husbands

The Abbé de Châteauneuf[1] told me one day, talking about Madame la Maréchale de Grancey, that she had been a very imperious woman; despite which, she had possessed remarkable qualities. Her greatest pride consisted in respecting herself, in doing nothing at which she might have cause to blush in secret; she never lowered herself to telling lies. She preferred to confess a dangerous truth than resort to easy dissimulation, maintaining that dissimulation was always a sign of cowardice. Her life was marked by a thousand generous deeds, but when praised for them she felt insulted; she used to say: 'So you think that such actions cost me an effort?' Her lovers adored her, her friends treasured her, and her husband respected her.

She dissipated her first forty years in that circle of amusements which for women count as the serious pursuits, having read nothing besides the letters she received, and having thought of nothing except the gossip of the day, the follies of her neighbours and the interests of her heart. At length, seeing herself reach the age when, as they say, women who have both beauty and wit pass from one throne to the other, she conceived a desire to read. She began with the tragedies of Racine, and was astonished to discover an even greater pleasure in reading them than she had felt in seeing them performed: the good taste inculcated in her mind by reading showed her that this man spoke only of things which were true and important; that his words were always in their right place; that he was noble and unaffected, without declamation, without anything forced, without any striving after effect; that his plots, like his thoughts, were all founded on nature. She rediscovered in her reading the history of her emotions and the picture of her life.

She was persuaded to read Montaigne:[2] she was charmed to find a man who seemed to converse with her alone, and who doubted everything. Then she was handed the *Lives* of Plutarch:[3] she asked why he had written only the history of great men, not of great women.

One day the Abbé de Châteauneuf found her in a state of high indignation. 'What is the trouble, madame?' said he. 'I opened by chance', she replied, 'a book which was lying about in my study; it is, I believe, some collection of letters, in which I came across these words: "*Wives, submit yourselves to your husbands.*"[4] I threw the book away.'

'What, Madame? Do you not know that these are the Epistles of St Paul?'

'I do not care who wrote them; the author is very ill-bred. My husband, Monsieur le Maréchal, has never written to me in such a style; I am persuaded that your St Paul was a very difficult man to live with. Was he married?'

'Yes, Madame.'

'Then his wife must surely have been a submissive creature: had I been the wife of such a man, I would have made him see a thing or two. *Submit yourselves* indeed! Now, had he contented himself with saying: "*Be gentle, complaisant, attentive, thrifty*", I should have said: there's a man who understands life. But why *submit yourselves*, may I ask? When I married Monsieur de Grancey, we promised to be faithful to each other: I have not kept my vows too punctiliously, nor he his; but neither of us ever promised obedience. Are we women slaves, then? Is it not enough that a man, having married me, has the right to give me a nine-months' illness, which is sometimes fatal? Is it not enough that I should bring forth with great pain a child who may appear in court against me when he comes of age? Is it not enough that I should be subjected every month to inconveniences which are most distasteful to a woman of quality, and that, to crown it all, the omission of just one of these monthly maladies may cause my death? Is not all this enough, without someone coming along and saying to me: *Obey!*

'No, nature has certainly said nothing of the kind; she has given us organs which differ from those of men; but, in making us necessary to each other, she has never pretended that our union should be a state of slavery. I can remember well what Molière said: "All power is on the side of the beard."[5] But that is a quaint reason, surely, for foisting a master on to me! What! because a man's chin is covered with an ugly rough skin which he is obliged to shave closely, whereas my chin was born smooth, it follows that I should humbly submit to him? I know perfectly well that men generally have muscles which are stronger than ours, and aim punches better than we do: indeed, I fear this may be all there is to their superiority.

'They claim moreover that their minds are better organized, and, in consequence, boast that they are more capable of governing; but I could show you queens who are worth many a king. I heard a few days ago of a German princess[6] who rises at five in the morning to work for the well-being of her subjects, directs the affairs of state, answers all letters, encourages all the arts, and dispenses benefits as numerous as her own abilities. Her courage equals her knowledge, because she was not brought up in a convent by idiots who teach us what we do not need to know, and leave us in ignorance of what we do need to know. For my part, had I a state to govern, I think I should be bold enough to follow her example.'

The Abbé de Châteauneuf, who was a very polite man, took care not to contradict Madame la Maréchale.

'By the way,' said she, 'is it true that Mohammed despised us so much that he maintained we were not worthy to enter Paradise, and should not be allowed beyond its gates?' – 'In that case', said the Abbé, 'the men would always stay near the door. But comfort yourself; there is not one word of truth in all that they say here about the Muslim faith. Our ignorant and wicked monks have thoroughly deceived us, as my brother, who was ambassador at the Porte[7] for twelve years, has testified.'

'What! Is it not true, sir, that Mohammed invented the custom of plurality of wives in order to have more control over the men? Is it not true that women are slaves in Turkey, and are forbidden to pray to God in the mosque?' – 'Not a word of truth in any of it, Madame. Mohammed, far from inventing polygamy, suppressed or restrained it. The wise Solomon had seven hundred wives. Mohammed reduced this number to just four. Ladies may go to Paradise, just the same as gentlemen; and, without doubt, they will make love there, though in a fashion different from how it is performed down here; for you must allow that we know love but very imperfectly in this world.'

'Alas, you are right,' said the Maréchale; 'mankind is truly of little account! But tell me, did your Mohammed not order wives to submit themselves to their husbands?'

'No, Madame; that is nowhere to be found in the Koran.'

'Then why are women slaves in Turkey?'

'They are by no means slaves; they have property; they can make wills; they are able to request a divorce on occasion; they have their times for going to the mosque – and to their rendezvous: one sees them in the streets with their veils over their noses, just as you used to wear your mask some years ago. It is true that they are not to be seen at the opera or the theatre, but that is because these do not exist. Can you doubt that, were there ever to be an opera house in Constantinople – the homeland of Orpheus – the ladies of Turkey would not fill the front boxes?'

'Wives, submit to your husbands!' said the Maréchale between her teeth. 'This Paul was a perfect savage.'

'He was a little hard,' replied the Abbé, 'and he greatly liked to be master: he looked down on St Peter, who was really quite a good fellow. Besides, we must not take all that he said too literally. He has been reproached with having a strong leaning towards the Jansenists.'

'I suspected all along that he was a heretic,' said the Maréchale; and she continued with her toilet.

Dialogue between the Cock and the Hen

COCK: Good Lord, my dear hen, you do look sad: what's wrong?

HEN: Dear friend, better ask what's *not* wrong with me. An awful servant took me on her knees, stuck a long needle up my backside, grabbed hold of my womb, rolled it around the needle, tore it out and gave it to her cat to eat. So now I can't receive the attentions of my favourite Chanticleer or lay an egg.

COCK: Alas! my dear, I've lost more than you. What they did to me was twice as cruel; you and I will no longer get any comfort in this world. They've neutered both of us. The only thing that consoles me in my desperate state is that the other day, near my hen-house, I heard two Italian priests saying that they'd suffered the same terrible fate, so they could sing to the Pope with a purer voice. According to them, men started out circumcising their fellow-men and ended up castrating them. They were cursing their fate and the human race.

HEN: What! you mean to say that they've taken away the best thing about us just so we could have a purer voice?

COCK: Alas! my poor hen, it's worse than that; it's to fatten us up and make our flesh more tender.

HEN: So . . . when we're fatter, will they be any better off?

COCK: Yes: because they're planning to eat us.

HEN: Eat us! oh, the brutes!

COCK: It's what they do. They lock us up for a few days, force us to swallow a mash of their own making, put our eyes out to keep our minds from wandering. Then, when the feast day arrives, they tear out our feathers, cut our throats, and roast us. We are carried in and put in front of them on a large silver platter. They all say what they think of us – it's our funeral oration. Someone says we smell of nuts, someone else how wonderful our flesh tastes. They praise our thighs, our arms, our rumps, and then our tale is told once and for all in this poor world.

HEN: What appalling villains! I feel faint. Oh no! they'll tear my eyes out, and cut my throat! I'll be roasted and eaten! Won't these ruffians suffer any remorse?

COCK: No, my dear. The two priests I told you about were saying that men don't ever have any remorse for things that they're accustomed to doing.

HEN: What a horrible race! I bet that even as they're eating us they start laughing and telling jokes, just as though there were nothing wrong.

COCK: You're right. But it might help a bit to know that these animals, who have two feet just like us but are much inferior since they have no feathers, have acted exactly the same way with their own kind times without number. I gathered from my two priests that the Greek and Christian emperors always took care to put out the eyes of their brothers and cousins; there was even, in our own country, a man named Debonair who had his nephew Bernard's eyes torn out. As for the matter of roasting human beings, there's nothing more common. My priests said that more than 20,000 people had been roasted for holding views that a cockerel would find it hard to explain and which I don't care about anyway.

HEN: So, I suppose they roasted them to eat them.

COCK: I'm not too sure. But I do recall very clearly being told that in lots of countries men have from time to time eaten one another.

HEN: Never mind about that. It's a good thing if the members of such a perverted species eat one another; then we can be shot of them. But what about me? I'm peaceable, I've never done any wrong, I've even fed these monsters by giving them eggs. Am I to be castrated, blinded, have my throat cut and be roasted? Are we treated like that in the rest of the world?

COCK: The two priests said No. They were sure that in a country called India, much bigger, more beautiful, more fertile than ours, men have a sacred law that for thousands of centuries now has forbidden them to eat us. One Pythagoras,[1] who had travelled amongst these just nations, introduced this humane law into Europe, and it was followed by all his disciples. These good priests were reading Porphyry[2] the Pythagorean, who wrote a fine book against roasting spits.

This Porphyry – what a good, divine man he was! With so much wisdom, forcefulness, tender respect for God he shows us that we are both the allies of men and related to them. God gave us, he says, the same organs, feelings, memory, the same mysterious germ of understanding that evolves in us to the point decreed by eternal law, which neither they nor we can ever infringe. Indeed, my dearest hen, wouldn't it be an insult to God to say that we have senses but cannot feel, a brain but cannot think? That fantasy, worthy of some madman they call Descartes,[3] wouldn't it be the height of ridicule and a worthless excuse for acting barbarously?

So the great philosophers of antiquity never roasted us on the spit. They made efforts to learn our language and to find out about the faculties we have that are so superior to human ones. We were as safe with them as in the Golden Age. Wise men don't kill animals, says Porphyry; only barbarians and priests kill and eat them. He wrote this marvellous book to convert a disciple who had become Christian out of sheer greediness.

HEN: Well then . . . did they put up altars to this great man who taught virtue to humans and saved animals?

COCK: No. He was detested by the Christians, the ones who eat us, and they still execrate his memory today. They call him a heathen and say his virtues weren't genuine, since he was a pagan.

HEN: What dreadful prejudices come from greediness! The other day, in this barn affair near our hen-house, I heard a man speaking; others were standing around saying nothing. He was holding forth that 'God had made a pact with us and these other animals called *men*; God had forbidden them to feed on our flesh and blood.' How then can they include in this stringent ban the right to consume our limbs when boiled or roasted? When they cut our throats, a lot of blood must still be left in our veins, and this must still be mixed in with our flesh. So they are visibly disobeying God by eating us. And also, isn't it a sacrilege to kill and eat creatures with whom God has made a pact? It would be a peculiar treaty indeed where the only clause is to deliver us up to die. Either our creator didn't make a pact with us, or it's a crime to kill and cook us. There's no middle way.

COCK: That isn't the only contradiction to be found amongst these barbarians, our undying enemies. They've been long since the object of criticism, because they never agree on anything. They make laws, only to break them; worse, they break them with a clear conscience. They have thought up scores of subterfuges, dozens of false arguments to justify their wrongdoing. They only apply their minds to excuse their injustices; they only use words to cover up their thoughts. Just imagine, in this little country of ours, it is forbidden to eat us two days a week. But they manage to find a way round that law. What's more, though on the surface it appears to help us, it is in fact barbarous. People are commanded to eat fish those two days, so they hunt down their victims in the seas and rivers. They devour fish which each cost them more than a hundred cockerels, and they call that *fasting* and *self-mortification*. In short, I don't think you can imagine a race both more absurd and more odious, more outrageous and bloodthirsty.

HEN: Oh, heavens! Don't I see that dreadful kitchen boy with his big knife?

COCK: This is it, my dear, our last hour has come; let us commend our souls to God.

HEN: If only I could give the rascal who is going to eat me a bout of indigestion that would kill him! But the weak can only take their revenge on the strong by making futile wishes, and the strong just laugh.

COCK: Ahhh! they've got me by the throat. Let us pardon our enemies.

HEN: I can't; they've grabbed me, they're carrying me off. Farewell, my dear Chanticleer.

COCK: Farewell, for all eternity, my dearest hen.

Conversation between Lucian, Erasmus and Rabelais, in the Elysian Fields

Some time ago, in the Elysian fields, Lucian[1] made the acquaintance of Erasmus,[2] despite his repugnance for everything that emanated from the German borders. He did not believe that an ancient Greek should abase himself by speaking to a Batavian, but since the shade of this particular Batavian struck him as worthy company, they had the following conversation together.

LUCIAN: So you used to pursue, in a barbarous land, the same profession which I pursued in the most civilized country the world has seen; did you too make a mock of everything?

ERASMUS: Alas! I should have dearly liked to; it would have been a great consolation for a poor theologian such as I was; but I could not take the same liberties as you.

LUCIAN: This astonishes me: generally men quite like to be shown their follies, provided one does not refer to a particular individual. Each applies his own absurdities to his neighbour, and all men laugh at each other's expense. Was it not the same with your contemporaries?

ERASMUS: There was a vast difference between the ridiculous men of your time and those of mine: you only had to deal with gods who were played in the theatres, and philosophers who had even less prestige than gods; I on the other hand was surrounded by fanatics, and I needed to be highly circumspect not to be burned alive by some or murdered by others.

LUCIAN: How were you able to laugh, with these for alternatives?

ERASMUS: The answer is that I laughed very little; even so, I was taken for more of a joker than was the case. I was thought to be very light-hearted and very clever, because everyone else at the time was so miserable. People were deeply embroiled in barren disputes which made them bad-tempered. Those who thought that a body can be in two places at one time were ready to cut the throats of those who explained the same idea after a different fashion. Worse still, a man of my profession who took no sides between such factions would have been considered a monster.

LUCIAN: What strange creatures, these barbarians among whom you lived! In my time even the Getes and the Massagetes tribes[3] were more amenable and sensible; and what was your profession in the horrible country where you lived?

ERASMUS: I was a Dutch monk.

LUCIAN: A monk! And what kind of profession is that?

ERASMUS: That of having no profession, and of taking an inviolable oath to be useless to the human race, to be ridiculous and a slave, and to live off others.

LUCIAN: Now there's a villainous profession! And how was a man of your wit able to embrace a state which dishonours human nature? Let's overlook the business of living off others, but to take a vow to forfeit common sense and lose one's liberty!

ERASMUS: The fact is that I was very young, and having neither parents nor friends I let myself be seduced by rogues who wanted to swell their numbers.

LUCIAN: What! There were many men of this persuasion?

ERASMUS: There were, throughout Europe, about six or seven thousand.

LUCIAN: Good heavens! The world has indeed become totally foolish and barbarous since I left it! Horace spoke truly that everything goes from bad to worse! *Progeniem vitiosiorem* (Bk. III, Ode VI).

ERASMUS: What consoles me is that everyone in my century had reached the lowest rung of folly; they had no choice but to get off the ladder, and for some of their number finally to recover a little human reason.

LUCIAN: As to that, I have strong doubts. Tell me, what were the principal follies of your time?

ERASMUS: Here, I keep a list which I always carry about with me; read it.

LUCIAN: It's long enough.

[*Lucian reads, and bursts out laughing; Rabelais[4] arrives on the scene.*]

RABELAIS: Gentlemen, wherever there is laughter I am welcome; what are you discussing?

LUCIAN AND ERASMUS: Eccentricities.

RABELAIS: Then I am your man.

LUCIAN [*to Erasmus*]: Who is this character?

ERASMUS: A gentleman who was bolder than I and more amusing; but he was only a priest, so he was able to take more liberties than I, a monk.

LUCIAN [*to Rabelais*]: Did you also take a vow to live off others?

RABELAIS: Doubly so, for I was both a priest and a doctor. I was born with native good sense, and I became as learned as Erasmus; and, observing that knowledge and wisdom commonly led only to the hospital or the gallows, and moreover that even this half-time joker Erasmus was sometimes persecuted, I decided to be even madder than all my compatriots put together. So I wrote a fat volume of cock and bull stories, awash with filth, in which I turned to ridicule all superstitions, all ceremony, all that was revered in my country and all stations of life, from that of the king and high pontiff down to the doctor of theology, which is the lowest of all. I dedicated my book to a cardinal, and I made even those who despised me laugh out loud.

LUCIAN: What is a cardinal, Erasmus?

ERASMUS: It means a priest dressed in red, who receives eight thousand écus a year for doing absolutely nothing.

LUCIAN: That at least was clever of these cardinals, you must admit. Not all your compatriots can have been as mad as you say.

ERASMUS: If Rabelais will allow me to put in a few words. Cardinals possessed a different kind of madness, that of power; and as it is easier to subjugate fools than men of sense, they attempted to knock senseless Reason itself, which at the time was beginning to raise its head. Monsieur Rabelais, whom you see before you, imitated the first Brutus,[5] who pretended to be mad so as to escape the suspicions and tyranny of the Tarquins.

LUCIAN: All that you say confirms me in the opinion that it was better to live in my century than in yours. These cardinals of whom you speak were therefore masters of the entire world, because they had control over the lunatics?

RABELAIS: No; there was one old fool higher than them.

LUCIAN: What was he called?

RABELAIS: A Popeye. The madness of this man consisted in declaring himself to be infallible, and believing himself to be the ruler of kings; and he talked so much, and repeated it so much, and had himself cried up so much by the monks, that in the end the whole of Europe was convinced.

LUCIAN: Ah! how much more advanced you were in the lunacy stakes! Our fables about Jupiter, Neptune and Pluto, of which I made such mockery, were perfectly respectable by comparison with the idiocies with which your world became infatuated. I cannot comprehend how you were able to turn to ridicule, with any degree of safety, individuals who must have feared ridicule even more than a conspiracy. For in the end one does not mock one's masters lightly, and I was prudent enough not to say a single word about the Roman emperors. What! Your natives worshipped a Popeye! You heaped on this Popeye all the ridicule imaginable, and they all endured it! They must have been very patient.

RABELAIS: I should explain to you about my native land. It was a compound of ignorance, superstition, folly, cruelty and absurdity. For a start they would hang and roast alive anyone who spoke out loud against Popeyes and cardinals. The French barbarians,[6] my compatriots, habitually swam in blood; but as soon as the executions were over everyone would dance, sing and make love, drink and laugh. I captured my fellow-countrymen through their weaknesses. I spoke to them of drink, I spoke of filth and by this secret means I was allowed to say anything. Men of intelligence saw through it and were grateful to me; the rabble saw only filth, and lapped it up; far from persecuting me, everyone loved me.

LUCIAN: You have filled me with a longing to read your book. Would you by any chance have a copy in your pocket? And you, Erasmus, would you also lend me your facetious pieces to read? [Here Erasmus and Rabelais give their works to Lucian, who reads some passages, and while he is reading, these two philosophers converse with each other.]

RABELAIS [*to Erasmus*]: I have read your writings, but you have not read mine, because I came a little after your time. You were perhaps a little too reserved in your mockeries, and I perhaps too crude in mine; but here and now we both think alike. For my part, I laugh when I see a Doctor of the Church arrive on these shores.

ERASMUS: For my part, I pity him; I say: 'Here is an unfortunate who has exhausted his life in deceiving himself, and who gains nothing here in leaving the path of error.'

RABELAIS: What! Does being undeceived count for nothing?

ERASMUS: It counts for little when you can no longer undeceive others. The greatest pleasure is to show the right path to friends who stray, and the dead ask their way from nobody.

Erasmus and Rabelais discussed the matter for quite some time. Lucian returned after having read Rabelais's chapter about the Arse-Wipers,[7] and a few pages of *The Praise of Folly*. Then, after encountering Doctor Swift, the four gentlemen went off to dinner together.

NOTES

Cuckoldage

1. *Cythera*: An Aegean island, where there was a temple to Venus.
2. *horns*: The traditional symbol of cuckolded husbands.
3. *Hymen*: The deity who presided over weddings.
4. *Iris*: The goddess of the rainbow.

The One-eyed Porter

1. *Tithonus*: Trojan prince who loved and married Aurora, goddess of the dawn.

Cosi-Sancta

1. *described in 'The City of God'*: Incorrect. The source is another work by St Augustine, *De Sermone Domini in monte* (Bk. 1, ch. 16).
2. *Hippo*: North African city of which St Augustine was bishop (AD 396–430).
3. *Jansenists*: Catholic sect founded in the seventeenth century, and noted for its rigorous moral code and hostility to the Jesuits. The anachronism is intended to demonstrate that St Augustine was considered to be its forebear.
4. *Venetian*: It has been suggested that Voltaire may have had Shakespeare's Othello in mind here.

Micromégas

1. *little Earth*: Voltaire mocks those who wish to make precise calculations – as well he might, for these and later figures are not correct, arithmetically!

2. *metaphysician*: Pascal, a Jansenist philosopher and scientist (1623–62), was frequently the target of Voltaire's satire.

3. *Mufti*: A Mohammedan priest. The disguised person is probably the Archbishop of Paris, who had condemned Voltaire's *Lettres philosophiques* (1734).

4. *mud-heap*: A metaphor frequently used by Voltaire to emphasize the contrast between man's earthbound wretchedness and the majesty of the heavens.

5. *repulsion*: Micromégas is evidently well acquainted with Newton's astronomical discoveries (*Principia*: 1686). Voltaire had already devoted to Newton four of his *Lettres philosophiques*, and the *Éléments de Newton* (1738).

6. *Derham*: William Derham (1657–1735) wrote a number of scientific works to prove God's existence through the wonders of nature, including *Aristotheology* (1715), referred to here.

7. *Lully's compositions*: Jean-Baptiste Lully (1632–87), born in Florence, spent most of his life in France, and was considered by Voltaire to be the father of French music.

8. *Secretary of the Academy of Saturn*: Reference to Fontenelle (1657–1757), Secretary of the Academy of Sciences, and particularly to his *Entretiens sur la pluralité des mondes* (1686).

9. *instructed*: Satirical allusions to Fontenelle's *Entretiens*, which Voltaire thought a frivolous discussion of a serious astronomical topic.

10. *five moons*: Only five satellites of Saturn were known until Herschel discovered two more in 1789.

11. *longing*: Voltaire has in mind Locke's concept of desire as the motive of action in the *Essay concerning Human Understanding* (1690).

12. *seven colours*: Discovered by Newton and reported in his *Optics* (1704).

13. *little globe*: Huyghens (1629–95), a Dutch astronomer who elucidated the nature of Saturn's rings.

14. *Castel*: Jesuit priest (1688–1757) who had attacked Voltaire's *Éléments de Newton*, defending Descartes's physics against Newton.

15. *new style*: The Gregorian calendar, adopted by France in 1582, but only much later by non-Catholic countries (1752 in Britain).

16. *Arctic Circle*: Maupertuis had undertaken an expedition to Scandinavia in 1737 in order to measure a meridian within the Arctic Circle.

17. *nothing more*: Voltaire has in mind here the Lilliputians in Swift's *Gulliver's*

Travels, which he had read admiringly on the novel's appearance in 1726.
18. *infinitesimally small*: A rather sarcastic allusion to the Grenadiers of Frederick II of Prussia.
19. *Leeuwenhoek and Hartsoeker*: Both Leeuwenhoek (1632–1723) and Hartsoeker (1656–1725) made significant discoveries about spermatozoa through their work with the microscope.
20. *bees*: Virgil, *Georgics*, Bk. IV.
21. *Swammerdam . . . Réaumur*: Swammerdam was a Dutch naturalist (1637–80), known mainly for his investigations into the structure of insects; Réaumur was a French naturalist (1683–1757), whose *Mémoires* on insects (1734–42) were a landmark in entomological studies.
22. *as I speak . . . turbans*: Reference to the Russo-Turkish War (1736–9).
23. *mud-heaps*: See above, n. 4.
24. *entelechy*: An immaterial substance which carries its own purpose within itself. Peripatetics were disciples of Aristotle.
25. *will never know again*: Voltaire's commonly expressed objection, following Locke, to Descartes's doctrine of innate ideas.
26. *Malebranche*: (1638–1715), disciple of Descartes.
27. *is clear*: The doctrine of pre-established harmony which Leibniz (1646–1716) elaborated, according to which body and soul are held together systematically by the principle of sufficient reason, as God had foreseen.
28. *'I do not know . . . we think'*: Voltaire's admiration of Locke's empirical philosophy is evident in the whole of this paragraph.
29. *for Man*: St Thomas Aquinas (*c.* 1225–74), whose *Summa Theologiae* represented the essence of scholastic orthodoxy. Voltaire concentrates here on one aspect: Aquinas's anthropocentrism.

The World As It Is

1. *entrance*: Voltaire is referring to the Faubourg Saint-Marceau, the old southern approach to Paris. Its foulness will be criticized again in 'Candide', ch. XXII.
2. *chantings*: Satire on Gregorian plainchant.
3. *deposited a corpse . . . stone above it*: The eighteenth century saw a gradual change from this practice with the establishment of Parisian cemeteries outside the built-up area.
4. *adore*: The statue to Louis XV here called for was not erected until 1763.
5. *armies*: The Hôtel des Invalides.
6. *mage*: An *abbé*.

7. *iniquity*: Voltaire regularly objected to the venality of judicial offices; the defence of venality later in the story is an exceptional case.

8. *profits*: The tax-farmers paid a fixed sum to the King but then raised whatever they thought appropriate from the people.

9. *machine*: A pulpit.

10. *could be seen*: The juxtaposition of this theatre with the preceding church underlines Voltaire's view that this is the house of true religion, with the actors as 'appointed preachers'.

11. *Any merchant . . . Empire*: This speech accords with the praise for commerce which Voltaire consistently displays in his writings.

12. *archimandrite*: The monastery's abbot.

13. *Great Lama*: The Pope; the anti-papist attitude indicates that the speaker is a Jansenist; his reference to the 'little girls' is an allusion to the notorious frenzies of the Jansenist convulsionaries at the time.

Memnon

1. *they are today*: The 'affliction' is syphilis, thought to have been brought back to Europe by the early colonists of America.

2. *poets and philosophers*: Pope and Leibniz in particular, both upholders of the doctrine of Optimism, which Voltaire demolishes in 'Candide'.

Letter from a Turk

1. *Gymnosophists*: Ancient Indian devotees, who lived a life of total austerity in the desert.

2. *Veda*: Ancient Sanskrit text (*c.* 500 BC).

3. *Zend-Avesta*: Sacred text of the ancient Persians.

Plato's Dream

1. *human nature . . . female*: The source is Plato's *Symposium*, 189d.

2. *there can only exist . . . mathematics*: Plato's *Timeus*, 55d.

3. *sleeping comes from waking . . . pond*: Plato's *Phaedo*, 99d.

4. *Phidias and Zeuxis*: Phidias was arguably the greatest sculptor of ancient Greece (d. *c.* 431 BC), and Zeuxis one of the outstanding painters of that period (464–398 BC).

5. *the Earth*: See above, 'Micromégas', n. 4.

6. *rings*: An error; Mars has no rings.

7. *a few hundred million years*: In his *Éléments de Newton*, Voltaire states that the English scientist had argued that with the passage of time the planetary motions and irregularities would diminish and the universe eventually disappear or be reordered (*Complete Works*, vol. 15, ed. W. H. Barber (Oxford: Voltaire Foundation, 1992), p. 218).

The History of the Travels of Scarmentado

1. *Candia*: Capital of Crete.

2. *Iro*: Anagram of Roi, the name of a poet with whom Voltaire had quarrelled.

3. *her lover*: Minos, King of Crete, was married to Pasiphaë, who committed adultery with a bull and gave birth to the monster Minotaur.

4. *Olympia*: Pope Innocent X's sister-in-law, who is about 20 years old when Scarmentado arrives in Rome in 1615. Her family connection enables her to organize an immense traffic in dispensations and benefits.

5. *Fatelo*: Italian for 'Do it'.

6. *Aconiti*: Aconite is a poison.

7. *Louis the Just*: Louis XIII (1601–43).

8. *the maréchal d'Ancre . . . wanted it*: The Maréchal d'Ancre was assassinated in 1617.

9. *Massacres*: This massacre of French Huguenots occurred in Paris in August 1572.

10. *heretics*: The Gunpowder Plot (1605).

11. *Queen Mary*: Reigned 1553–8.

12. *St Patrick's well*: Commonly supposed to be the entrance to hell.

13. *Cardinal Nephew*: Nephew of the reigning Pope.

14. *Barneveldt*: Executed in 1619 for a Protestant heresy.

15. *preacher*: A Calvinist.

16. *the galleons had returned safely*: From the American colonies with their rich cargo.

17. *flames*: These references are all to the rituals of an *auto-da-fé*, organized by the Spanish Inquisition; alguazils: police officers.

18. *Hermandad*: Spanish police; familiars: Inquisition officials, with the power to arrest.

19. *Bishop of Chiapa*: Las Casas (1474–1566), whose *Brevisima Relación de la destrucción de las Indias* (1552) gives a trenchant account of these massacres.

20. *Divan*: Turkish judicial court.

21. *Allah, Illah, Allah!*: 'Only Allah is great!'
22. *Cadi*: Turkish judge.
23. *Aureng-Zebe*: Moghul Emperor of India (1619–1707).
24. *Muley Ismaël*: Sultan Sherif of Morocco (1646–1727).

The Consoler and the Consoled

1. *daughter of . . . Henri IV*: Henrietta Maria (1609–69), queen consort of Charles I.
2. *Mary Stuart . . . eighteen years*: The musician, David Rizzio, was murdered (1566) by Mary's husband Darnley and others. Elizabeth sent Mary to the executioner's block in 1587.
3. *Queen of Naples . . . strangled*: Queen Joan of Naples was murdered in 1382 by her successor, Charles de Durazzo.
4. *Hecuba*: Wife of Priam, King of Troy, who saw most of her children die in the Trojan War and was thereafter taken into slavery.
5. *Niobe*: Queen of Thebes, whose many children were murdered. She wept for nine days and nights, and remains a poignant literary symbol of grief.

The Story of a Good Brahmin

1. *if Brahma . . . they are both eternal*: An indirect allusion to the theological debate on the nature of the Christian Trinity.

Pot-Pourri

1. *Brioché*: A marionette presenter (d. 1680). He represents St Joseph, Jesus' father.
2. *Punchinello*: An Italian marionette.
3. *Brioché's actual father . . . Fat-René*: A parody of the differing genealogies of Jesus in the Gospels (Matthew and Luke).
4. *Almanac of the Fairground*: A fictitious journal.
5. *Monsieur Parfaict*: In fact two brothers, François and Claude, authors of a history of fairground theatre (1743).
6. *Tabarin . . . Big-William . . . John-the-Sausage*: All seventeenth-century comic actors who specialized in farce.
7. *Father Daniel*: Jesuit historian, author of a 17-volume *Histoire de France* (1758).

8. *parricide in Portugal*: The assassination of Joseph I (1758).

9. *fomenting a rebellion in Paraguay*: The Jesuits had encouraged a rebellion by the Indians in 1750 which was still going on several years later.

10. *in France*: An anti-Jesuit campaign was to lead to the expulsion of the Order from France in 1767.

11. *faction*: Cf. above, 'Cosi-Sancta', n. 3.

12. *he never mastered the use of a pen*: A reference to the illiteracy of Jesus Christ, who left no written documents behind him.

13. *read it*: John 8: 2–11; a somewhat tendentious reading of this episode.

14. *orvietan*: The allusion is to the Temple of Jerusalem; orvietan was considered a miracle cure. Cf. below, Ch. VII, where the pedlars of orvietan stand for activists in the competing religious sects.

15. *magistrate*: Jesus appeared before the Jewish courts, who passed on their condemnation of him to Pilate.

16. *It was also claimed . . . sorcerer*: Voltaire appears to have in mind Christ's actions against the merchants in the Temple (Mark 11: 15; John 2: 13–17) and the miracle at the Cana wedding feast (John 2: 1–12).

17. *We do not know . . . Brioché*: The Gospels do not mention St Joseph's fate.

18. *Dumarsais*: Grammarian and *philosophe* (1676–1756).

19. *Urbain Grandier*: Burned at the stake in 1634 for practising witchcraft with the nuns of Loudun.

20. *Gaufredi*: Burned in 1611 as a sorcerer.

21. *since you are a Dutchman*: The Catholic Italian cannot imagine that a Protestant could be considered a Christian: a signal example of the sheer ignorance which underlies religious intolerance.

22. *Socinian*: Socinians did not believe in the Holy Trinity.

23. *Mansebo*: An anagram of one Böseman, a Jewish merchant.

24. *On this particular day . . . exchange*: This recalls Voltaire's famous description of the London Stock Exchange in the sixth *Lettre philosophique*, where all religious sects trade together peaceably. The wax medals were blessed and distributed by the Pope.

25. *Ahmed III*: Reigned as Sultan in Constantinople (1703–30), where Christianity was tolerated. In contrast, neither Islam (next paragraph) nor Protestantism (Ch. VI) was accorded open toleration in France at this time.

26. *janissaries*: Turkish soldiers.

27. *Unigenitus*: A Papal edict imposed on the Catholic Church by the Jesuits in 1713, which instigated deep unrest amongst the Jansenists, since it condemned over a hundred Jansenist propositions.

28. *Cévennes Massacres*: The Protestant peasants in the Cévennes, whose rebellion was brutally suppressed (1702–4).

29. *"Wake up . . . beauty"*: Allusion to the Protestant custom of singing psalms (like Psalm 136, quoted below) to popular airs and in French.

30. *"Happy . . . heads"*: This appears to be a free development of Psalm 137: 9: 'Happy he who seizes thy children and crushes them on the rock!'

31. *hills that skip like rams*: Psalm 114.

32. *Racine junior*: Louis Racine (1692–1763), son of the dramatist and great defender of the Catholic faith.

33. *I find it very bad . . . interference*: Protestants who refused marriage by Catholic priests were denied marital rights under the law.

34. *went from village to village*: As did the Apostles.

35. *Nostradamus*: The sixteenth-century astrologer, famed for his cryptic prophecies; this is a veiled allusion to the Old Testament prophesying of the coming of Christ.

36. *Madame Carminetta*: Represents the Emperor Constantine, whose protection the Christians sought through the Edict of Milan (AD 313).

37. *Madame Gigogne*: A traditional character in fairground theatre, she comes to represent the Catholic Church in this story.

38. *orvietan*: See above, n. 14.

39. *he elected himself leader of the troupe*: Refers to the establishment of the Bishop of Rome as the Pope.

40. *he had the door . . . her face*: Refers to quarrels between Pope and Emperor.

41. *Father La Valette*: (1707–62), a Jesuit missionary in Martinique, whose bankruptcy was considered the responsibility of the Order; the subsequent lawsuit led to its suppression.

42. *Polyeucte*: Play by Corneille (*c.* 1642). The eponymous hero, an early Christian martyr, is seen by Voltaire as a fanatic.

43. *Lubolier . . . Urieju*: Lubolier is an anagram of Boullier (1699–1759), a Protestant enemy of the *philosophes*; Morfyré = Formey (1711–97), a German Protestant; Urieju = Jurieu (1637–1713), a Huguenot extremist.

44. *the scene . . . husband*: Act V, sc. 5: the preceding quotation is an approximate version of lines in Act II, sc. 2.

45. *Polyeucte . . . I now am*: Act III, sc. 5; this quotation is more correct.

46. *provincial . . . Paris Opera*: Alludes to payments made to the Catholic Church for various indulgences and ceremonies.

47. *a servant . . . Good-Deed*: Luther's rebellion against the Catholic Church (1517), which led to the Wars of Religion.

48. *The English . . . over him*: Allusion to Henry VIII (1494–1547) and his establishment of the Church of England.

49. *Simon Bar-jona*: St Peter (see Matthew 16: 17).

50. *Porentru*: Near Colmar; refers to Voltaire's dispute with the Bishop of Colmar since 1754 in trying to obtain permission for the peasants to work on feast days.

51. *bills of confession*: The Archbishop of Paris had demanded that those on their deathbed produce a certificate testifying that they had *not* been confessed by a Jansenist priest, before they could receive the last sacraments.

An Indian Incident

1. *Pythagoras*: Greek philosopher (*c*. 550–*c*. 500 BC), about whom little is known. He bequeathed a way of life rather than a specific doctrine, based upon asceticism and the kinship of all living things. Plato was probably influenced by Pythagoreanism; after Plato, the movement became a form of neo-Platonism.

Lord Chesterfield's Ears

1. *a dreamy fellow . . . Channel*: Voltaire.

2. *Schools*: The Faculties of Theology; the biblical reference is to St Paul's First Epistle to the Corinthians, 15: 38.

3. *Gloucester*: Bishop Warburton (1698–1779), whom Voltaire attacked virulently in a pamphlet addressed to Warburton.

4. *Philips*: John Philips (1676–1709), author of *The Splendid Shilling*, a well-known burlesque poem.

5. *his book . . . ever written*: Locke's *Essay concerning Human Understanding* (1690), a work consistently praised by Voltaire.

6. *Rabelais's characters*: Panurge and Thaumaste converse by signs, *Pantagruel*, Bk. I, ch. xix. Cf. also below, *Conversation between Lucian, Erasmus and Rabelais*, n. 4.

7. *Apollonius and Archimedes*: Apollonius of Perga (fl. 250–220 BC); Archimedes: arguably the greatest mathematician of ancient Greece (*c*. 287–212 BC).

8. *Likewise he*: In this and the preceding sentence Voltaire is quoting himself.

9. *Epictetus*: Greek Stoic philosopher (fl. first century AD), one of Voltaire's admired predecessors as 'apostles of Reason'.

10. *Banks and Solander*: Sir Joseph Banks (1743–1820), President of the Royal Society, and Daniel Solander (1736–82), a distinguished botanist and secretary to Banks, were companions of Cook on his expedition to Tahiti (1768–71) and wrote an account of the voyage.

11. *Bonneval*: A French officer (1675–1747) who served the Sultan of Constantinople and was converted to Islam.

12. *MacCarthy*: An Irish priest who was said to have become a Muslim (*c.* 1730).

13. *Ramsay*: (1686–1743), a Scottish nobleman who was a convert to Catholicism (not to Islam).

14. *Malagrida*: Gabriel Malagrida (1689–1761), a Portuguese Jesuit, had been implicated in a plot in 1758 against King Joseph II; he was later condemned and executed.

15. *domicile*: The latter baptism was for foreigners living in Palestine, whereas baptism of justice was complete, including circumcision.

16. *such as are to be found . . . Jesuit Fathers*: Letters by several Jesuits, published in the *Journal de Trévoux* from 1702 onwards.

17. *Dr John Hawkesworth*: (*c.* 1715–73), Director of the East India Company.

18. *Dawkins and Wood*: James Dawkins (1722–57); Robert Wood (*c.* 1717–71), author of *Ruins of Palmyra* (1753) and *Ruins of Balbec* (1757).

19. *Vesuvius*: Sir William Hamilton (1730–1803), British Ambassador to Naples, wrote on Vesuvius and Etna.

20. *Wallis*: Samuel Wallis (1728–95), a naval officer, visited Tahiti in 1767.

21. *Bougainville*: Circumnavigated the globe and published an account of it, *Voyage autour du monde* (1771).

22. *It has been said*: By Voltaire in 'Candide', ch. IV.

23. *Finxit . . . deorum*: 'He fashioned [us] in the image of the gods who control all things' (Ovid, *Metamorphoses*, i. 83).

24. *Lord Rochester's noble verse: 'Love . . . to God'*: John Wilmot, Earl of Rochester (1647–80). Voltaire had respectfully translated a passage of Rochester's verse in his 21st *Lettre philosophique*. This line, which also appears in the article 'Amour' of the *Dictionnaire philosophique*, does not seem to exist as such in the original, and is probably the digest of a complex phrase in the letter-poem 'Artemisa to Chloë': 'Love, the most generous passion of the mind . . . On which one only blessing God might raise / In lands of atheists subsidies of praise' (*Rochester: Complete Works*, ed. F. H. Ellis, Harmondsworth, Penguin, 1994, p. 50).

25. *Pecquet's reservoir*: Jean Pecquet, a well-known doctor of Dieppe (d. 1647).

26. *together with his brother*: duc de Guise (1550–88) and cardinal de Guise (1555–88), both assassinated on the orders of Henri III at Blois.

27. *St Bartholomew's Day Massacre*: Massacre of Protestants (1572), ordered by Charles IX (1550–74), but at the instigation of his mother, Catherine de Médicis, and the Guise family.

28. *demi-lune*: Fortified outwork.

29. *'Now . . . write history'*: In fact, a verse from Voltaire's play *Charlot*, Act I, sc. 7.

30. *six burghers of Calais . . . necks*: Edward III (1312–77) captured Calais in 1347 after a year's siege. Voltaire's sceptical comments run counter to the traditional view that the action of the six burghers constituted a glorious sacrifice.

31. *pitchers*: Judges 7: 16–22.

32. *a Burnet, a Whiston or a Woodward*: All three produced accounts of the Earth in the late seventeenth century: Thomas Burnet (*c.* 1635–1715), *Telluris Theoria Sacra* (1680–89); William Whiston (1667–1752), *New Theory of the Earth* (1696); John Woodward, *Essay toward a Natural History of the Earth* (1695). Voltaire disliked their dependence on the Bible, especially regarding the Flood.

33. *a Maillet*: Benoît de Maillet (1656–1738), *Telliamed* (1748).

Account of the Illness, Confession, Death and Apparition of the Jesuit Berthier

1. *Berthier*: Guillaume Berthier (1704–82), editor of the Jesuit *Journal de Trévoux* (1745–62). This satire by Voltaire marks his definitive break with the Order, which had attacked his works over a long period of time and also the *Encyclopédie*.

2. *Coutu*: Probably fictitious.

3. *Mead and Boerhaave*: Richard Mead (1673–1754), Fellow of the Royal Society, whose *Mechanical Account of Poisons* (1702) was much admired by Voltaire; Hermann Boerhaave (1668–1738), Dutch Professor of Medicine, who had turned Leiden into one of the most prestigious medical schools in Europe.

4. *Lemoine's 'Louisiade'*: Pierre Le Moine (1602–71), Jesuit author of the unsuccessful epic *Saint Louis* (1651–3).

5. *Ducerceau's . . . dressing*: Jean Du Cerceau (1670–1730), Jesuit poet, whose verses are mocked elsewhere by Voltaire.

6. *Reflections*: *Pensez-y bien, ou Réflexions* (1710), a proselytizing work by Father Paul de Barry (1585–1661).

7. *Bougeant*: Guillaume Bougeant (1690–1743), a professor in the Jesuit College of Louis-le-Grand where Voltaire was a schoolboy; his *Amusement philosophique sur le langage des bêtes* (1739) was considered by Voltaire to be full of extravagant fantasies. No trace, however, has been found of any condemnation of the work by the Parlement or the Archbishop.

8. *Father Berruyer ... in France*: Isaac Berruyer (1681–1758); his *Histoire du peuple de Dieu* (1728–53) had caused a great scandal and been condemned by two Popes and a wide range of ecclesiastical authorities in Paris and elsewhere for its improprieties. *Clélie*: a 10-volume romance by Madeleine de Scudéry (1654–60).

9. *Brother Busenbaum and Brother Lacroix*: Voltaire attacked both Hermann Busenbaum (1600–1668) and Claude Lacroix (1652–1714) as authors of the *Theologia moralis* (1707–11), which defended regicide and was condemned by the Parlements of Paris and Toulouse, as well as being disavowed by the Jesuit Order.

10. *Guignard, Guéret*: Jean Guignard had been executed in 1595 for writings proposing the murder of Henri IV. Jean Guéret (1559–1639) was indicted for his part in the attempted assassination of Henri IV and suffered banishment for life.

11. *Garnet, Oldcorn*: Henry Garnett and Edward Oldcorn, both English Jesuits, were implicated in the Gunpowder Plot and put to death in 1606. Neither, however, appears to have actually advocated regicide in writing; the same is true of Guéret (n. 10).

12. *Jouvency*: Joseph de Jouvency (1643–1719), whose *Histoire de la Société de Jésus* (1710) was condemned by the Paris Parlement, the Sorbonne and the Pope for supporting the right of regicide.

13. *Harlay*: Achille de Harlay (1536–1616), a leading magistrate of the Paris Parlement, who had opposed the Jesuits.

14. *Pascal's eloquence ... merciful*: Reference to Pascal's swingeing attack on the Jesuits in his *Lettres provinciales* (1656–7).

15. *Sanchez ... dared to say*: Thomas Sanchez (1550–1610), a Spanish Jesuit, had provoked a scandal by the lubricious nature of the anatomical remarks in his *De Matrimonio* (1598), including the question as to whether semen had been produced in the copulation of the Virgin Mary with the Holy Ghost. Pietro Aretino (1492–1554) was an Italian poet whose verses were notoriously obscene; as was also the *Histoire de dom B., portier des Chartreux* (*History of Father B., the Carthusian Porter*, 1715–18), by Jean de La Touche.

16. *hell fire*: Matthew 5: 22.

17. *Abbé Velly*: Paul Velly (1709–59), criticized by the *Journal de Trévoux* for misusing source materials in his *Histoire de France* (1755–86).

18. *Abbé Coyer*: François Coyer (1707–82), attacked by the *Journal de Trévoux* for purportedly defending the *philosophes* in his *Lettre au R. P. Berthier sur le matérialisme* (1759).

19. *Abbé d'Olivet*: Pierre d'Olivet (1682–1768), one of Voltaire's former teachers, who attracted unfavourable comment in the *Journal de Trévoux* for his criticisms of Jesuit commentaries and alleged tendencies towards scepticism.

20. *Francis Xavier . . . crab*: Père Dominique Bouhours (1628–1702) recounts this tale in his *Vie de Saint François Xavier* (1682) as evidence supporting Xavier's claim to sainthood.

21. *St Francis . . . one time*: Voltaire tells how Xavier was seen simultaneously on two ships 150 leagues apart (art. 'François Xavier', *Dictionnaire philosophique*, Moland ed., xix. 203–4).

22. *accomplices*: See above, Lord Chesterfield's Ears', n. 14.

23. *intentionality*: This refers to the Jesuit doctrine whereby an evil act may be remitted if the original contribution was pure. Pascal fiercely attacked this doctrine as casuistical in the *Lettres provinciales* (1656–7), esp. VII and IX.

24. *Nouvelles ecclésiastiques*: The Jansenist journal, published weekly since 1724.

25. *fox . . . wolf*: Voltaire frequently refers to the Jesuits as foxes and to the Jansenists as wolves.

26. *Lettres . . . curieuses*: See above, 'Lord Chesterfield's Ears', n. 16. The source of the *History of Convulsions* is unknown.

27. *Garasse*: François Garasse (1585–1631), a particularly fanatical Jesuit preacher. *Garassise*: probably fictitious.

28. *Paradise Open to Philagie*: Another work (1636) by Father Paul de Barry (see n. 6), referred to mockingly by Pascal in the ninth of his *Lettres provinciales*.

29. *Provincial Letters*: See n. 14 above.

30. *Port-Royal*: A Jansenist abbey near Paris which became the centre of Jansenist activity, until it was destroyed on orders from Louis XIV in 1712.

31. *Le Tellier*: Michel Le Tellier (1643–1719), the Jesuit confessor of Louis XIV from 1709, and a ruthless enemy of the Jansenists.

32. *the Worthiest Archbishop . . . France*: Cardinal de Noailles (1651–1729), whom Le Tellier accused of having Jansenist sympathies.

33. *condemned in Rome*: Le Tellier's *Défense des nouveaux chrétiens* (1687–90), dealing with converted Christians in China and Japan, was placed on the Papal Index in 1700 for its readiness to syncretize the Catholic faith with local Oriental beliefs.

34. *Desfontaines*: Author of the *Voltairomanie* (1738), a fierce attack on Voltaire.

35. *Paraguay grass*: Reference to tea from Paraguay, where the Jesuits had established a theocratic state.

36. *Année littéraire*: The editor was Élie Fréron (1718–76), one of Voltaire's bitterest enemies.

Dialogue between a Savage and a Graduate

1. *the War of Acadia, which you do know about*: The Seven Years War, during which the French lost their North American empire; this included Acadia, now Nova Scotia and New Brunswick.

2. *Unigenitus*: See above, 'Pot-Pourri', n. 27.

Dialogue between Ariste and Acrotal

1. *Acrotal*: The name means 'high-placed'; he represents the opponents of the *Encyclopédie*.

2. *Ramus*: Pierre de La Ramée (1515–72), a famous scholar, was murdered during the St Bartholomew's Day Massacre; cf. 'Lord Chesterfield's Ears', n. 27.

3. *Charron*: Pierre Charron (1541–1603), author of *De la sagesse* (1601), a work designed to exploit philosophy in defence of the Catholic faith.

4. *Montaigne*: Michel de Montaigne (1533–92), the renowned essayist and sceptic.

5. *Bayle . . . inhabitants*: Pierre Bayle (1641–1706), philosopher exiled in Rotterdam from 1680 because of his Protestant convictions.

6. *one of our great ministers . . . doing*: This is thought to be Louis XIV's war minister, the marquis de Louvois (1641–91).

7. *priest*: The Abbé Étienne de Condillac (1715–89), whose 'Lockean' *Traité des sensations* appeared in 1754.

Wives, Submit Yourselves to Your Husbands

1. *Abbé de Châteauneuf*: François de Châteauneuf (1645–1708), diplomat and godfather of Voltaire, who had introduced him into the libertine Société du Temple.

2. *Montaigne*: See above, 'Dialogue between Ariste and Acrotal', n. 4.

3. *Plutarch*: Greek historian and biographer (*c*. AD 46–*c*. 120). The *Lives* contain 46 portraits of eminent Greeks and Romans.

4. *"Wives . . . husbands"*: Epistle of Paul to the Ephesians, 5: 22; Epistle of Paul to the Colossians, 3: 18.

5. *"All power . . . beard"*: Molière's *L'École des femmes*, Act III, sc. 2. This remark is made by Arnolphe, whose obsessive vanity is ridiculed throughout by the playwright.

6. *a German princess*: Empress Catherine the Great of Russia (1729–96), born in Stettin and originally Princess of Anhalt-Zerbst.

7. *Porte*: The (Sublime) Porte was the name given to the Turkish government in Constantinople.

Dialogue between the Cock and the Hen

1. *Pythagoras*: See above, 'An Indian Incident', n. 1.

2. *Porphyry*: Greek philosopher and neo-Platonist (*c.* AD 232–*c.* 305).

3. *Descartes*: René Descartes (1596–1650) had argued in his *Discours de la méthode* (1637) that animals were fundamentally different from human beings, in that we were possessed of reason where they were simply machines (Part V).

Conversation between Lucian, Erasmus and Rabelais, in the Elysian Fields

1. *Lucian*: Greek author (*c.* AD 117–*c.* 180).

2. *Erasmus*: Dutch humanist and a leading Renaissance writer (*c.* 1466–1536), author of the celebrated satire *In Praise of Folly* (1509).

3. *Getes and Massagetes*: Both these tribes were Scythian; they migrated from the Russian steppes to the Black Sea region *c.* 800 BC.

4. *Rabelais*: (*c.* 1494–*c.* 1533); French writer, whose *Pantagruel* and *Gargantua* present a lively, comic and sometimes vulgar view of the whole spectrum of the society in which he lived.

5. *Brutus*: Lucius Junius Brutus who, according to traditional accounts, led the Romans to overthrow the Tarquin monarchy and found the Roman Republic (*c.* 500 BC).

6. *barbarians*: Voltaire uses the term 'Welches', which for him represented all that was intolerant and bloodthirsty in the French nation. (The *Discours aux Welches* (1764) is one of his most virulent satires.) The contrast which he goes on to point out between this murderous tendency and the French love of frivolity is a common theme in his writings at this time.

7. *Rabelais's chapter about the Arse-Wipers*: *Gargantua*, Bk. I, ch. XIII.